# SAVING OWEN (SPECIAL FORCES: OPERATION ALPHA)

## SAVING SEALS, BOOK 3

### JANE BLYTHE

Dear Readers,

*Welcome to the Special Forces: Operation Alpha Fan-Fiction world!*

If you are new to this amazing world, in a nutshell the author wrote a story using one or more of my characters in it. Sometimes that character has a major role in the story, and other times they are only mentioned briefly. This is perfectly legal and allowable because they are going through Aces Press to publish the story.

This book is entirely the work of the author who wrote it. While I might have assisted with brainstorming and other ideas about which of my characters to use, I didn't have any part in the process or writing or editing the story.

I'm proud and excited that so many authors loved my characters enough that they wanted to write them into their own story. Thank you for supporting them, and me!

READ ON!
    Xoxo
    Susan Stoker

*I'd like to thank everyone who played a part in bringing this story to life. Particularly my mom who is always there to share her thoughts and opinions with me. The wonderful Cat Imb of TRC Designs who made the stunning cover. And my lovely editor Lisa Edwards for all her encouragement and for all the hard work she puts into polishing my work.*

# CHAPTER 1

August 3$^{rd}$

10:54 P.M.

It was supposed to get easier the more time that passed.

That was what everyone said anyway.

Lies.

It was all lies.

No amount of time was going to ease the constant ache in his heart, the constant pressure on his chest, the constant bone-crushing grief every time he thought of his wife.

Maya was gone, and she wasn't coming back, somehow he had to find a way to accept it.

Owen "Fox" LeGrand sighed and ran a hand through his messy brown hair, he had no idea how he was supposed to do that. How did you accept that the woman you loved with every fiber of your being was never coming back? How did

1

you accept you would never touch her again, never kiss her again, and never make love to her again? That you would never get to have the future you had dreamed about?

He and Maya had met in high school, for him it had been love at first sight, for her it had come more slowly, but they'd married just after he learned he made the SEAL team, and they'd thought they had the rest of their lives to spend together.

With a growl, Fox slammed his fist into the brick wall of the apartment building where he'd moved to live, unable to go back into the house he and Maya had shared without her bright, cheerful, sunshiny self. It wasn't fair. *He* was a SEAL, *he* was the one who risked his life to save others. It should have been *him* who died, not his sweet, caring, big-hearted wife.

Watching Maya fade away as cancer slowly stole her from him was worse than facing armed militants that wanted him dead, worse than getting shot, worse than being tortured, worse than anything his job could throw at him. He would gladly have taken all of that rather than watch the woman he adored face an agonizing battle he couldn't fight for her.

Because the only way he knew he'd get any sleep was to keep his body on a brutal regime of PT with his team, then his own punishing workout, he bypassed the lifts and headed toward the back of the building to take the stairs up to the twelfth floor. He paused with a frown when he passed the last apartment before the door to the stairwell.

The door was partially open.

His gut stirred.

In his line of work, trusting your gut saved lives.

Fox moved closer. He had a concealed carry permit and never went anywhere without a weapon, now his hand strayed to hover above it.

A muffled scream echoed through the apartment and that

2

was it, there was no way he was walking away from someone who needed help.

Quietly, he crept into the apartment, the living room was dark, but he could see a light on down the hall so he headed in that direction.

As he reached the bathroom, he saw a naked woman shoved up against the wall, held in place by a man dressed all in black with a ski mask covering his face.

The man was raping her.

Fox saw red.

Men who hurt women and children were the lowest of the low.

Not wanting to risk hurting the woman who was crying and doing her best to fight the much larger man off, he left his weapon in its holster, he didn't need it anyway. He could kill a man a hundred different ways without needing any weapon other than his hands. This man didn't deserve a quick death though, he would pay for what he'd done to this woman, but he'd do it by serving time in prison.

The rapist didn't notice Fox as he approached and slammed a well-aimed fist into the side of the guy's head.

He dropped instantly.

The tiny woman—who couldn't be more than an even five feet—turned terrified blue eyes in his direction and screamed.

Holding up his hands palms out, he tried to look as non-threatening as a six-foot-two man could look to a naked woman who had just been brutalized. "It's okay," he said soothingly. "I'm not going to hurt you. I live in the building, I heard you screaming. He can't hurt you again. I'm Fox—uh, Owen," he corrected. He had gone by Fox for so many years now he sometimes forgot he had another name.

Her brow crinkled. "Fox?"

A small smile tugged at his lips, after everything she'd just been through that was what she chose to focus on. "It's my nickname," he told her.

She nodded slowly. She was trembling, but she made no move to cover herself, and her eyes had taken on a glassy look. She ran a shaky hair through her wild mess of blonde curls, and when he looked at her more closely it was like a punch to the gut.

She looked unnervingly like Maya.

At around five-five, Maya had been taller, but she'd had the same shade of blue eyes as this woman, and a mop of blonde curls that had more often than not driven her crazy. They had the same delicate features and the same milky white complexion.

The woman's shaking had intensified, and her teeth were chattering, and she was looking at him warily. Fox realized he'd been staring and quickly shoved aside all thoughts of Maya. He'd call the cops, stay until they came and then get as far away from here as he could, looking at this woman was freaking him out.

Forcing away his own discomfort, he reached for a towel and wrapped it around the woman's shoulders. "Can you tell me your name?" he asked.

"Evangeline ... Evie," she said her voice soft, teeth still chattering.

Eyeing Evie's attacker, he grabbed the hairdryer from the vanity and used the electrical cord to bind the man's hands behind his back. Since he didn't want Evie to have to stay in her assailant's presence a second longer, Fox grabbed a robe hanging on a hook on the door, passed it to her, then lightly touched her shoulder and gestured to the door. "Let's go wait in your living room and I'll call the cops. Maybe get you something to drink too," he added. He'd see if she had juice or something in her fridge, something to get her blood sugar

4

up before the adrenaline crash he knew would be coming hit her.

He was switching the lights on in the living room and pulling out his phone when Evie threw herself at him, wrapping her thin arms around him and burying her face against his chest. "Thank you. How can I ever thank you enough? You saved my life. I don't know what he would have done when he finished ... if you hadn't come, if you hadn't stopped him, he probably would have killed me."

Surprise at the woman seeking comfort from him, it took a moment for his arms to close around her. When they did she sighed through her tears and pressed closer until she was practically plastered against him. "Hey, now," he said awkwardly. It wasn't that he couldn't handle a woman's tears—especially well deserved ones—but he didn't know this woman and she'd just been through a traumatic ordeal. "Everything is okay now."

"Thanks to you," she said, gripping him with a strength that belied her small size.

She was a tough one, Evie. She'd fought against the man assaulting her, and she was holding it together now remarkably well. He was proud of her, he could feel her inner strength and knew that she would need it to get through this.

"Come on, go sit down. I'll get you something to drink and call this in," he said gruffly, uncomfortable with her praise. Saving people was what he did, was who he was, protectiveness was ingrained in him.

"Stay with me, please," she said, looking up at him with tear-drenched eyes.

How could he say no to that pretty face?

"Let's go sit down, see if we can get you to stop shaking," he said, guiding her to the sofa. When he would have sat on the other end of the couch to give her space, she placed herself beside him and rested her head on his shoulder. She was clearly someone who was warm and open with their emotions, one of those touchy-feely people. Maya had been too.

The similarities between the two women were striking, and he found himself now wanting to linger, not go running up to his stark, lonely apartment. He hated that place. He wanted to be back in his home with his wife. He couldn't have that, but he could be here for Evie now, support her like he'd supported Maya through round after round of debilitating chemo and radiation. In the end, he hadn't been able to save Maya, but he had saved Evie, and he found some small measure of redemption in that.

Instead of putting some distance between them, he wrapped an arm around her shaking shoulders and drew her closer as he pulled out his phone and called for cops and an ambulance. If his presence made this even a tiny bit easier for Evie then he wasn't going anywhere.

# CHAPTER 2

One Year Later
August 3rd

6:43 P.M.

It had been a long year.

A weird year.

Some of the lowest moments of her life but also some of the highest. A strange mix of some days feeling like she was trudging through the bowels of Hell, and other days it felt like she was floating through Heaven.

One year.

One year ago, in just a couple of hours, she had been getting ready to take a bath after a long day of work, only to have a man break into her apartment and rape her.

Evangeline Walter stood now in the bathroom of her old apartment, tears tumbling silently down her cheeks. How

7

could the most horrific thing that had ever happened to her have led her to the best thing that had ever happened to her?

Owen LeGrand had saved her life, and then he'd stolen her heart.

She wasn't even sure how it had happened. She'd expected him to leave as soon as the cops and ambulance had shown up, he didn't owe her anything, and his only obligation was to give the cops his statement. Nothing more. He could have gone and never had to see her again, but he hadn't done that. He had insisted on riding with her to the hospital, he'd insisted on holding her hand while she endured the rape kit, he'd insisted on driving her back home and staying with her so she wouldn't be alone.

From there they'd developed a firm friendship.

A friendship that over the last twelve months had grown into something more.

They'd been a couple now for the last three months, and it had been amazing. For all his tough alpha maleness, he was surprisingly gentle and sweet, he never complained if she cried or had flashbacks, and the first time they had made love he had been so careful to make it good for her.

She loved him.

Completely and with her entire being.

She felt so lucky, and now she wanted to lay the bad parts of the last year behind her. It was why she had come here after work. While she still leased the apartment, once they'd gotten together, they moved to Owen's house, which was about ten minutes away from the apartment building where he'd been living a year ago. Today she had to come back here, she had to stand here, had to set the past where it belonged so she could focus solely on the future.

"You shouldn't have come here by yourself."

Evie startled at the voice and the large hands that settled

on her shoulders but immediately relaxed when she realized it was just Owen.

"I would have come here with you if you'd told me you needed to be here," Owen reprimanded gently.

"I know." She leaned back against his chest, and his arms moved to circle her waist, drawing her closer. Evie soaked in his warmth and strength, she wasn't sure how she would have made it through the last twelve months without his steady presence. "I just needed to … I can't even explain, it just seemed important."

"You don't need to have an explanation, not for me and not even for yourself," Owen said, touching a light kiss to her temple. "What do you need from me?"

Evie smiled. How had she gotten so lucky that this amazing man had come running to her rescue and that he had stuck around? "I just need you to be here. Hold me."

"That I can do." Owen turned her in his arms so she was snuggled against his chest. One of his hands stroked the length of her spine, and his other hand cradled the back of her head as she pressed her cheek above his heart.

"I love you," she whispered as more tears rolled down her cheeks.

"I love you too, fairy."

She giggled at the nickname, she knew Owen only called her that because it always made her smile, and she was quickly coming to learn that there wasn't much that Owen wouldn't do to make her smile. Her arms slid around his waist, and she held onto him tightly. She was so grateful to have him in her life. Evie wasn't used to anyone putting her first. It was the complete opposite of the way she had grown up, always in her older sister's shadow.

"You ready to get out of here?" Owen asked.

"Yeah, I am." As Owen took her hand and led her out of the apartment, she knew that she was never coming back here. She had the closure she needed, there was no need to step foot in this place again. When the lease ended, she was going to give it up.

"I'll meet you at home," Owen said, pausing at her car to pull her into his arms and kiss her.

"Home," she echoed, unable to stop smiling. All her life she had dreamed of a happy home, a home where she wasn't always failing to live up to expectations, always being compared to someone else, always being a disappointment.

Owen beat her home, his car in the driveway when she pulled in. Pressing the button for the garage door, she waited till it opened then drove her car inside and turned off the engine. She was exhausted. It had been a long day—a long year—and all day today she'd felt like she was balancing on a knife's edge, waiting to see if the anniversary of her assault was going to trigger a meltdown. Now that the day was mostly over and there had been no freak-outs all she wanted to do was eat dinner with her boyfriend, curl up in his arms and chill out before making love to him and falling asleep with his warm body beside her.

Evie paused, a small frown creasing her forehead when she went to open the door leading inside and found a red ribbon tied around the doorknob.

What was Owen up to?

Her frown turned into a smile, and she opened the door to see that the ribbon disappeared off through the dark, quiet house. Evie flipped on the light and took hold of the ribbon, following it as it wrapped around various pieces of furniture throughout the living room and the dining room, through the kitchen, and then winding its way upstairs. It went to the door to the master bedroom and then disappeared inside.

Unable to stop smiling, Evie opened the door to the bedroom and gasped. Owen had strung up fairy lights across the ceiling and around the headboard of the large sleigh bed they shared. The end of the red ribbon was tied around Owen's waist as he knelt in the middle of the room on one knee.

Evie gasped, her hands flying to cover her mouth.

Was he about to do what she thought he was about to do?

"Evie, my sweet little fairy, you're so full of smiles, so full of life, with those big blue eyes and those wild blonde curls you remind me of a fairy, flying through life, making people's lives better just by being there. From the first night you crept into my apartment, into my bedroom, because you were scared to be in your apartment alone, you also crept into my heart, and you've been there ever since. I've loved every second of getting to know you over the last twelve months, and I'm honored that you wanted me there beside you while you rebuilt your life, making it stronger than it was before. I'm so proud of you, in awe of you really. You are so strong, an inspiration, nothing can take you down. Will you do me the honor of letting me call myself your husband?"

She just stared at him.

She knew they were serious about each other, they were living together after all, and she'd never lived with any man she'd been dating other than Owen. He'd been amazing these last twelve months, and for her that first night she'd used the key Owen had given her to slip into his place because she'd been terrified on her own he'd won her heart. She'd intended to sleep on the floor, not wanting to disturb him, but he'd gotten up, gotten dressed, and made her sleep in his bed while he slept beside her on top of the covers.

From that moment, she'd been all in, and even though it had been another eight months before he asked her out, they'd spent most of the time when he wasn't away on some mission, together, getting to know each other better. That their relationship had grown from friendship made it so much deeper, so much more real, and she wanted nothing more than to marry Owen and spend their lives together.

Evie flew across the room and threw her arms around Owen's neck. He caught her and drew her against him as she pressed her face into his neck and held him tight.

"Is that a yes or a no?" Owen asked, sounding uncharacteristically nervous. Owen was a big, tough Navy SEAL, he was never nervous, and she liked seeing this hint of vulnerability in him, it made him seem more human.

"Of course it's a yes," she said with a laugh as if there would be any doubt.

Owen's hands spanned her waist, and he set her on her feet in front of him and took her left hand. He opened the little red velvet box and took out the ring, sliding it onto her finger, making their engagement official.

She couldn't be happier.

Finally, she'd found someone who thought she was special. Special enough to marry.

Owen stood and captured her lips as he guided her toward the bed. Evie didn't think that her life could get any better than it was in this moment.

# CHAPTER 3

Seven Months Later
March 12<sup>th</sup>

4:12 P.M.

Fox was glad to be back home after a particularly horrific mission, but there was an underlying tension rippling through him as he pulled into his driveway.

As always, he'd sent Evie a message letting her know the second he had arrived safely home. He hated that she worried about him while he was gone and he always put her mind at ease as soon as he could. They were still newlyweds, they'd married just a month after he'd proposed, he knew how fragile life was and hadn't wanted to wait, and Evie had been all too happy to go with a small and simple wedding.

Usually, he couldn't wait to get her into his arms, kiss her, reassure himself that she was okay, because while he was the one who was off risking his life on a mission, the fear of losing the second woman he had fallen in love with never really faded. Today, though, he felt like something was off in the message she'd sent in reply to his. He couldn't quite put his finger on it, but he'd felt a distance between them, she hadn't been her usual bright and bubbly self, and he had no idea why.

What could possibly have gone wrong in the two weeks he'd been gone?

Had something happened to her?

Had she been hurt?

Raped?

His blood turned to ice at the thought of Evie suffering again. She was his sweet, kind-hearted, shining light in the dark that had been his grief, he couldn't imagine not having her in his life.

With hands that were shaking—yes, actually shaking—he got out of his car and let himself inside his house.

He froze as soon as he stepped through the door.

Boxes.

There were boxes stacked neatly beside the front door, and when he looked over he saw Evie sitting stiffly on the couch. Her knees were pressed together, her hands folded primly in her lap, her usually smiling face was a blank mask.

"What's wrong?" he demanded, already storming across the room.

When he reached for her, intending to pull her into his arms and fix whatever problem had put that expression on his wife's face, she flinched away from him, and he knew whatever this was it was bad.

More worried now, he dropped to his knees in front of her. "Evie, honey, what's wrong?"

Instead of answering him, she tilted her head to the side, looking at something hanging above the fireplace.

Fox turned to see what she was looking at, and the moment he saw it his heart seemed to stop beating.

This was worse than he had thought.

Above the fireplace was a painting—no doubt done by Evie who was an amazing artist—of him standing at Maya's gravesite. She had captured the exact emotions he'd been feeling as he stood there, talking to his wife and promising her he would make it home alive from this mission. It was something Maya had made him do every single time he left. They both knew he couldn't actually promise that he wouldn't get killed, but it was their ritual, and he had continued to go by the cemetery to make that promise to her.

"Why didn't you tell me?" Evie asked, her voice tortured.

How did he explain that when he himself didn't really know the answer?

At first, he'd never told her about Maya because Evie had just been violated and his entire focus had been on helping her deal with that. How could he have known he would end up falling in love with her?

Finding love again hadn't even been on his radar back then, they'd just been friends, and then out of that something more had grown.

By then, it seemed irrelevant to mention Maya, he and Evie were navigating the changes in their relationship, and again that had been his focus. By then he'd been in deep, but part of him had also recognized that he'd made a mistake by not telling her right away because then he was worried that she would take it exactly as she appeared to be taking it now.

Like he'd deliberately kept it from her.

And knowing her past, he knew exactly why she thought he'd done it.

"I'm sorry, I should have told you," he said. There was no point in making excuses, he had messed up and he'd own it.

Basically, he would do anything to wipe the devastation off Evie's face.

"Why? Why didn't you?" she asked, tears streaming, seemingly unnoticed, down her pale face.

"I don't know," he said simply. "The time never seemed right."

She looked disappointed by his answer, and he hated he had done this to her. Made her doubt herself and her worth, been just another person to let her down, to not value her. Evie never complained, but he knew how badly she'd been hurt in the past, and he respected how she didn't let it make her bitter. She loved wholly and openly, she was the sweetest, most generous person he'd ever met. He had promised to always love and protect her and yet he had failed her.

"I'm sorry, Evie," he said, reaching out to her, but when she shied away he let his hand drop back down to his side. "What can I do to make this up to you?"

"Nothing," she said softly. "I'm leaving. I've already contacted a lawyer to have divorce papers drawn up. I don't want anything, you can keep your house, and everything in it. I've already packed up the things I brought with me when I moved in."

Now his heart felt like it wanted to beat its way right out of his chest.

No.

He couldn't lose her.

Couldn't accept that this was over.

No way was he losing another woman he loved.

"Sweetheart, whatever you're thinking about why I didn't tell you about Maya you're wrong. It wasn't about you at all."

She flinched at his words, and he realized how she'd taken them. "I know," she said, her eyes impossibly sad. "Nothing is ever about me."

"No, honey, that's not what I meant. How did you find out?"

"I was at the cemetery visiting my sister's grave, and I saw you there. You told me you'd left on a mission. I waited till you left and then went to see whose grave you were visiting. You can imagine my surprise when I found out it was your wife's. I did a little research, and I found out about her, how she battled cancer and eventually passed away, how I look just like her." She shuddered as she said that as though the pain inside her was so great it was trying to find a way out. "When I saw a picture of her, I knew. Knew why you married me. I was Maya's replacement. You couldn't have her so I was the next best thing."

"No," he said viciously, hating that Evie believed that with every fiber of her being.

"Yes," she countered. "This isn't about you still loving Maya, I would never have been jealous of her if you'd told me. I wouldn't have minded sharing your heart with her. If you'd told me, I would have shared that love with you. I would have found out everything I could about Maya and the things she liked, so I didn't accidentally do them and hurt you, or if you wanted me to do them then I would have. I would have celebrated her with you, but you didn't want me to. You wanted to shut me out because what you feel for me isn't the same thing as what you feel for her. I'll always be second, I'm just the replacement, I can't do that again. I'm tired of always being second, I want to be first for once. I want someone to look at me the way you're looking at Maya's grave."

Fox felt like he was drowning. He was a SEAL, the water was like a second home to him, but right now waves were washing over his head, and he couldn't seem to find his way up. He was losing Evie—feared it was already too late and it

17

was a done deal—and he didn't know what to say to make things better.

How did he convince her that she was wrong?

That while he would always love Maya he loved her too.

Loved her every bit as much as he had loved his first wife, and losing her would devastate him just as fully.

"Tell me what to do to fix this," he begged because he wasn't too proud to do that, the alternative was accepting that his marriage was over.

"You can't fix it," Evie said. The tears brimming in her eyes told him that she didn't like this, didn't want to do it, but was trying to protect herself against more pain. "I should go. I would have left right away, but that didn't feel right. I owed it to you to tell you in person."

"Don't go," he pleaded. This time he did grab her and drag her into his arms. He held her tightly, willing her to feel his love for her. She was stiff in his hold, and he knew that anything he said or did right now was only going to make things worse. Asking Evie to stay was asking her to put herself once again in a position where she felt like she was second best. It was asking her to willingly endure more pain.

How could he do that to her?

It seemed like the only option was to let her go.

While he might allow her to walk out the door of their home, he wasn't giving up on her. He loved her, and he wasn't interested in ever looking for love anywhere else. Either he found a way to win back Evie's heart or he spent the rest of his life alone.

\* \* \*

4:39 P.M.

.  .  .

Evie felt like her heart was broken.

She'd been walking around in a daze for the last two weeks, ever since she'd caught sight of Owen at the cemetery and learned the huge secret he was keeping from her.

Why?

The question had echoed through her head nearly constantly and even having finally had her chance to speak to Owen she wasn't any more clear about why he wouldn't tell her that he'd been married and that his wife had died. They'd been friends for nine months before they started dating, dated for three months before getting engaged, then married a month later. That was plenty of time for him to have mentioned it.

Especially since he had moved her into the house he and his wife had shared.

He hadn't told her because he didn't want her to know that she was nothing but a replacement for Maya. A way to pretend that he had the woman he loved back. And while her heart wanted to insist that she stay because she knew that Owen did care about her, she was so tired of coming in second and knew she could never be completely happy if she remained married to Owen.

For once, she wanted to be first in someone's eyes.

Maybe that made her selfish, it certainly wouldn't be the worst thing someone called her, but she couldn't stay. Her heart may tell her to stay, but her head knew she had no choice but to leave.

For once, she was going to listen to her head.

No one would accuse her of being naïve and stupid this time.

"I have to go," she told Owen, who was still holding her desperately, afraid to loosen his hold because he knew when he did she was going to move away.

"At least just take some time. Let me prove to you that I love you."

The sad thing was she did believe that he loved her, but he would always love Maya more. It wasn't a competition. She had no problem with him forever loving his wife, he *should* forever love her, but how could she not feel like she was just a substitute when he had lied to her?

"I know you love me, but you're not *in love* with me."

Owen leaned back to stare down at her, and she took advantage of that to move out of his hold, it was too hard to think clearly when he was touching her. "So you know how I feel, do you?" he demanded.

"Yes, because your actions have shown me. I don't want to rehash it, I'm not angry with you, it was up to you to decide whether to tell me about Maya or not, but that doesn't mean there aren't consequences to your choices. You know about my family, how I was always in my sister's shadow. She was the smart one, the pretty one, the one who was good at sports, played musical instruments, and had a lot of friends, and I was just … me. You know that when she died, my parents told me what a loss she was to the world, how she would have gone on to do great things, how it should have been me instead. I don't want to live the rest of my life like that. Always knowing that Maya is who you want and feeling like you would trade me for her in a heartbeat. Don't ask me to do that. Please."

The brown eyes that looked down at her were so sad that she nearly crumbled, nearly promised to do whatever it took to make him happy, but for once she had to put herself first. She had brushed off so many things in her life, never stood up to her parents, never yelled at her popular high school boyfriend who had been embarrassed about her and kept her secret, told her parents to hire her college boyfriend who was using her to get a job as a chef at one of her family's

SAVING OWEN (SPECIAL FORCES: OPERATION ALPHA)

many restaurants. She'd been a doormat most of her life, allowing people to use her for their own personal reasons, but no more.

No more.

While her heart may feel like it was broken right now, she would bounce back. She always did. She had great friends, a job as an emergency room nurse that she adored, and she was only twenty-five, she still had plenty of time to find the man who would look at her with stars in his eyes, like she was it for him, the most precious thing he had.

She wasn't going to settle.

She'd been settling for whatever scraps someone doled out to her for twenty-five years, but she wasn't going to spend the rest of her life doing it.

"Please, Evie, give me a chance to fix this," Owen begged, and she could see the toll it took on him to actually beg another person for anything. He was a SEAL, a warrior, a protector who would never hesitate to put himself between anyone else and danger. He had saved her life, been her rock as she recovered from her assault, and given her a wonderful eighteen months of fun and laughter and love.

But he couldn't give her what she needed.

Not while he hadn't moved on from his wife's death.

He might never move on, but she wasn't selfish enough to want him to remain alone forever. If she couldn't be the woman for him, she prayed he met someone else, someone who would never take Maya's place in his heart but have her own place, someone who could give him children and grow old at his side.

"I don't want you to think that I'm walking away because I'm angry. I was angry at first that you lied, but now I'm just sad to find out I was a replacement for your wife." She winced as he did, realizing that neither option was better than the other. "I want you to be happy, I want you to move

21

on, I want you to always love Maya but find someone else that you can love just as much. I want those things for you even if that woman isn't me." She stood on tiptoes and kissed his cheek. "I love you, Owen, like you love Maya, but I can't stay married to a man who doesn't love me that same way. I hope you can understand that."

Since there didn't seem to be anything left to say, she walked quietly over to the table by the front door and picked up her purse. Tears rolled down her cheeks, this might be the hardest thing she'd ever had to do, but it had to be done.

"I'll be staying in a hotel until I find a new place. I hope it's okay to leave my things here until then," she said, eyeing the boxes and finding herself too weary to deal with them today.

"Of course."

"Thank you," she murmured. Then she straightened her spine, grabbed the suitcase with her clothes and toiletries, and walked out the front door.

As she climbed into her car she half expected Owen to come running after her, plead with her not to go, but he didn't. She cried the whole drive to a nearby hotel, then wiped her face as clean as she could get it and managed not to cry again until she was checked into her room.

Sagging onto the bed, Evie kept expecting Owen to call or text or track her down here. But again, he did none of those things. She couldn't be mad at him about it, he was only doing what she had asked him to do, but that he could let her go so easily, without putting up any real fight, hurt but also assured her she had done the right thing.

Somehow she managed to strip off her clothes and stagger to the bathroom where she turned the shower on as hot as she could stand and then sank down to her bottom under the spray. Her legs to her chest, she buried her face in her hands and cried.

She would allow herself this time to vent her emotions, heartbreak was messy, and she knew she needed to get everything out because it was the only way she could move forward. Tomorrow was a new day, and while it sucked that it wouldn't be started with a kiss from her husband, she was strong enough to weather anything life threw at her. Right now, things might seem dark and gloomy and soul-crushing, but she would get up tomorrow, face the day, search for happiness, and she was confident that one day she would find it.

One day it would be her turn to find that fairytale, soul mate, forever kind of love and she wasn't going to settle until she did.

Until that day came, she was going to make darn sure that never again would anyone accuse her of being a doormat.

## CHAPTER 4

Two Years Later
April 1st

12:23 P.M.

"I should have driven," Fox muttered, as Grayson "Chaos" Simpson slowed to a near stop to turn the corner. "I thought your name was Chaos. Why do you drive like an old lady?"

Chaos just laughed. "I like to get there in one piece, man. How can I continue to make the world a better place with my sparkling personality and famous wit if I wrap the car around a telephone pole?"

Fox rolled his eyes at his friend and teammate. While sparkling personality might not be something you associated with a Navy SEAL, it was true about Chaos. The man had a huge heart, he was full of life and energy, and despite the horrific things they'd all seen, it didn't seem to affect Chaos.

The man was as charming as they came, between his dimples, his sandy blond hair, and light green eyes, he had women falling all over themselves to get into bed with him. Most days Fox had no idea what had made Chaos decide to join the military. He'd come from the perfect family, parents still married, mother a schoolteacher, father an accountant, two siblings, they were the epitome of the middle-class, suburban family. Although he looked and seemed like someone more suited to a career as a model, Chaos was exactly who you wanted watching your back.

Actually, Chaos reminded him a lot of Evie.

His sweet little fairy who he had missed like a piece of himself had been severed and thrown away, was also full of life and energy, the sunshine you needed on a cloudy day, and loyal to a fault.

He missed her so much he'd been walking around with an ache in his chest for the last two years.

Now she was in trouble, and instead of reaching out to him, she had reached out to his friend and teammate Logan "Shark" Kirk. Shark was the opposite of both Evie and Chaos. The huge man was six-foot-six, built like a tank, hair as black as coal with eyes to match. Cool and calm under pressure, rarely smiled, more often than not silent, observing not participating in what was going on around him. It killed Fox to know that even when she needed help she wouldn't turn to him, and he hated even more that he had no one to blame for that but himself.

"Tell me again what she said," he demanded, twisting in his seat to look at Shark who sat in the backseat.

"Exactly what I already told you. She said she was at the police station and she needed help, that she would explain more once I got there," Shark repeated calmly.

"Was she arrested?" He couldn't imagine Evie doing anything illegal, but that didn't mean she hadn't accidentally got herself mixed up in something. She was far too trusting, she had a big heart and cared about others, and she had a tendency to think that everybody was just like her.

"She said she didn't need to be bailed out," Shark replied.

"Stop stressing about it, we'll be at the station in five minutes, and you can ask her yourself what's going on," Chaos said as he took another turn ridiculously slowly.

"No," Shark said firmly. "You stay in the car. She didn't call you, Fox. She could have but she chose not to. Let me handle this."

Promising to stay in the car was how he had convinced Shark to agree to let him tag along, but he had no intention of honoring that promise. This was his Evie. The woman he still loved. There was no way he wasn't going to help her with whatever had happened that had her reaching out to his team.

He knew she was still friends with fellow teammate Ryder "Spider" Flynn's wife Abigail, and Eric "Night" McNamara's fiancée Lavender, but other than that she tried to avoid him and his team for the most part.

At least he thought she did.

But she'd reached out to Shark of all people, and he couldn't figure out why.

"You sure you're telling me everything?" he asked Shark. The man had said that he wasn't romantically involved with Evie, and it wasn't that he thought his friend was lying, it was just he wasn't seeing the connection between Evie and Shark.

"Why wouldn't I?"

"You tell me. I just think it's strange that she would reach out to you. No offense, man, you're just not the most approachable of people. I'd get it if she called Spider or Night, since she's friends with Abby and Lavender, but why would she call you?" Fox demanded, hating it came out a little accusatorial. It wasn't really Shark he was angry at, it was himself. If he had just told Evie about Maya, she would never have left him, and she wouldn't be in whatever trouble she was in now.

Shark sighed. "Look, she didn't want me to say anything, but her rapist was let out of prison a couple of months ago. My brother's new partner was one of the cops who worked Evie's case, and Shawn reached out to me because he recognized Evie's name. She was your woman, and I know you loved her, so I called her up, told her that even though you two weren't together anymore if she ever saw him hanging around, or if she ever needed anything, that she could reach out to me. To be honest, I never expected that she would because of her history with you, but she called today, so obviously I was wrong."

That was the most he'd ever heard his friend say in one go, and Fox was touched that Shark would reach out to Evie for him even though the man avoided most contact with people. "Thanks, man," he said, and Shark nodded in acknowledgment.

"Let's go get this mess with your girl sorted out so we can go to the hospital and find out if Spider and Abby are getting a son or a daughter. Who knows, maybe we can convince Evie to come with us, and you can use this opportunity to win your girl back," Chaos said with a wink.

What he wouldn't give for another chance with Evie.

And to be honest, he wasn't above using the impending birth of Spider and Abby's baby to do it. He and his team had been having lunch together when Evie's phone call and Abby going into labor had broken things up. Shark and Chaos had come with him to deal with Evie's problem, while Spider, Abby's brother Night, his three months pregnant fiancée Lavender, and their other teammate Charlie "King" Voss, had all gone to the hospital with Abby. Since Evie was Abby's friend, he was pretty sure he could persuade her to go with them to meet the new baby once they found out what was going on with her.

"We're here," Chaos announced as he parked across the street from the police station, and sure enough there was Evie standing on the sidewalk waiting for Shark to show up.

"You stay here," Shark ordered. "If I need help I'll let Chaos know and he can join us."

Fox merely nodded at Shark as he climbed out of the car, but he couldn't tear his eyes off his Evie. She looked the same. Her blonde curls were pulled up into a ponytail. She was dressed in a skintight pair of black jeans and a sparkly blue sleeveless top that definitely wasn't warm enough for the cool spring day. She had on heels that added a couple of inches to her height but still had her coming in at shorter than most people.

Shark strode across the street, and when she caught sight of him, she lifted a hand and waved. Evie wrapped her arms around her middle, huddling in on herself, it was clear she was cold. Shark shrugged out of his jacket and draped it around her shoulders when he reached her side.

That was it.

He wasn't sitting back and letting someone else take care of his woman.

Evie was his. He still loved her, still wanted her back, and he wasn't going to stay here and allow Shark to help her through whatever problem she was facing.

"Whatcha doing?" Chaos asked when Fox opened his door.

"Taking care of what's mine. You got a problem with that?" He scowled over his shoulder at Chaos.

"Nope," Chaos said cheerfully. "Just surprised you lasted this long in the car without storming over there to save the day. Let's go help your girl."

He intended to. Maybe if he helped Evie with her

problem big enough that she would reach out to his team, he could prove to her that she was wrong, that he had always loved her every bit as much as he loved Maya, that he had made a mistake in not telling her about his first wife, but that it was a mistake he wanted to rectify.

Letting her walk away had been one of the hardest things he'd ever done, but he had done it because she'd asked him to. This time she could beg until she was blue in the face, but he wasn't going to let her walk away a second time.

* * *

12:38 P.M.

Evie lifted a weary hand to wave at Shark when she saw him crossing the street. She was exhausted, all she wanted was to go home, take a shower, and crawl under the covers to sleep for a week.

But she couldn't.

She was afraid, scared enough to reach out to one of Owen's teammates.

"You look cold," Shark said bluntly when he reached her, and shrugged out of his jacket to drape it over her shoulders. Immediately warmth seeped into her. She didn't have a jacket on her, she hadn't thought she'd need one at the club last night. She had no way of foreseeing the disaster that last night had turned into.

"Thank you," she murmured, drawing the jacket tighter around herself. She was about to just jump on in and tell him what was going on when movement in her peripheral vision caught her attention.

Her body turned to ice when she saw who it was.

Owen was storming toward them.

She didn't think, she just reacted, turning on her heel and intending to head back inside the police station to call a cab to take her back to the club to get her car. A hand snaked out and caught her wrist, halting her escape. Shark held her firmly but gently, and reluctantly, she turned back to face him.

"Why is he here?" she asked.

"Because he loves you," Shark replied simply.

But he wasn't *in love* with her which was why she hadn't called him. As it was, it had been a big enough risk to reach out to Shark knowing that he might tell Owen. She had assumed he would and that at some point she would have to face her ex, but she hadn't expected to have to do it so soon. It had been two years since she left Owen, and he hadn't made a single move to reach out to her, to fight for their relationship, so why did he have to be here now?

"He doesn't love me, and he shouldn't be here," she reprimanded the giant man.

"You are the only one who thinks that," Shark said.

"What's going on, Evie?" Owen demanded as he joined her and Shark on the sidewalk.

People were milling around, and to be honest, she was ready to get as far away from the police station as she could so she shook her head, accepting that for the moment she was going to have to deal with her ex. "Not here. Can we go somewhere quieter to talk?"

"Sure," Shark said before Owen had a chance to no doubt demand she tell him everything on the spot.

"The park is just down the street. How about we go hang out there while you tell us what's going on," Chaos suggested in his easy manner, and she shot him a smile, she hadn't even realized he was there.

"Hey, Chaos," she greeted the easy-going member of Owen's team. Perhaps if she thought of him as Fox the SEAL it would make having to tell him what was going on easier. She did know he loved her and would go all out to protect her and keep her safe.

"Hey, gorgeous." Chaos pulled her in for a hug, then wrapped an arm around her shoulders and guided her toward a black truck on the other side of the street.

Evie was aware of Owen glaring at Chaos, but he didn't say anything, and a moment later, they all piled into the car. She didn't pay much attention to the guys as they drove, she was too busy trying to wrap her head around the situation she had found herself in. How she wished she could go back in time about twelve hours. If she could, she would never have gone outside. She would have just left when her best friend ditched her to leave with a guy.

"We're here," Owen announced, and Evie blinked and realized that the car had stopped and the guys were all standing around her open car door.

She nodded and got out of the car, following the others over to an empty picnic table. The park was quiet, there were some people out walking dogs, and running, a few moms with kids on the playground, but there was no one nearby so she didn't have to worry about being overheard while she said this.

"So, what's up?" Owen asked as soon as they sat down like he couldn't stand to wait another second to find out what problem he had to fix for her.

But this wasn't something he could fix.

No one could.

She was in this mess, and she had to find a way to deal with it.

"Floor's yours, sweetheart," Chaos said, shooting her a supportive smile.

She looked from him to Shark who had his arms crossed over his chest and was watching her closely, his calm mask in place. Owen was also watching her, although with a lot less calm, he looked about a second away from grabbing her and shaking answers out of her.

May as well get on with it.

"I went out with Lacey last night. She'd been bugging me to go to a club with her because it had been about a month since she last hooked up with a guy. We had been there for about an hour when she found some guy she liked and they left."

"She just left you alone at a club?" Owen groused.

Evie nodded. "I didn't mind, I just intended to finish my drink and head home, but I ... uh ... I got a little ... panicky." She hated that, it had been a long time since her assault had made her panic in large groups, but knowing her rapist was now out of prison had her a little jumpy. "Anyway, I needed fresh air so I went outside, into the back alley." Owen made a sound like he couldn't believe she would do that, but she ignored him and kept talking. "As soon as I got out there I realized it was a mistake. I wasn't alone. There were two men with guns, and they had another guy on the ground. He looked like he'd been beaten. I hid behind a dumpster so they didn't see me, but I heard them yelling at the injured man, and then they shot him." She dragged in a breath so she didn't throw up, no way she wanted to embarrass herself in front of these SEALs who had seen and heard a lot worse.

"Did they see you?" Owen asked tightly.

She shook her head. "I heard them leave and I climbed into the dumpster. I was scared they might come back so I stayed there. They left the body behind, and it must have been reported because some cops found me in there. They thought that I might be ... involved, so they took me down to the station to question me."

"Did they cuff you?" Owen asked, or growled would

probably be a better word for the sound that came out of his mouth.

Evie nodded, her eyes fixed firmly on her lap. She startled when Owen reached out and tugged her hands out from inside Shark's jacket, his fingertips tracing lightly over the red marks still circling her wrists. Being patted down and cuffed then thrown in the back of a police car had been terrifying, as had being locked up in an interrogation room while two detectives peppered her with questions.

"They checked my hands for gunshot residue, and when the test came back clean, they stopped looking at me as a suspect and started looking at me as a witness." That didn't seem to mollify Owen whose fingers moved from her wrist to curl around her hand, holding it gently in his. "When I told them that one of the men I saw with the guns had tattoos that looked like knives on his temples they were particularly interested."

The shocked gasps of the three men at the table told her that they, unlike her, knew what that meant. She hadn't known until the cops told her, but apparently, that was the mark of a cartel based in Mexico that trafficked drugs, weapons, and women.

"The Perez cartel," Owen said, then swore. "You witnessed a hit by the Perez cartel."

"Yes." She finally met his eyes and was shaken by the raw fear she saw there. If he was afraid for her, then she was in a worse spot than she thought she was. "The other man with the gun was dressed in a suit, he was maybe my age, and his clothes looked really expensive. The cops think that it might have been Miguel Perez."

Owen swore viciously. "You witnessed the *son* of the cartel boss kill someone?"

"That's what they think," she confirmed. Shark and Chaos looked as unhappy by that as Owen did. She wasn't stupid, she knew this was bad, but their concerns were putting her even more on edge. How had she gotten herself mixed up in this? And how was she going to get out of it?

"They want you to testify," Shark said. It sounded like a statement, not a question, but she nodded anyway.

"They have an arrest warrant out for Miguel. Apparently they've been trying to get him for a while now," she said.

"The cartel doesn't know you were there otherwise you'd already be dead," Owen said, his hand tightening around hers until it was almost painful.

"The cops said that as long as the cartel doesn't find out about me then I shouldn't be in any danger, but … I was scared, and I trust you guys, so … I called Shark," she finished. She didn't really know what they could do to help her. They were SEALs, they weren't bodyguards, but she didn't know what to do, and she couldn't face this alone.

Owen squeezed her hand again, his thumb brushing lightly across the inside of her wrist. When she looked at him his face was deadly serious. "Evie, you did the right thing in calling."

The right thing for her life, but probably not for her heart.

* * *

1:23 P.M.

The Perez cartel.

This was so much worse than he'd thought.

Fox didn't have an actual idea on what he thought might have been going on with Evie, but he certainly hadn't been expecting this. If the cartel found out that she had witnessed the son of the cartel boss murder someone, they would put a hit out on her.

How was he going to protect her if that happened?

He could keep her safe when he was here, but he could get sent on a mission at any time and be gone for days, weeks, or even months. Maybe he needed to look into hiring personal security for her. Even if the cops were able to find and arrest Miguel Perez, she would have a target on her back until the trial. And even if he was found guilty, Luis Perez might still want to take her out just for messing with his only son.

This was a nightmare.

Both Chaos and Shark looked as concerned for Evie's safety as he felt, and he knew when the rest of his team found out what was going on they were all going to freak out as well. Especially Spider. Although he hadn't been directly responsible for her abduction and imprisonment, Luis Perez had allowed Abigail to be kept locked in a cage on his Mexican compound for fourteen months. It was only just under a year ago that they had stumbled upon her, close to death, while on a mission to rescue three kidnapped girls.

No way was he letting the Perez cartel get their hands on Evie.

If they did, she would be raped, tortured, and eventually killed.

Or perhaps worse; sold.

The cartel was particularly vicious and bloodthirsty and had a thing for knives and carving people up.

That wasn't happening to his Evie.

Offering her what he hoped was a reassuring smile, he laced his fingers with hers. "We'll figure this out, okay?"

Relief was stark in her blue eyes. "Thank you. Do you really think the cartel will come after me?"

He didn't want to scare her, but he also needed her to

know that this was serious so she knew to make sure she kept herself safe. "If they find out that you're a witness to a hit, even if it wasn't Miguel, then they're likely to try to take you out to stop you from testifying."

Her fingers tightened around his. "What am I going to do?"

"For now, let's not worry about it. They won't know about you until Miguel is in custody and his lawyer gets a look at the evidence against him." While they had time Fox had no idea how much time, but today he wanted to try to alleviate some of the stress that was rolling off her in waves. She'd had a really rough night, witnessing a murder, being cuffed and hauled down to the police station, being questioned for hours, but he knew what would cheer her up. "Hey, how about you come with us to the hospital to see Abby? She's in labor."

Evie's eyes brightened. She and Abby were good friends, she'd even stayed with Abigail, who had been put on bed rest after a pregnancy scare, earlier in the year when Spider and the rest of the team had gone to look for Night's girlfriend Lavender who had gone missing. "Abby is in labor?"

"Yep, her water broke about the same time you called Shark," he said, trying not to be jealous that his ex-wife hadn't reached out to him personally. In the end it didn't matter, he was here now, and he was going to personally oversee her safety.

"She's probably going to call you as soon as the baby's born anyway, may as well show up and surprise her," Chaos said, shooting her one of his most charming smiles.

"Well ..." Evie said slowly, clearly undecided.

He wanted her to come, wasn't ready to say goodbye to her yet, and it had nothing to do with being worried for her safety. He wanted back into her life, hadn't wanted out of it when she'd left, but then he hadn't had a choice. He hadn't dated in the two years since they'd broken up, hadn't even touched another woman. There wasn't any woman he wanted bar the one whose hand he was currently holding.

"Come on, you know Abby will be thrilled to have you there," he said, prepared to use Abby and the baby to get her to agree. He needed more time with her and needed to find a way to show her that she was wrong and that he had always loved her.

"Yeah, I guess I could come by for a while. I can't wait to see whether they have a boy or a girl." A smile touched Evie's face, the first he'd seen on her this afternoon, and as it always did it lit up her entire being.

He'd missed her so much.

Wanted her back so badly.

He'd had a lot of time to reflect, and he realized that maybe there had been some truth to what Evie had believed. Just a tiny bit. He had known that keeping Maya a secret wasn't the best move, even though he had excuses as to why he'd done it, and perhaps deep down he had wondered if what he felt for Evie was trying desperately to get back what he had with Maya.

Two years of living without Evie had convinced him that wasn't true.

His love for Evie was equal to his love for Maya, both relationships were different because both women were different, but he loved them equally.

Maya was gone, but Evie wasn't, and he was determined to find a way to convince her that she was no replacement. No second place.

"Let's get over there then. Knowing Spider and Abby I'm sure this little one isn't going to take his or her time to make their entrance into the world," Fox said, standing and bring Evie up with him.

"Abby is going to be so thrilled to have that little one out so she isn't stuck in bed or on the couch anymore," Evie said as the four of them headed back toward Chaos' car.

"I bet, give her a week or two of sleepless nights she's going to be wishing she was back in bed with nothing to do but rest," Chaos joked as he climbed into the driver's seat.

When Shark went to get in the back Fox fixed a glare on him. No way was he not sitting with Evie, she'd just had her entire world tipped upside down, and she needed him. Easing Shark's jacket off Evie's shoulders, he handed it back to his teammate. "Thanks for letting Evie borrow this," he said as he took off his jacket and wrapped it around her, and helped her into the car. He didn't care that he was being obvious and a little possessive, Evie was his, and she needed that reminder more than anyone else.

"Men," Evie muttered as she slid into the car and buckled up. Still, she didn't take the jacket off, and when he got in beside her and took her hand she didn't protest or pull it away.

Baby steps.

He was going to have to accept that he couldn't just force Evie to accept that she was wrong and that he loved her. He might have spent the last two years dispelling any doubts he had about his feelings for Evie, but she had spent the last two years believing she was right and she was nothing but a poor imitation.

If it was the last thing he ever did, he would prove to her that she was wrong.

But before he could do that, they had to get a handle on the Perez situation. He wasn't going to bury another wife. No way, no how.

There was a friend he had served with who owned Prey Security, the best security firm in the country. Besides running hostage recovery and black ops missions the government couldn't send any other team on, they also did personal security. Fox would reach out to them, see if they would take on Evie's case, he was sure that Eagle would, they were friends, brothers, and he knew that family was the most important thing to the Oswald family. There wasn't anyone else that he would trust Evie's safety to than the Oswalds. No one matched them when it came to skills or resources, they only hired the best, and they were the best at what they did.

For the next few hours though, he just wanted to hang out with Evie and his friends, enjoy the impending birth of the first baby to join his SEAL team family. For now, Evie was safe, so long as the cartel didn't know about her, he didn't have to worry, and this was exactly what they needed if he was going to win her back. They needed time just to be together, with their friends so there wasn't any pressure, and maybe when Evie saw that he was willing to do whatever it took to protect her from this threat, she would realize it was because he loved her.

# CHAPTER 5

April 2nd

12:00 A.M.

"We have a baby."

Evie and everyone else turned as Spider walked into the waiting room with a tiny bundle in his arms.

"Boy or girl?" King asked as they all went to meet the new little one.

Spider waited until they all gathered around, then with a face that was beaming with pride he shifted the baby so they could all get a better look at his child. "It's a boy, I have a son." From the look on Spider's face, he could barely believe that his baby was here now.

"What's his name?" Night asked. Not only was Night the only biological relative to the baby, but he and his fiancée were also expecting a child. He was no doubt imagining himself and Lavender in Spider and Abby's place in six months' time.

"His name is Ryder Flynn Junior, RJ," Spider told them.

"I love that," Lavender said, resting a hand on her still flat stomach as though she were thinking of possible names for her and Night's little one.

"I dibs first hold," Chaos announced, reaching for the baby.

"Hey, I'm the uncle, I should go fist," Night said, managing to scoop RJ up before Chaos could.

Evie watched as everyone took turns holding the baby, who didn't seem to mind being passed around from person to person. She'd never really thought much about having kids. She knew she wanted to, but the only time she'd ever been in a place where it might happen was during the six months she had been married to Owen.

"Here you go," Owen said as he set RJ in her arms.

The tiny little baby blinked sleepily, his dark lashes fanned out on his little red cheeks, and she felt her entire body melt. How amazing would it be to hold her own baby in her arms? With her child, she would never have to worry about coming in second, but until she found a man who thought she was the most important thing in his life she could never have a baby.

She was done with coming second.

Over the last two years, she'd hardened her heart a little. She still cared about others, would still do anything for any of her friends, still tried to see the best in people, but she wasn't as naïve or as open as she used to be. She'd learned the hard way that when you were too trusting people took advantage of you and she was sick of that happening.

"You look good holding a baby," Owen said softly, and she looked up to see him watching her with a smile on his face.

She had no idea what game he was playing, they were

divorced, they'd both moved on, for all she knew he was involved with someone else. What they'd had was over, and while she would take whatever protection or advice he and his team could offer, she wasn't going to be sucked back into another game, she wasn't going to be used again.

"He's a cutie," she said, pasting on a smile and passing RJ back to his daddy.

"I better take him back to his mommy, Abby is probably missing him," Spider said. "Thanks so much to all of you for being here for us."

His team waved off Spider's thanks, they were a close-knit group, and they were there for one another no matter what, no questions, no explanations. She liked that, wished she had a group of friends like that in her life.

She and Lavender had hung out most of the day here in the waiting room, popping in briefly to see Abby before her labor had progressed too far along, and she knew that Lavender and Night would give her a ride back to the club to get her car, but she needed some time alone. So while everyone was distracted, Evie slipped quietly away, hurrying down from the maternity ward and out into the night.

Thankfully she'd had her purse with her when she'd gone out of the club for fresh air, so she had her cell phone to call a cab and her credit cards to pay for it. Luck was on her side and someone was just climbing out of a cab as she walked outside. She hurried over to get in, gave the address, and then sunk back down against the seat.

It had been a long and exhausting twenty-four hours. She wanted to just go to bed and wake up and have all of this fixed, have it all be better, but she had a feeling that things were going to get a whole lot worse before they got any better.

She had a cartel after her.

Or at least she would as soon as they learned there was a witness to Miguel Perez committing murder.

How had she found herself in this mess?

She hadn't even wanted to go to the club, she was only there for her friend, but while Lacey had no doubt enjoyed a night of hot sex she'd been thrown into a nightmare that she may very well not survive.

Evie wasn't stupid, the cops and Owen and his team had told her just how vicious the Perez cartel was and how ruthlessly they would hunt her down as soon as they knew about her, there was a very good chance they would get their hands on her and make her wish for death before it came for her.

It wasn't until she got back to her house that she finally allowed herself to shed a tear. She'd held it together with the cops and the SEALs, they were all so strong and tough, and she hadn't wanted to break down in front of them. Now she was alone she could let go, let everything that was swirling around inside her come out. Evie had long ago learned that tears were cleansing, there was no use in bottling things up. It was so much better for her mental health to let it go. Cry it out, process it, and then put her efforts into moving forward.

Now moving forward included a shower and sleep. Her clothes still smelled from the hours in the dumpster, which had thankfully been empty when she climbed inside it, and she couldn't wait to get them off and wash away the horrible day.

She muddled through the shower, tossed her clothes into the washing machine, and then when she finally felt human again she crawled under the covers. She felt drained, empty, and another round of crying ensued.

Exhaustion tugged at her and Evie was just drifting off when she heard something.

Immediately she bolted up, her fingers curling into the

covers. Was she imagining things because she was on edge or was someone really inside her house?

Straining to hear through the quiet night, Evie was just about to lie back down, sure what she'd thought she had heard was just a product of her emotionally strung-out imagination, when she heard it again.

Someone was in her home.

She didn't second guess herself, didn't hesitate, just flew out of bed, threw on a pair of sweatpants and a hoodie over her sleep shorts and tank top, then shoved her feet into a pair of sneakers, grabbed her cell phone, and opened up her window. Her sweet little cottage was only one floor so she didn't have to worry about breaking a leg or worse as she dropped down from the second floor.

Knowing she didn't have time to hang around, as soon as her feet hit the ground she didn't even bother closing the window, the intruder would know as soon as he got into her bedroom she had been there and wasn't any longer so there was no point trying to trick him.

Instead, she ran.

Evie didn't look back, didn't slow down. She'd never been much of a runner but knowing it was run or die gave her legs strength they wouldn't usually have. She didn't even notice the burn in her side or the fact that she was wheezing loudly, out of breath but forcing herself to keep going. She certainly wasn't being quiet, but it was one in the morning, and there weren't really any people about.

She'd made it about five blocks when she heard a car coming. Of course it could be nothing, just someone out and about minding their own business, but because she knew one mistake was all it took to find herself in the cartel's hands, Evie threw herself into a bush in someone's front yard, shoving herself down underneath the branches, barely noticing as she got scratched up.

A car came slowly down the street, crawling along as though it was searching for someone.

Searching for her.

It had to be the cartel.

Tears streamed silently down her cheeks, and she pressed her hands to her mouth, afraid her ragged breathing would alert the driver to her presence.

Gripped by fear and panic, Evie lay there in the bush long after the car had disappeared down the street.

Why was this happening to her?

Exhausted and strung out, Evie knew she couldn't go back to her house, there would no doubt be someone watching it, she knew she was out of options. There was only one thing she could do, pulling out her phone she called for help.

* * *

1:16 A.M.

The chirping of his phone dragged him from sleep.

Fox rolled over and grabbed his cell from the night-stand. It wasn't unusual to be woken at any time with a call to go on a mission, but he really hoped that wasn't what this call was about. No way he wanted to leave Evie alone right now when they didn't have a handle on her situation yet. She'd slipped away from the hospital when no one was looking, and he wasn't pleased knowing she was alone and unprotected, but given their history he could hardly go storming over to her place and insist that she not leave his sight.

It was Shark's name on the screen, and that didn't make him feel any better. Evie had reached out to Shark last time, and there was every chance she had reached out to him again if something bad had happened.

"What's wrong?" he demanded as soon as he answered the call.

"Evie called. Someone broke into her house," Shark said with equal bluntness.

"Is she hurt?" He knew he should have gone over there and disregarded the fact that Evie wouldn't like it, but he'd been too caught up in not wanting to anger her to give himself a better chance at winning her back. Now he'd take angry because the alternative was dead and he wasn't losing her. He'd rather ruin his chances at a reunion than he would bury her. Living without her was a sacrifice he'd make in a heartbeat because she came first.

"Don't know, not there yet. She said she's not, said she heard someone in her house and went out the window, then ran and hid. She was near a gas station when she called. I didn't want her alone so I told her to go there and wait for me. I'm on my way to pick her up and then I'm taking her to the police station so she can report what happened. Meet us there."

"Already getting ready," he said as he got out of bed and rummaged around for clothes.

"I'll take care of her until you get there," Shark promised.

"Thanks, man."

"I'll text when I have her," Shark said before hanging up.

Fox was dressed and in the car when he got Shark's text, and he relaxed a little. Evie was safe for now, Shark wouldn't let anyone get to her, but he hated that she was still bypassing him to go to his team instead of coming to him.

That was stopping now.

If she needed something she should reach out to him, he was going to make that clear. Not that he planned to let her out of his sight after this. He was sticking to her like glue, and as soon as he spoke with his team he was reaching out to Eagle.

He arrived at the station first and parked his car, pacing out the front of the building while he waited for Shark and Evie. They arrived about ten minutes after he did, and Fox didn't hesitate, as soon as he saw Evie, he stalked toward her, taking in the scratches on her face, the dirt on her clothes, and the fear in her eyes. Wrapping his arms around her, he pulled her against him and held her tight. This wasn't supposed to happen. She should be safe here in her own community. He was the one who spent his life dancing with death, and yet he always survived while the women in his life didn't.

Well, he wasn't losing Evie like he'd lost Maya.

Whether she liked it or not, he was going to do whatever it took to keep her safe.

"Are you okay?" he asked. She hadn't pulled away from him, and she had put her arms around his waist, but she hadn't really relaxed into him. It drove Fox crazy that it was his own fault that she no longer trusted him.

"Yeah, I'm okay."

Placing his hands on her shoulders, he leaned down so they were eye to eye. "Next time you need help you call me. Not Shark, not anyone else on my team. Me. You call me. Got it?"

Evie's blue eyes widened and her mouth opened, no doubt to tell him where he could put his order, but then resignation flickered in her gaze, and she nodded. "Fine. Next time I'll call you, but let's hope that there isn't a next time."

"Amen," he muttered. "Come on, let's go and get this done so we can get you somewhere you can get some rest."

Taking Evie's hand—pleased when she accepted his comfort and support—he guided her up the steps and inside the station. As soon as they stepped through the doors two people walked toward them. One was an older man, probably in his fifties, who looked to be in great shape for his age, the other was a middle-aged woman with brown hair streaked with gray pulled back into a bun at the nape of her neck.

Evie stiffened when she saw them and edged a little closer to him. "Detective Coughlan, Detective Dannel," she greeted the cops that must have been the ones who interrogated her yesterday.

"Ms. Walter," the man said, nodding at her then shifting his gaze to Fox and Shark. "I'm Detective Coughlan, and you are?"

"We're Evie's friends," he replied.

"Military?" Detective Dannel asked.

"SEALs," Fox confirmed.

The two detectives exchanged looks but didn't comment further. "All right, Ms. Walter, let's go and you can tell us what happened."

Evie didn't let go of his hand as they followed the cops, and he threaded their fingers together, trying to let her know without words that he was here for her, that he had her back, that she didn't have anything to be worried about as long as he was around.

"You can wait out here while we interview Ms. Walter," Detective Dannel told them.

"Not happening. Where she goes, I go," Fox said, and Shark crossed his arms across his massive chest and fixed the two detectives with his best glower, the kind of look that froze fire.

Again, the cops exchanged looks but didn't stop them from following Evie into the room and flanking her when she took a seat on one side of the table.

"Floor is yours," Detective Coughlan said as he and his partner sat at the other side of the table.

"I don't know much, just that someone was in my house tonight. I heard him and climbed out the window then ran. I hid in some bushes when I heard a car coming, and it was going really slowly like the driver was looking for someone. I was scared, and I called Shark, he came and got me and said we should come here and report it. Do you think it's related to the cartel? Do they know about me already?"

"You have a leak," Fox said, glaring at the cops. Not only had they treated Evie like a criminal, upsetting her on top of what was already a traumatic ordeal, but they hadn't done their job in making sure she was safe and protected. He hadn't either, he'd thought that the cartel couldn't have known about Evie yet, but it was a mistake he didn't intend to repeat.

"Someone in the department is on Perez's payroll," Evie said, quickly figuring out what was going on. "It's the only way they could know about me this quickly. You said that they wouldn't know until you had Miguel in custody and his lawyers asked for what evidence you had against him. But someone broke into my house almost as soon as I got home, so they were watching it, waiting for me." Evie turned in her chair to look up at him. "How am I going to stay safe when I can't trust the cops?"

"You listen to me," he said fiercely, crouching before her and taking her cold hands in his. "You don't trust me anymore, I get that, you have doubts about me and my motives, but one thing you know without a shadow of a doubt is that I would do literally anything it took to make sure you were safe. Trust that, Evie." He lifted one hand and cupped her cheek, letting his fingers trace across her soft skin, caressing her temple, wishing he could pull her into his arms, kiss her and hold her and make it so she was never afraid again. "I let you down once, Evie, but I won't *ever* make that mistake again."

"I do trust you in this," she told him, her fingers curling around his and squeezing tightly. "But I'm scared. I don't trust them." She threw a quick look over her shoulder at the two detectives. "And you could be called up at any moment. When that happens, I'll be all alone facing a cartel."

"No," he said firmly. "You will never be alone. I would never leave you unprotected if I couldn't be there to watch over you myself." Fox turned to the detectives. "If you haven't already, send a forensics team to Evie's house. We're taking her out of here and will be making arrangements for her protection. You better find your mole because if she gets hurt I'll have your badges." With that, he tugged Evie to her feet, tucked her in between him and Shark, and led her out of the station. He might not trust those two detectives as far as he could throw them, but he and his team would do whatever it took to protect her from the Perez cartel.

\* \* \*

2:23 A.M.

Exhaustion was crashing over her in waves, and Evie sunk into the passenger seat of Owen's car. She'd wanted to go with Shark, it was why she'd called him in the first place since she just wasn't ready to deal with Owen yet, but he had insisted, and right about now she just wanted to take the road of least resistance.

She just wanted to find somewhere to lie down and get some sleep, but she didn't know where to go. She had her phone so she could use her credit card. Maybe she'd ask Owen to take her to a hotel, but she wasn't sure she would feel safe enough there to let go and get the rest she knew she needed. There was only so long she could last without getting proper rest, but Evie wasn't sure that she would feel safe enough anywhere to let go enough to sleep.

"We're here, honey," Owen announced.

"Here?" She looked out the window and saw they were parked outside the hospital. "What are we doing back here?"

"Easiest place for my team to meet up since Spider is here with Abby and RJ."

"Why do we need to meet with your team?"

"Because we need to figure out a plan on how we're going to keep you safe."

It was amping up her anxiety to know that Owen was truly afraid for her safety. With what she'd been told about the cartel, she knew his fears were well-founded. If the cartel got their hands on her, they wouldn't just kill her, they'd rape her first, maybe torture her, no doubt keep her for days, maybe even weeks before finishing her off.

If that was what they decided to do.

The Perez cartel was involved in human trafficking so there was always the possibility that they would decide to sell her when they were finished with her.

Evie shuddered at the thought.

"Hey," Owen said, and she realized he'd exited the car and come around to open her door for her. "We won't let them get you, okay?"

"Okay." Evie nodded her agreement. She *did* trust Owen and his team, even if things between her and her ex-husband were strained and awkward. Owen was a protector to his core, and he would do whatever it took to make sure the cartel didn't get to her, but she was worried about what was going to happen when he and his team got called out.

Shark joined them, and like they had when they'd been at the station, they flanked her on either side as they walked her inside, and that really drilled into her how worried they were. If they thought that the cartel was tailing them, that they might take a shot at her in a public place, even if it was the middle of the night the hospital was reasonably busy, then it meant that there was no way that Luis Perez was going to give up on taking her out. She could potentially get his son sent to prison for first-degree murder. He couldn't allow her to live.

"Hey, sweetheart," Spider said when they walked into the otherwise empty cafeteria where the rest of Owen's team was waiting for them. "I'm so sorry you got mixed up in this."

"Me too," Evie said, hugging Spider back. Besides Owen, she was probably closest to Spider just because he was married to Abby and she and Abby were such good friends. If they hadn't been about to have their first baby any day she would have reached out to him instead of Shark. "How's RJ?"

"He's perfect," Spider said, beaming with pride at the mention of his son. "Come sit down." Spider guided her to a chair and set a mug of coffee down in front of her.

"Catch us up," King said when everyone was seated.

"Evie was out at a club and went outside for fresh air, she saw a man in a suit and a man with knife tattoos on his temples, with a third man who was beaten and on the ground. The man in the suit shot him. Evie hid, was found by the cops who questioned her and told her that they believe she witnessed a hit by the Perez cartel. Tonight when she went home someone broke into her house, we have to assume that it was the cartel trying to take her out," Owen explained.

Spider swore, looking furious. "I wish we'd killed Luis Perez when we went to rescue Abby from Alex. That man knew she was there, allowed her to be kept prisoner, and since we never got a chance to question Alex we don't know if he was involved in what happened to her. She is far from over her ordeal, she's doing better, but she still has nightmares, she still has days where she struggles in large groups of people, she still sees her therapist regularly, when she hears about this she's going to freak."

"She doesn't have to hear about it," Night said. "No need to upset my sister by telling her."

"She's going to find out eventually," Chaos reminded them. "This problem isn't going anywhere anytime soon. Miguel is probably out of the country already, and they obviously already know about Evie. All they have to do is take her out, and the case against Miguel goes away. Luis Perez is ruthless, and there's no way he's letting his son go down. Sorry, Evie." Chaos shot her an apologetic look, but she waved it off. She'd already heard this from the cops and Owen and Shark.

"There is obviously a leak at the station because someone gave the cartel Evie's name and address. We can't trust her safety to them, so I'm going to have Evie come and stay with me," Owen announced.

Evie gaped at him in shock. "Yeah, that's not happening."

"You can't go back home," he reminded her. "And you can't go to your family even if I thought you wanted to."

"I'll stay in a hotel. The cartel won't try to go after me there, and I'll be safe when I'm at the hospital working as well," she protested. She was already dealing with this whole cartel mess, no way she could throw dealing with her ex-husband into the mix.

"I don't want to worry you more, but you won't be safe at a hotel," Owen said gently. "Luis Perez is wealthy, he has the resources to do whatever he wants, and he has a mole somewhere in the police department. He will track you to a hotel, we need to put you somewhere safe. Where could you be safer than with me?"

"But ... but ..." she stuttered, looking around at the other men at the table. Okay, she couldn't stay with Spider or Night since Lavender was pregnant and she wouldn't endanger her friend, but maybe she could stay with Shark, Chaos, or King. None of the men offered her any reprieve from Owen's plan, and she knew they weren't going to get involved in their team leader's relationship. "Well, what about your training? Even if I stayed with you while you're here you have PT every day."

"I can keep up my training at my place, I have a gym, and this isn't a long-term arrangement." Owen turned his attention to his team. "I'm going to call Eagle, get him and Prey on this. He doesn't do a lot of personal security, but I know he'll help us with this. And he has a lot of connections, what we really need to make sure Evie is safe is to eliminate the head of the snake. Luis."

"Who is Eagle?" Evie asked.

"Someone we used to serve with, he and his five siblings own a security firm, they do jobs for the government, hostage recovery, they consult and work with law enforcement agencies. Other than my team there's nobody I would trust your safety with more than Eagle and his company," Owen explained. "For now, I want you to stay with me. Let's give the cops a chance to find Miguel and bring him in, find whoever the leak is. I'll call Eagle and let him know the situation, then when we get called out we'll have one of his team take over your security. Bottom line, Evie, you and I have a history, and I'm not having you go through this alone."

She didn't know what to say to that.

There didn't seem to be any point in arguing about it, and what other choice did she have anyway? Owen's team weren't going to step in when Owen had obviously made up his mind, she couldn't trust the cops, she didn't have the skills to protect herself from a cartel, and she had no idea where to go to find a security firm to hire. Which meant that she could either be stubborn and refuse to let Owen help her on principle, or she could stay with him until he had a chance to work out something with this friend of his.

She could deal with spending a few days around Owen.

She *had* to deal with spending a few days around Owen.

"Evie?" Owen asked. "You said you trusted me to keep you safe, well this is how I'm going to do it."

"Okay," she agreed. "I'll come and stay with you, and I'll work with your friend Eagle when you bring him in."

"You don't have to sound so enthusiastic about it," Owen teased.

She huffed a chuckle. "You're right. You're putting yourself out to help me when you don't have to. All of you are. So thank you, I'm sorry I wasn't more grateful for the sacrifices you're making because I got myself stuck in this mess."

Owen's hand cupped her chin, making her meet his gaze. "Let's get one thing straight right now. This isn't a sacrifice, Evie. *You* are never a sacrifice. My team and I will protect you, and Eagle is the best. It might not feel like it right now, but one day this will all be just a bad dream."

He was right.

She had to hold onto that.

One day this would be over and then once again she would have to walk back out of Owen's life. It had nearly killed her last time, forced her to reevaluate her life and make some changes about how she allowed herself to be treated by others. Even though this was different than walking away from her marriage, she had a feeling it was going to be every bit as hard.

\* \* \*

5:32 A.M.

. . .

Miguel Perez pounded into the woman in his bed, emptying himself inside her as he came with a grunt.

The woman was barely moving, her face was shoved into the pillow, her arms spread out at her sides. He had her hips gripped in his hands, but he let go as he pulled out of her, letting her droop down so she lay awkwardly with her backside in the air. He slapped at it absently as he got off the bed and stretched, walking naked across the bedroom to the attached bathroom.

His phone was chirping incessantly, but he ignored it as he turned on the shower and stepped under the spray. It was probably just his father, and he wasn't in the mood to listen to anything he had to say.

How many times should he have to listen to his father tell him what a disappointment he was?

No matter how many times his father said it, it didn't change anything. He still had no interest in taking over the cartel. He didn't want to spend his days locked up in the compound because he was on so many hit lists from various world governments, rival cartels, and mercenaries out to make some cash. He just didn't care about all the intricacies involved in coordinating drug deals, weapons deals, and human trafficking deals.

The only thing he cared about was having fun.

He was only twenty-six, way too young to be training to take over one of the most feared cartels in the world. He was much more interested in getting his fill of women. His father had tried to arrange a marriage for him with some woman whose family ran some major trafficking ring and who owed his father, but Miguel had flat out refused.

No way was he limiting himself to one woman.

And even though the idea of cheating on a wife didn't faze him in the least, he wasn't interested in even putting in the energy it took to pretend to be interested in a woman. He wasn't going to be forced into providing an heir just because his father wasn't happy with him and how he chose to live his life.

The only thing he was grateful to his father's cartel for was the money. He could do whatever he wanted, he traveled the world, he slept his way through the female population, and he bought anything his heart desired.

A spoiled child, his father called him, and he wasn't wrong. He had been pampered and spoiled since he came out of the womb, and he wasn't giving that up for anyone, not even his father.

When he finished up in the shower, he toweled off then stalked back into the bedroom. It was early, but he was a night owl, he usually went to bed when the sun rose and slept the day away. His stomach rumbled, and he left the hooker on the bed where she looked like she was passed out from the drugs he'd shot her up with, and headed for the kitchen.

Miguel didn't bother to get dressed first, he was comfortable with his body, he worked out every day, followed a strict diet, and he preferred to walk around without clothes on in his home. The only people here to see him anyway were the staff and his father's men, the ones he insisted stay with him round the clock as a security detail.

It was insulting.

He was a black belt in Taekwondo, he was proficient with firearms, and he was an expert with a knife. The only way someone would even stand a chance at taking him out was with a rifle from a distance, striking without any warning.

"Sorry, to interrupt, sir, but your father is on the phone."

With an irritated growl, Miguel looked up from making his sandwich. "I'll talk to him later."

The man stood firm, not backing down. His father's men were well trained, their loyalty lay firmly at Luis Perez's feet,

JANE BLYTHE

not his. "I'm sorry, sir, but he says he's not taking no for an answer. He's been trying to contact you for the last twenty-four hours, and you aren't answering or returning his calls. He says you either speak with him on the phone now or we're to take you to him using whatever means necessary."

More annoyed than afraid at his father's threats, Miguel sighed dramatically and rolled his eyes. Okay, so that was childish, but he had already earned the reputation with his father and his father's men for being immature, more child than man. "Fine," he snapped, tossing the knife onto the counter and snatching the phone before stalking off to throw himself down on a couch in the living room. "What do you want?"

"Respect, chico," his father's stern voice came down the line. It was clear whatever he had to say he was angry. A lesser man would be afraid of the icy tone of Luis' voice, a smarter man would not provoke him.

Miguel was neither.

Instead, he infused as much scorn into his tone and said, "I'm not one of your minions, I'm your son, I don't answer to you."

"The only reason you're still alive is because you are my son," Luis snapped. "Even as my flesh and blood, you're toeing the line, hijo. Someone saw you."

"Saw me do what?" he asked, bored. He wanted to eat and then head back up to the bedroom and finish up with his hooker. He was good-looking and rich, he didn't have to pay for sex, but the thing about hookers was you offered to pay them whatever they asked for, and they would do things most other women wouldn't.

"Kill a man."

That had him straightening in his seat. That was impossible. The only one who had been there when he'd made that hit was the only man on his father's payroll who was loyal to him and not Luis. Antonio was the same age as Miguel, the son of Luis' right-hand man, the two had been best friends since childhood, and if there was one person in this world he trusted, it was Antonio. No way would his friend have turned him in, so how did his father even know about the hit?

The cartel didn't sanction it, he was doing his own thing as he always did. The man, Cameron Holt, had been a thorn in his side for long enough. Cameron was engaged to the one woman that Miguel couldn't seem to get out of his head. She was a socialite, a model, a stunning, tall blonde with beguiling green eyes, and she was hot, but no matter how many times he tried to pick her up she always rebuffed him.

No one rebuffed him.

He was Miguel Perez.

That man deserved to die, he was in the way, an obstacle between him and his goal of getting to Ellie Kennedy.

"No one was there except for Antonio," he snapped.

"Wrong," Luis said. "There was a woman there, she saw everything."

"So, take her out," he said, not understanding what the big deal was. If there was a witness to the murder then eliminate them. No witness no way to charge him with the crime.

"Do you think I'm a novice, chico?" Luis demanded. "She managed to slip away, and we haven't been able to get eyes on her again. She will be taken care of, that's not why I'm calling. I'm calling to tell you it's time to stop playing around, I've given you time to mature, but you're getting stupider by the day. Killing a man over some woman you don't even know? Foolish. I've grown tired of waiting, it is time for you to come home and start learning how to take over the empire I've built. That is not a request, hijo. As soon as this issue with the woman is resolved I am bringing you home. Until then, you are to stay at the beach house, you don't leave for any reason. The house isn't easily connectable to me so they won't be looking for you there, it will be easier to get you out of the country if you haven't been arrested. Let me make myself clear, Miguel, you leave that house, you get yourself arrested, you make yourself a liability to me and everything I've worked hard to build, and I will take you out even if you are my son."

With the threat delivered in a coldly serious voice, his father disconnected the call.

Furious about his father ordering him around and trying to control his life, Miguel tossed the phone across the room, satisfied when it hit the wall and shattered.

No one told him what to do.

No way was he going to Mexico and working with his father.

Maybe it was time someone knocked Luis Perez down a peg or two. What a coup it would be for it to be his own son to topple the empire feared around the world.

No longer hungry for food, Miguel stomped up the stairs to find the hooker groggily trying to climb off the bed and stumble toward the bathroom.

Miguel grabbed her, picked her up, and threw her onto the bed. In one swift thrust he buried himself inside her, growing harder at her cries of pain. Without mercy, he pounded into her over and over again until he found his release.

His father thought he was immature, pathetic, weak, but there was one thing Miguel had inherited from him that made him the perfect person to tear Luis Perez down; a complete lack of conscience.

\* \* \*

8:41 A.M.

. . .

"Here we go, let's get you inside, and you can finally get the rest you need," Fox said as he pulled into his garage.

Evie offered him a tight smile. There were dark smudges under her eyes, her hands trembled slightly, and she was sagging in her seat. She needed sleep, and he hoped that now that she was at his place she'd be able to relax enough to crash.

"You head on in, I'll grab the bags," he said as they both got out of the car. After they'd talked through everything with his team at the hospital, he had taken Evie shopping to buy some clothes and toiletries to hold her through the next few days. Since there was every chance her house was being watched, he hadn't wanted to risk taking her back there, but once they had a better idea of what the cartel was going to try he'd organize to have some of her things packed up and brought here.

For now, he just wanted her comfortable and safe.

Grabbing the shopping bags, he headed inside to find Evie hovering awkwardly in the middle of the living room. She had her arms wrapped around her stomach, and she was rocking ever so slightly. Fox knew she'd reached the end of her rope and that a crash was imminent and he longed to go to her, pull her into his arms and hold her, but he didn't think he would be welcome.

As far as Evie was concerned, he was helping her because of their past. She believed he cared about her but didn't believe that he loved her, and he honestly had no idea how to convince her she was wrong. Didn't mean he wasn't going to figure it out. He'd had two years to figure out exactly what his feelings for Evie were, but she didn't know that, which meant he had to somehow undo two years' worth of doubts.

"Make yourself at home," he said, hoping to set her at ease, as he put the bags on the table.

She nodded but looked around the open plan living space as though she had never seen it before. He saw her stiffen when her gaze fell on the painting of him at Maya's grave that she had painted after discovering his lies. He had kept the painting not just because it was stunning but also because it was a reminder of Evie. She was the sweetest woman, and he hadn't needed her assurances that she wasn't walking away out of hatred or anger, he knew she had walked away because he'd hurt her, made her feel less valuable like she was second place to Maya.

Fox hated that she had doubted his feelings once she learned the truth.

What he should have done was be honest with her as soon as he realized he was falling for her, then they could have dated for a while and built a solid foundation for a relationship that would last. Instead, he'd jumped in and not thought about the consequences, he'd known keeping Maya a secret was wrong, but he'd been afraid of losing Evie if she learned about his wife.

In the end, he had lost her anyway.

And now he had to figure out a way to undo the damage that he'd caused.

"I kept the painting as a reminder of how badly I hurt you," he said, walking up till he stood behind her, close enough that she could feel him but not touching her.

"Why?"

"Because it's my biggest regret," he answered honestly. "You're the sweetest, kindest, most generous woman I've ever met, and I hate that I hurt you, that I dimmed your bright light."

"I'm not the same woman I was when you knew me," Evie said, turning to face him. "What happened with you finally taught me that I needed to stop being so naïve. I had to harden my heart a little, not only see the good in people."

"I won't ever forgive myself for doing that to you." He tucked a stray curl behind her ear that had fallen loose from her ponytail. "Do you want to eat something or go take a shower and go to bed?" As much as he wanted to sit her down and discuss their past and what he wanted to be their future, Evie was wiped out and needed to sleep, what they had to talk about needed them both to be at their best, and right now, neither of them were.

"I'm not really hungry," she replied, a flash of hurt flaring in her eyes, obviously she had expected him to take that conversation in a different direction. And he would, but not when she was dead on her feet, and he was responsible for keeping her alive.

"Okay, then I'll show you to your room." It felt odd to be leading Evie through the house since they had lived here together. Now Evie was a guest, and if he wanted a chance at rekindling their relationship he had to play this just right, one wrong move and he'd push her away forever. "I'll put you in the room next to the master, that way I'll be close just in case anything goes wrong." As unlikely as it was that the cartel would get inside, especially with one of his team watching the house at all times, he had to think worst-case scenario just as he would with a mission. Only no mission he'd ever been on had had stakes this high. The life of the woman he loved was hanging in the balance which meant there was zero room for error.

"I thought you had that room set up as a home theater," Evie said.

"I renovated the basement last year, built a custom home theater down there as part of the renovations," he explained.

"Oh." The look on her face clearly communicated the

JANE BLYTHE

awkwardness she felt. "I guess a lot has changed since I moved out."

That was both true and untrue. He'd renovated the basement, but other than that, things were pretty much as she'd left them. "As you know the bathroom is just across the hall, the fridge and pantry are both well stocked, so if you wake up and you're hungry you can go make yourself something to eat. I want you to be comfortable here, Evie, I know things between us are weird—"

"Way beyond weird," she muttered, but some of the tension simmering between them eased.

"Okay, way beyond weird," he amended with a chuckle. "But I will keep you safe, and while you're here I want you to be comfortable. I don't want things to be weird between us, Evie."

"I don't know if I can be friends with you, Owen. I'm not sure I'm that strong," she admitted.

"Sweetheart, I don't want to be friends with you either." Leaving it at that, Fox took her face between his hands, kissed her forehead, and then set the bags of clothes on the floor. "Relax, take a bath if you need it, then get some sleep, your body needs it."

Walking away went against his instincts which were to hold her, comfort her, protect her even if the protection he was offering was merely an illusion, a Band-Aid, a momentary reprieve from the deep hole she had been tossed into. But he knew Evie wasn't ready to hear it yet. Words weren't going to convince her of his feelings, he was going to have to show her.

In the kitchen, he popped a couple of slices of bread into the toaster, he was tired, but he'd gone a lot longer than twenty-four hours without sleep, and he needed to call Eagle, apprise him of the situation and ask him to fly out here and set up a more permanent protection detail for Evie. While the bread was toasting, he made himself a cup of coffee. He used to drink instant, but Evie was a coffee connoisseur and she'd converted him. Now he only drank percolated coffee made from specialty beans he ground himself.

Since they hadn't done PT yesterday he was feeling edgy, he had extra energy that needed to be worked out, but he had to talk to Eagle and then explain the situation to his commander. Maybe once he and Evie had both gotten some sleep he'd take her down to his gym, and they could work out together. He wanted to run her through some self-defense moves so she at least stood a chance at protecting herself if the cartel managed to get their hands on her.

The toast popped up, and he buttered it then sat at the table and pulled up Eagle's number. Watching Maya waste away as she valiantly battled cancer had been one of the hardest things he'd ever had to do, wishing he could fight the battle for her but knowing he couldn't struck deep at his protector's heart. But somehow this was worse. Evie was in danger, and he hated that he had to reach out to someone else, put her safety in their hands, just because he trusted Eagle and Prey Security implicitly didn't change the fact that he wanted to be the one to save her. The one to fix this mess for her.

"Hello?"

"Eagle, it's Fox."

"Fox, good to hear from you. Although from your tone I'm guessing this isn't a social call."

"It's not. I have a situation with Evie."

"Evie? Your Evie?" Eagle knew all about the disastrous ending to his marriage, as did most of his friends, so he wasn't surprised to hear the shock in his old friend's voice.

"Yeah, my Evie. We have a situation, and I need your help."

# CHAPTER 6

April 3<sup>rd</sup>

6:07 A.M.

Evie yawned and rolled over to check the time on the clock on the nightstand. Just after six, so she'd slept another eight hours straight. She had collapsed into bed a little after nine yesterday morning and slept for eleven hours, waking around eight in the evening. Not hungry and wanting to avoid Owen at all costs, she had crept across the hall to the bathroom and run herself a hot bath. Two hours later and still not hungry, she'd come back to bed and immediately passed out.

Now she finally felt well rested again, her body had caught up the missed sleep of the previous two nights, and some of the anxiety of her situation had receded a little. It was still there, she knew she was in no way out of danger, nor would she be for probably a long time yet, but at least she knew she was safe here with Owen in the next room and one of his team watching the house. And from what she'd heard about Prey Security, there was no one who would do a better job at making sure the Perez cartel didn't get to her. So for now, although she might not like being in Owen's house, at least she didn't have to worry about someone breaking in and killing her while she was vulnerable in sleep.

Owen.

The man confused her.

He'd kept from her the fact that he had been married to a woman who looked a whole lot like her. The only reason to do that was because he had a reason to hide it. What other reason could there be other than that she was a poor replacement for the woman he really wanted?

Evie had heard so many times that she was too soft, too naïve, always looking for the best in everyone even when it was hard to find, but that didn't mean she was somehow impervious to pain. She'd cried herself to sleep more times than she could count as a kid because she knew her parents didn't love her as much as they loved her sister. And when they'd told her that it should have been her who died instead of her sister because what was she ever going to contribute to society, it had just about destroyed her.

Nothing had hurt more though than learning the man she loved completely was using her as a substitute for the woman he truly loved.

The proverbial straw that broke the camel's back, she had finally realized she had to toughen up a little or be used and walked over for the rest of her life.

But now she was stuck in Owen's house, forced to spend time with him when she'd rather be anywhere else, and he was saying sweet things like hurting her was his biggest regret, and telling her he didn't want to be friends with her then tenderly kissing on the forehead.

What did he want?

Why was he playing with her emotions like that?

She could never be Maya.

Annoyed with herself for even caring, Evie threw off the covers, pulled out a pair of jeans and a sweatshirt from the bags of clothes they'd bought yesterday morning, and then eased open her door. It was early, but Owen was usually up early, and even if he was still in bed he was such a light sleeper that the slightest sound would wake him up. She knew it was because of his training, because when he was on a mission he had to sleep when and where he could then be alert at a moment's notice, but right about now, she wished he didn't possess that skill.

When the hallway looked clear, Evie tiptoed to the top of the stairs and hurried down them. She hated this, having to creep through a house that she used to call her home, feeling so awkward and out of place that she almost would rather be back at her house even if she knew she'd be a sitting duck.

The downstairs was quiet, and she padded over to the kitchen but stopped short of making herself some breakfast. This wasn't her home, and she found that she couldn't just go through the pantry or the fridge to get herself something to eat. It felt wrong, impolite, she was a guest here, it was bad manners to go through somebody else's kitchen like she owned the place.

"You gonna stand there or get something to eat?"

Evie startled at the voice, managed to hold in the scream that bubbled up, but couldn't stop herself from spinning around and almost losing her balance.

Owen was there in a second, placing a steadying hand on her elbow. "Relax, sweetheart, you're safe here."

Yeah, but only physically. She couldn't think of a more

dangerous position she could have put her heart in. She wasn't over Owen, and her body clearly still reacted to his touch because right now there was heat between her legs that she hadn't felt since she and Owen had divorced.

It seemed that since her rape, Owen was the only man her body responded to. There'd been two others since the divorce, but neither had been anything special. The men hadn't been able to get her to come, and she'd been embarrassed, they'd been annoyed, and the relationships had been over. It was because she didn't love them, the only way she could get any pleasure from sex now was with a connection to the man she was with, and the only man she loved was Owen.

Yep.

Staying here definitely had disaster written all over it.

"Were you going to make yourself some breakfast?" Owen asked. His hand still cupped her elbow, and whether he was doing it on purpose or subconsciously, his thumb was brushing across the sensitive skin on the inside of her elbow.

A mini firework exploded inside her from the simple touch, and embarrassed, Evie quickly moved away, scuttling over to the other side of the kitchen. Why was she getting turned on from one little touch? Why did he have to have such control over her body? Why did he have to soothe her soul in a way that meant she could get past all the old hurts just because he loved her?

*But he doesn't love you*, she reminded herself.

She'd do well to remember that.

"I'm, umm, not hungry," she stammered, fixing her gaze on the floor and trying to figure out an escape route. She wasn't sure how long she'd be staying here, but it was unlikely she could avoid Owen the entire time. What she wanted was for things to at least be normal between them, like it had been when they'd just been friends, but she'd meant it when she said she wasn't strong enough to be friends with him again. She might have been working on hardening her heart, teaching herself to keep some emotional distance between herself and others, but she knew herself well enough to know that too long in Owen's company, and her walls would crumble.

Then she'd wind up hurt and alone again.

Owen frowned at her. "You haven't had anything since yesterday morning at the hospital cafeteria, you need to eat." He started for the pantry then stopped. "I don't want you to be uncomfortable while you're here. You can use anything that's here, eat anything you want, watch TV, use the Wi-Fi, whatever you want. And I can try to stay out of your way as much as possible if that will make it easier for you."

It would make it easier—marginally—but this was Owen's home, she could hardly ask him to stay in his room so things would be better for her. "I *am* uncomfortable here," she said sadly. Her eyes met his, and she pleaded with him for … she didn't even know. To love her like she loved him? To fix this problem so she could go home and work on forgetting him all over again? To make it like they'd never fallen in love so he could go back to being the best friend she'd ever had?

"I'm sorry, Evie, I'm so damn sorry for hurting you." There was so much pain, so much sadness, and even a tinge of desperation in his light brown eyes that she staggered backward.

"It's okay," she said quickly, dropping her gaze once again to the floor.

"It's not. Don't let me off the hook so easily. Make me work to earn your forgiveness and your trust again."

Her eyes jerked up at his words, but he had already turned and was pulling out a loaf of her favorite cinnamon raisin swirl bread. She knew he hated the stuff, he had a real aversion to dried fruits, so he must have gotten it for her. That was so sweet.

She frowned when he walked over to the high-end coffee maker, and then her mouth dropped open when he started grinding his own coffee beans. "You always used to drink instant coffee."

"I started drinking real coffee with you," he said, grinning at her over his shoulder.

"But I just assumed when I left you'd go back to drinking instant."

"Then you assumed wrong," he said, his easy smile never wavering. "You converted me."

When she looked closer, she saw that the grinder and coffee machine were both the ones she'd bought when they were married. He'd kept them. All she'd taken with her when she left were her clothes and personal belongings, everything else she hadn't cared about but instead of getting rid of the coffee maker he'd kept it, and obviously used it.

Her gaze scanned the kitchen, and she spotted the magnetic shopping list notepad on the fridge. It was a different one than she'd had but he obviously still used her system even though he'd complained about it at first. The silly dog magnet with the long dangly legs was still on the fridge too. It had been a running joke between them, he would twist the legs around in different ways and stick the little feet back onto the fridge, then she would undo it when she noticed so all four legs hung straight down. The gigantic bright yellow cookie jar she'd bought at an antique store still sat in a corner of the counter, and beside it sat the fruit bowl with brightly colored fruit painted on it.

He'd kept so many of the things that they'd bought together.

Why?

She was so confused.

But mostly she was confused about his statement that she make him work to earn her forgiveness and trust. Why did it matter? They weren't together, she could never be his former wife, and she could never stay with him knowing she was always going to be second place. As soon as this cartel matter was resolved they'd both go back to their lives.

So why did it matter?

And why did she care?

* * *

7:10 A.M.

Their first meal together back in this house had been every bit as awkward as Fox was expecting it to be.

Even without her outright admitting it, he'd known how awkward Evie felt being back here. She hadn't come down to eat anything last night even though he knew she'd been up and taken a bath, and this morning she had tried to sneak down without alerting him. Of course that was ridiculous, he was trained to wake at the slightest of noises, and he'd heard her the second she climbed out of bed. Throwing on sweatpants and a t-shirt, he'd headed downstairs and just about scared her to death when he'd found her standing in the kitchen looking lost and unsure of herself.

He wanted so badly to wipe that look off her face.

He wanted her to feel safe here, relaxed and comfortable, but he knew that was asking a lot given this was the home they used to share together and how their marriage had ended.

She'd been shocked when he'd told her to make him work to earn her trust back, and he knew she wanted to ask him what he meant, but other than answering any direct questions he'd asked, she'd been quiet throughout breakfast. Her eyes had been constantly on the move though, roving the room and noticing every single thing that she'd left behind that he'd kept. The thought of boxing her things up and getting rid of them never even crossed his mind. Evie was a part of him just like Maya was and he would never try to—or want to—erase her presence from his home or his life.

Every time she spotted something her gaze would whip around to him, and she'd study him as though he were an equation she was struggling to figure out. He'd be happy to explain it to her, but she had to be the one to ask. She had to be willing to listen to him and really hear him, otherwise, he was only going to push her further away. Knowing her, she'd think he was telling her he loved her and wanted her back just as a way to try to keep her close and keep her safe from the cartel when that couldn't be further from the truth.

"I've got a surprise for you," he told her as he picked up their empty plates and stacked them in the dishwasher.

"A surprise?" Evie asked, sounding hesitant and borderline suspicious.

"Yep," he said cheerfully. "And trust me you're going to love it."

"Okay." Still looking doubtful, she stood up, pushed her chair in, and then followed him to the door that led to the basement steps.

Switching on the light, he led the way downstairs and into the large space that had taken over a year to fully renovate. Evie gasped when she saw it. Over to one side was a large home gym, fitted out with more equipment than a lot of public gyms. There was a pool table, an air hockey table, a foosball table, and a couple of arcade games. A large screen TV was on one wall, a couple of couches positioned around it. There was a kitchenette well stocked with drinks and snacks for when he had his team over to hang out. There were also two doors, one led to the home theater with comfortable chairs, better than those in a theater, and a huge screen. He'd also bought a popcorn machine, snow cone maker, ice cream maker, pretzel maker, and a pizza oven.

But it was what was through the second door that he wanted to show her.

"Wow, this is amazing," Evie said as she spun in a slow circle taking everything in.

"Come see the best part." Because he couldn't resist, he rested his hand on the small of her back, noting the way she immediately stiffened and sucked in a breath, and knew she wasn't unaffected by his touch. Pleased by that revelation, he guided her across the room and through the other door.

"Oh, you did it, you put in a pool," she gushed as she stepped into the specially designed space. The pool was only about a quarter the size of an Olympic pool but still big enough to swim laps. He'd extended the basement specifically to put it in, and had a special roof installed that could be retracted, opening the pool up so you could enjoy a beautiful summer's day while also making the space usable in the wintertime.

"Yep." The smile on her face as she looked at the water sparkling as the spring sunshine streamed through the glass ceiling was exactly why he'd spent the exorbitant amount of cash it had taken to put the pool in. He was a SEAL so it went without saying that he loved being in the water, but Evie loved it every bit as much. In the early days after her assault when she'd struggled to leave her apartment, he used to take her to the pool, and they'd swim laps side by side. Being able to do something on autopilot that wore out her body and allowed her mind to check out had really helped her, and when she'd moved in he'd always wanted to put in a pool for her.

"Oh." Evie's smile dipped.

"What's wrong?"

"I don't have a swimsuit so I can't go swimming."

Fox just nodded at a white box tied with red ribbon sitting on one of the lounges around the pool.

Evie arched a brow but walked over and picked up the box, opening it to find a brand new one-piece bathing suit. He'd wanted to get her a bikini but thought that might be a little inappropriate given their history, so he'd gone with this instead.

"You really thought of everything, didn't you?" When she looked up at him, tears shimmered in her big blue eyes. "Why? Why are you doing this? I know we have history, and it's one thing to let me stay here, but why do these little things like have my favorite toast and a swimsuit ready to go swimming?"

"Because you're important to me," he said simply. "Now go change, there's a changing room through there." He pointed to a door at the end of the pool room. "I'll throw on some board shorts and swim laps with you. Just like old times."

"Yeah, just like old times," Evie echoed, a thoughtful look on her face.

While Evie went to change, he grabbed the board shorts he'd left out yesterday while Evie was sleeping, intending to bring her in here to swim as soon as her body had recharged. By the time he was ready to dive into the pool, Evie had come out of the change room with a towel wrapped around her. She stood awkwardly halfway between the change room and the pool as though she was half debating how good a plan this was and bailing and throwing her clothes back on and retreating to her room.

"I've seen you naked a time or two before, sweetheart, we were married," Fox teased. "I think I can handle you in a bathing suit."

Evie's cheeks turned pink, but she nodded and slowly unwound the towel, folding it up and setting it on a chair. Fox had to school his features so he didn't react, didn't let on just how amazingly stunning he thought she was because if Evie knew how badly he wanted to tangle his fingers in her curls and kiss her senseless, then rip that swimsuit off and make love to her, it would have her running for the hills.

"You going to get in or just stand there?" he asked with a teasing smile.

She looked over at him, her eyes roving his naked chest, and her cheeks turned a brighter shade of pink. Good to know she found him every bit as appealing to ogle as he found her. Her hands smoothed across her stomach and down her legs as though she found herself lacking in comparison to him.

He wasn't having that.

"Evie." He waited until she met his gaze. "You are without a doubt the single most beautiful creature on the face of the earth. I lie awake at night, hard as a rock, berating myself for hurting you and pushing you away instead of holding you close because if I had, I'd have you in my arms and be able to kiss you, touch you, and make love to you. Never think for one moment that I'm not insanely attracted to you."

With that, he dived into the water, staying under until he reached the other end of the pool, then settling into a smooth, easy freestyle stroke that he knew Evie would be able to match. A moment later he heard a splash, and then Evie's little body settled in beside his as they swam laps of the pool. He'd rather burn off steam between the sheets, but swimming together was one of the ways they had bonded when they'd first met, and he hoped it might help regain what he had so carelessly ruined.

* * *

8:23 A.M.

Her arms and legs were trembling with exhaustion, her chest starting to burn, but Evie wasn't ready to stop swimming yet. There was something soothing about gliding through the water. She'd been swimming since she was two, she'd never been fast enough to win races, but she had a smooth, easy stroke, and rather than compete in swim meets she'd just used it as a way to stay in shape and to decompress and relax.

When she and Owen had been together, they'd discussed the possibility of putting in a pool. Since she loved to swim and Owen was a SEAL, it had seemed like something they could enjoy together. That he had put in the pool after they had divorced was bittersweet.

The more she spent time with him the more his behavior confused her. He said such nice things about her, and it was almost like … maybe he wanted to get back together?

But that was crazy.

Right?

Owen was the reason they had gotten divorced. His secrets had eroded any trust she had in him, and how could you stay married when there was no foundation for the relationship?

Maybe he was being so nice just to make sure he could keep her close and therefore safe while a cartel was after her?

Shoving away thoughts of Owen, Evie focused on blanking her mind, letting the simple kicking of her feet and movement of her arms lull her into a peaceful zone where she just existed. Swimming had been a lifesaver after her assault. She'd felt alone and hadn't wanted to rely too heavily on Owen who was new to her life.

She went another few laps before her arms and legs started to feel like they weighed a hundred pounds each. She pushed through, not ready to go back to real life yet. With the water around her, nothing to do but swim, she could almost forget that she was temporarily living in her ex-husband's house, that a cartel wanted her dead, that she had seen someone die.

Ruthlessly she pushed herself harder, willing her shaking limbs to keep moving. Her kicking got bigger, her stroke more clumsy, she had to take a breath with almost every turn of her arms, and she knew it was time to call it quits but couldn't seem to make herself stop.

Strong arms closed around her, pulling her upright. "That's enough, fairy, you're going to hurt yourself if you keep going."

Evie stared at Owen. He'd called her fairy. She'd laughed the first time he'd called her that, thought it was a silly nick-name, but he'd told her how her small stature, wild blonde curls, bubbly personality, and constant need to look out for others made him think of a sweet little fairy. The name had grown on her, but she didn't want to hear it fall from his lips now. He'd taken the person she was and done what nobody else had been able to. Not her parents, not her past boyfriends, not even her rapist, it hadn't been them it had been Owen who finally crushed her.

She fought against his hold. She didn't want him touching her, he'd lost that right when he decided not to tell her about Maya. Time had dulled the pain of his betrayal but being here with him now made it all come rushing back. Evie struggled harder, but Owen just held her, taking her weight, and swam them to one end of the pool where he sat on the steps and pulled her into his lap.

"It'll be all right, Evie," he said, holding her and rocking her slightly. "I'll find a way to fix this, I promise."

She didn't know if he was promising to fix her current problem or their relationship, and she didn't want to ask.

Didn't want to shatter the illusion that he meant he wanted to fix them. There wasn't a them, she knew that, even knew that there never could be, but she longed to think there could be.

Giving up fighting against Owen, he was too strong, and there was no way she could get out of his hold anyway, she sagged against him, suddenly completely spent. She felt exhausted down to her very marrow. It wasn't just because of the murder she'd witnessed, it was everything, her entire life. She was tired of looking for the bright side, sometimes there just wasn't one. Maybe that was something she had to learn.

"I hate seeing you like this, beaten down, that's not you, Evie." Owen turned her sideways so he could tuck her head under his chin, one of his hands rubbing circles on her back.

"Maybe I just accepted that the world isn't always the place I wish it was," she said softly.

"No." He said it so forcefully that she straightened abruptly, surprised to see fire flaring in his brown eyes. "The world needs people like you. It needs people that look for the good, that think of others, that truly care. You will get through this. I know you, I've seen you at your lowest, I saw you fight to make it through what happened to you. You can do this, Evie. I believe in you, just don't give up. Promise me you won't."

The sincerity in his words shook her. He seemed to care so deeply. Evie nodded and made herself smile. If you didn't feel like smiling you did it anyway, and sooner or later, it became real rather than forced, that had always been her outlook. "You're right, I can't give up. No matter what, no matter how I'm feeling or how hard it is to see a way out, I have to keep fighting, keep searching."

"You can do this," he said again, like the more he said it, the more it was true.

"I can," she agreed. If she could survive life with her

parents and being raped, then she could certainly survive this. And sure, it was awkward here with Owen, but at least she was alive, she had got away from the man who broke into her house, and she had an entire team of SEALs plus a security firm willing to commit to keeping her alive. She had a lot to be thankful for, and it was time she started focusing on that rather than the negatives in her life.

"I'm proud of you, Evie."

Maybe they shouldn't, but Owen's words warmed her. "Do you think you could teach me some self-defense?" Back when they'd been friends he and his team had run her through the basics, but that was three years ago now, and she'd become complacent, gone back to forgetting there were evil people in the world. She definitely needed a refresher course now that her life was on the line. While she might prefer one of the other guys to work with her so things wouldn't be awkward, she couldn't spend her whole life worrying about it. So she and Owen had gotten divorced, and maybe she wasn't strong enough to be his friend, but they were stuck together, and she trusted him not to go easy on her and help her learn what she had to learn.

Owen grinned at her then scooped her up and walked out of the pool, setting her on her feet but keeping an arm loosely around her waist. "Great minds think alike. I was thinking when I brought you here yesterday that I should run you through some self-defense training, brush up on what you already know, make sure that you feel comfortable defending yourself if it comes down to it."

"We were often on the same page," she said wistfully, wishing they had been on the same page when it came to what was important, but she shrugged off the sadness.

"We are. Why don't you go up, shower, get into something comfortable, and then meet me back down here in the gym."

"Okay. I'll meet you down here in thirty minutes."

"Thirty minutes?" Owen grimaced. "If you can take a shower and be back down here in thirty minutes, then I'll buy you that gigantic six-foot tall teddy bear you were always mooning over."

Evie laughed, she did have a bit of a penchant for getting lost in the shower and spending way more time in there than she should. "I wasn't *mooning* over it, I just thought it was cute, and it would be a great addition to my collection." Evie owned almost three hundred teddy bears. A lot of them were from places she had vacationed, she had some from some of the most well-known cities in the world, and others were gifts from birthdays, graduations, and anniversaries.

"It would be a great addition to your collection," Owen agreed.

Her eyes grew wide when she realized he was serious. "You aren't joking, are you?"

"Nope," he said, smiling at her. "So you want that bear you'd better hurry. Your thirty minutes start now." He swatted playfully at her backside, and she squeaked and took off upstairs, she'd have to hurry if she wanted to be done in thirty minutes. All thoughts of exhaustion were gone, the black cloud that had been gathering above her had vanished, and she knew she could get through this because there wasn't really any other option.

One thing she had long ago learned was that hard times were a part of life. You couldn't go around them, you couldn't go under them or over them, you had to go through them, and you could do it complaining the whole time or you could make the best of things. She'd always chosen to work through the hard times while making the best of things. This time shouldn't be any different. She might even get the teddy bear of her dreams out of it. It wasn't as good as getting the *man* of her dreams, but still pretty cool.

# CHAPTER 7

April 4<sup>th</sup>

12:39 P.M.

Fox swung at Evie, who ducked and swiped with her leg, just as he'd taught her. She caught him as he was moving and effectively overbalanced him, sending him tumbling to the floor where he landed flat on his back.

Evie darted up and clapped her hands delightedly as she bounced from foot to foot above him. "I did it," she squealed. "And it worked. I actually made you fall over. *You*. A Navy SEAL, if I can knock you down then maybe I really do stand a chance at getting away if something happens."

He smiled up at her, pleased not only with her confidence but that she was working hard to learn what he was teaching her and was going all out to make it work. He obviously wasn't going one hundred percent, there were dozens of ways he could incapacitate or kill a grown man with his bare hands, let alone a small woman, but he also wasn't going easy on her, and she had managed to take him down.

"I told you if you worked hard you'd be able to do it," he told her.

She held out her hand to him and even though he was more likely to pull her over than her be able to help him up, he loved the gesture, and he clasped her hand but used his own momentum to stand. As he did, he tugged gently on her hand to bring her closer, then curled an arm around her waist. Her hands planted against his pecs and she looked up at him uncertainly like she wasn't sure that what she was feeling simmering between them was real.

But it was.

They'd worked on self-defense training for a couple of hours yesterday morning before breaking for lunch. He'd called Eagle again, and given Evie the chance to talk to him since the man and his company would be responsible for her security, then they'd spent a few more hours running self-defense moves. Although they had both been focused on what he was teaching her—they were in too serious of a situation to not be—he couldn't deny that he felt a spark ignite every time he touched her.

"Can we try it again?" Evie asked.

"We can, but first we need to break for lunch. We've been going at this for three hours now. You need a break and to refuel."

"Three hours?" Her eyes went wide. "It feels like we couldn't have possibly been doing this for more than an hour tops. You made this fun and interesting, you pushed me hard but not hard enough to make me feel like I'm too small to ever do anything, so thank you. I remember you made me feel confident in my ability to defend myself when you trained me after my assault too, you're a good teacher."

Fox cupped her cheek in his hand, his other arm still anchoring Evie against him. "I'm pretty sure you taught me a whole hell of a lot more than I could ever teach you." He'd intended to wait until Eagle was here and they had her long-term security in place as well as a possible plan to permanently eliminate Luis Perez as a threat before he sat her down to discuss them, but his gut said to do it now.

Apparently, the universe had other ideas.

His phone rang, and since it was the ringtone associated with the members of his team, he knew he had to answer. Leaning down, he kissed the tip of Evie's nose, drawing a startled indrawn breath from her, then released her. "Go shower then we'll have lunch and relax for a few hours before we come back at it. I don't want you to pull a muscle or injure yourself by over-extending yourself doing too much too quickly."

Evie looked at him hesitantly, her brows drawn together in confusion, but nodded and hurried up the stairs.

"What's up?" he asked as he answered his phone.

"There was a fire at Evie's house," Chaos announced without preamble.

Fox cursed under his breath. "How bad?"

"Fire isn't out yet, but from what I heard whoever started it used an accelerant, there isn't going to be anything left. King and I are on our way there, we'll let you know more when we get there. Shark is still on guard outside your place."

Helpless rage washed over him. Evie didn't deserve this, she'd just been in the wrong place at the wrong time, and now she'd lost everything. Yeah, she could always buy a new house and new furniture and clothes, but there would be things in there that were irreplaceable, mementos and keepsakes from the special people and moments in her life that were now going up in flames. It wasn't fair, Evie was so sweet, a ray of sunshine for anyone she came into contact with, and yet bad things kept happening to her. From her parents to her old boyfriends, to being raped, to what he'd done to her, and now this.

"She's going to want to go and see for herself," Fox said.

"It could be a trap," Chaos warned.

"I know, but I also have to balance her mental wellbeing with her physical safety."

"Try to convince her to stay at your place, but if she needs to come we'll make it work."

"Thanks, man. I better go tell her."

"Good luck."

Yeah, good luck, Fox thought as he disconnected the call and trudged up the stairs. His feet felt weighed down as he went in search of Evie. He knew she was strong enough to get through this, every time life knocked her down she found a way to scramble back up, but it took a toll on her. There was a wariness about her that hadn't been there when they'd been together. She'd learned how to dial back her natural openness, life had taught her over and over again that it didn't matter how nice she was, how caring, how much she did for others, the bad things were going to keep coming at her. He hated to see his sweet little fairy hurting, especially when it was something he couldn't fix. He could keep her alive, physically protect her from the Perez cartel, but he couldn't bring back her belongings, and he couldn't make this better.

Upstairs he heard the shower in the family bathroom running, and he paused to draw in a breath. He'd much rather face an army of insurgents outmanned and outgunned than he would go in there and cause pain to the woman he loved and adored.

"Evie?" he called out, knocking and opening the door.

"What are you doing in here?" she squealed, clutching the shower curtain close as she peeked around it.

"Turn the shower off, honey, and get dressed, I have something I have to tell you."

"What's wrong?" she asked, quickly picking up on his demeanor.

"Get dressed," he said. He wasn't having this conversation with her naked in the shower.

She looked like she was about to argue but then nodded and ducked back behind the shower curtain and the water turned off.

"I'll meet you in the kitchen," he said and retreated to give her space to get herself together before she joined him.

In the kitchen, he dragged his hands through his short dark hair. This was a nightmare that just kept getting worse. He hadn't expected the cartel to give up, he knew that Evie was a problem they couldn't allow to stay alive, but he hadn't expected them to take out her house. He'd thought they would try to track her down and then either kidnap her or kill her on sight. Instead, they were trying to destabilize her world, make her more vulnerable, now she had no belongings, no home to go to. She was left dangling alone.

Only she wasn't alone. She had an entire team of SEALs and the best security firm in the world at her back.

"Owen, what's wrong?" Evie's worried voice asked behind him as she came galloping down the stairs.

"Come and sit." He pulled out a chair, but she shook her head.

"Just say it," she begged.

Since there was no way to sugarcoat it, no way to make it better by saying the words gently, Fox nodded. "The phone call was from Chaos. I'm sorry, Evie, but your house is on fire."

She stared at him blankly as though his words hadn't penetrated. "My house ... what?"

"It's on fire. I'm so sorry, Evie." Impotence raged inside him, and he had to curl his hands into fists so he didn't slam one through the nearest wall. No one deserved this, but Evie even less so, she was everything good in the world, and he was afraid this would destroy her.

"H-how bad?" she asked, tremors rippling through her body.

"Chaos said it's bad, that you'll probably lose everything."

The shaking intensified and her knees buckled. Fox got to her before she hit the floor and dragged her close, scooping her up into his arms and cradling her against his chest. She pressed her face against his neck and he felt her tears against his skin.

"I'm so sorry, sweetheart. What do you need from me?"

Her arms curled around his neck, and she burrowed closer. "Just hold me," she whispered through her tears.

That he could do. "Always, honey, I'll always be here to hold you."

* * *

1:30 P.M.

Owen stood in his kitchen holding her in his arms as she felt like her entire world was spinning further out of control.

She'd lost everything, all she had left was her life.

Was she going to lose that too?

Evie pressed closer against Owen, attempting to absorb his heat. She knew seeking comfort from him wasn't a good idea, he wasn't going to be a part of her future. When this

87

situation was resolved, they would go back to their lives, but right now she was too lost to care.

She had no one else.

Her relationship with her parents was nothing more than strangers being polite with one another over dinner once a month and Thanksgiving and Christmas. She had friends at the hospital who she would go out with, and she was friends with Owen's teammates' women Abby and Lavender, but she couldn't take her problems to any of their doors.

Which left her alone blowing in the wind with nothing to anchor her to earth.

It was a horrible feeling, and she wanted it to go away.

"Deep breaths, sweetheart," Owen's voice rumbled through his chest, and Evie realized she was sucking in air at an alarming rate.

She was hyperventilating.

The more she tried to calm her breathing, the harder it seemed to be to get air into her lungs.

Panic flooded her system, and black dots began to dance in front of her.

"It's okay, Evie, you're okay, you can do this. Breathe with me. In and out, in and out." Owen coached her, and she latched on to his steady presence, allowing it to guide her through the fog of loss and fear, and out the other side.

"I'm okay," she murmured a few minutes later when she could breathe again. "Thank you."

"Don't thank me for being here for you," he rebuked, then leaned down and pressed the lightest of kisses to her lips.

"I want to go and see my house," she announced.

"I don't think that's a good idea." Owen set her on her feet but didn't let go of her, keeping an arm around her waist.

Evie planted her hands on his chest. "Let me rephrase. I *need* to go and see my house. I have to see for myself how bad it is."

"It could be a trap, a way to get you out in the open so they can take you out," he warned.

"I won't go alone."

"Damn right," Owen said fiercely. "I'll take you, Shark will come with us, and Chaos and King will meet us there."

"Thank you." She wrapped her arms around Owen and hugged him hard, grateful that he understood that she needed to see the fire to begin processing it. She'd always been that way, it was like her mind could only accept what she could see with her own two eyes.

"You're welcome." He kissed the top of her head and held her until she felt composed enough to go outside and see Shark. "You good to go?"

"Yeah." She just wanted to go and get it over and done with then come back here to this little bubble of safety Owen had managed to create for her. She'd thought it would be weird being back here, sleeping in the guest room, and showering in the family bathroom, and it had been, but she'd also felt protected here, and Owen had been going out of his way to make her feel welcome.

"Grab a coat, it's chilly today. I'll just go up and change, and we'll go in Shark's car."

While Owen went to change, Evie slipped on a coat over her blue sweater and shoved her feet into a pair of converse sneakers. Then she grabbed her purse and waited by the door. Owen returned two minutes later in jeans and a sweater and immediately took her hand as he led her outside.

The drive to her house was quiet and tense, she didn't need either of the guys to tell her that the cartel had set her house on fire. They were trying to destroy her, chip away at her foundation to make her an easier target. She was so glad that her ex-husband had stepped up to help her and she regretted that she hadn't reached out to him directly when she first landed in this mess. She'd thought it would be too awkward and she was still too hurt, but the last couple of days had erased most of the hurt, and while she didn't completely trust him when it came to their relationship, it was nice to have him back in her life even if it was temporary.

When Shark turned into her street, she saw the fire trucks and the police cars and the flames and smoke, and reality settled heavily over her.

This was really happening.

Her house had really been set on fire.

If she hadn't reached out to Owen's team then she probably would have been in it at the time.

A shudder rippled through her and Owen immediately enfolded her in an embrace. "I know how hard this is, Evie. If you change your mind we can turn around and go straight back to my place."

Evie allowed herself to lean against him for just a moment, let herself pretend that things were different, and then she straightened and reached for the door handle. "I can do this. I can't explain … I just need to see."

"It's okay, you don't need to explain," Owen told her. "Wait till Shark comes round and opens your door. If anyone is here we don't want to make it easy for them to take a shot at you."

She scanned the chaos of the street fearfully. "You really think they would try to shoot me here?"

"Probably not. I think it's more likely they want to make sure they can interrogate you before they kill you, so they're looking at a situation where they can abduct you. They can't do that here. Still better safe than sorry," Owen said.

King and Chaos appeared outside the car and when Shark opened her door, the three of them surrounded her. Owen got out and stood behind her, effectively blocking any attempts to take her out.

Unfortunately, they couldn't protect her from the pain of seeing her house engulfed in flames.

Nothing was going to survive, that much was clear. The fire was raging even with the firefighters working hard to put it out. Everything she owned was gone. She could always buy another house, and more furniture and linens and things, but there was no way she could replace the mementos of her life. Things from her childhood, jewelry she had inherited from her grandparents that had been in her family for generations—her parents would no doubt blame her for that loss—and little things she'd kept from her marriage to Owen.

Gone now.

All of them.

She sagged backward without even realizing it, but Owen was there to hold her, offering his support not with words but with the way his body seemed to curl around her. The way he tucked her head underneath his chin and sporadically touched a kiss to the top of her head or to her temple.

Evie barely noticed when Shark's phone rang, she was mesmerized—almost hypnotized—by the dancing flames, watching with an almost morbid dedication as they destroyed everything in this world that she owned other than the few clothes she'd bought when she moved into Owen's place.

She felt rather than saw the change in demeanor of the man on her left and managed to drag her gaze away from the fire to look at Shark, whose own gaze was fixed on Owen.

"I'm so sorry, man," Shark said, sympathy replacing his usual calm blank expression.

"What?" Owen asked.

"Somehow the cartel must have found out about you and that Evie was staying with you. I don't know if they knew we were here or if they thought you two were still at your house and it was a good time to strike while we were distracted with this, but your house is on fire too," Shark said.

What?

The cartel had destroyed not only her home but Owen's too?

That was the house that Owen had shared with Maya. He'd have all of her things there, all he had left of the woman he loved. And now it was all gone—because of her.

Horror ripped through, and she jerked herself out of Owen's arms and staggered away, needing to get away from the crushing guilt she felt. Her stuff could mostly be replaced, and even what couldn't it wasn't like it belonged to someone who was dead, only the jewelry that had belonged to the grandparents she had never met, and that wasn't the same thing at all.

Owen reached for her, his expression dark, but she stumbled backward, almost losing her balance. King grabbed her elbow and steadied her, but she quickly yanked herself free from his hold. Tears were burning her eyes, and she wrapped her arms around herself, icy cold now as shock descended.

She spun around in a slow circle, desperately seeking a safe harbor that didn't exist. All she saw were flames, people pointlessly trying to put them out, and four sets of angry eyes from the only people she'd thought she had on her side.

But Owen's team's loyalty was to him.

And because he'd tried to help her, he had lost all he had left of his wife.

Evie had never felt as alone in her life—and loneliness wasn't anything new to her—as she did in this moment with her house burning behind her and a cold, dark expression on the face of the man she had loved. The man she had destroyed. The man who now hated her guts.

# CHAPTER 8

April 5<sup>th</sup>

12:22 A.M.

"All right, Eagle, thanks. Tonight I'll check into a hotel with the credit card you gave us so Evie can rest, and then we'll head out to the cabin you arranged for us," Fox said to the dark-haired man on the computer screen.

"I'm organizing two of my guys to come and work security for her, and we'll find a more permanent place to keep her, but it will be a couple of days before they can get there," Eagle said. "I also have something in the works to solve our problem permanently."

Fox hoped whatever black ops mission Eagle was planning was set to happen soon because the reality was that as long as Luis Perez was alive, Evie was going to be in danger. Miguel getting arrested, even found guilty and imprisoned,

JANE BLYTHE

didn't necessarily mean the threat would be gone. Luis could still want to seek revenge against Evie, which meant that she would most likely be looking at witness protection. Being given a new name and sent away somewhere meant that any chance he had at winning her back would be gone.

For good.

The worst kind of closure when closure was the last thing he wanted.

"Keep us updated," he said to Eagle, who nodded once, and then the screen went black as he disconnected the call. "This better work," he muttered to his team, who had gathered at Shark's apartment after they'd spoken with the cops and visited both fire scenes.

His gaze moved over to Evie, who was fast asleep. She had been quiet and withdrawn, barely speaking to any of them, and while they had gathered around the table, Evie had placed herself in an armchair in the far corner and not looked their way once. He was worried about her. He knew she was on emotional overload, the last few days had been beyond rough, and she was struggling to get her feet beneath her, but he wanted her to come to him.

It was unfair because he was the one who had ruined what they had, but he had been married to Evie, and he still loved her, still wanted her, and was wishing that he had fought for her instead of giving her the space she said she wanted. How different would things have turned out if he hadn't given up on them? On her?

"I better wake her and get her to the hotel," he said, standing and stretching his back.

"You're welcome to stay tonight," Shark offered.

"If they know about me then they know about you guys, and if they think Evie is here I wouldn't put it past them to set the building on fire," he said. "I think it's safer if we check into the hotel, they won't be able to track us there, and then

94

once Evie gets some sleep we'll be heading out to the safe house."

"You let us know if you need anything," Chaos said.

"I will," Fox promised. And he would, but he was hoping for a couple of days alone with Evie before Eagle's team came in to take over her protection. He crossed the room and crouched in front of Evie, gently placing a hand on her knee. "Wake up, honey," he said softly as he brushed a lock of hair off her cheek.

Evie startled awake, her fearful gaze scanning the room before settling on him. Immediately she shuttered her eyes and seemed to shrink away from him even though she physically didn't move.

"We're going to go to a hotel for the night, well, the rest of the night," he amended.

She nodded stiffly and got to her feet without a word. Fox stood too, wanting to do something to help her but not knowing what it was. For now he thought the best he could do was get her somewhere where she could rest properly, decompress a little without having an audience.

"Lavender went shopping and picked up some clothes for us, so you don't need to worry about that. You can crash as soon as we get to the hotel," he said.

She just nodded again. He took her hand, and while she didn't pull away, she didn't curl her fingers around his. Fox led her to the door and picked up the suitcase with his free hand, then he turned and surveyed his team, they had dropped everything to help him and Evie with this situation and he couldn't be more grateful for them. They weren't just his team, they weren't just his friends, they were his family, his brothers.

"Thanks, guys," he said.

"No need for thanks," Night said. "We have each other's back on a mission or here at home. You guys were there for me when Lavender went missing, and you all helped look for Abby when she was abducted. We're here for you and Evie, whatever you need."

"We appreciate it," Fox said for both himself and Evie, who seemed stuck in shock.

He led Evie down through the apartment building and out to his car, careful to keep watch in case they'd been followed here. He didn't see anyone, and he quickly bundled Evie into his SUV. She didn't say anything, just slumped against the door once it was closed, and Fox focused on making sure they didn't have a tail.

The drive was uneventful, and by the time they got to the hotel, he checked them in and got Evie up to the room he was getting freaked out by Evie's zombie routine. She wasn't speaking, was barely reacting to her surroundings. She had completely checked out and was buried away inside herself where she didn't have to deal with the mess her life had become.

Fox was putting a stop to that.

Evie was a survivor, it was what she did. She could get through this, he knew it, but she had to know it too.

Setting the suitcase on one of the beds, he stalked over to where Evie was standing in the middle of the room, looking so lost and alone it broke his heart.

"Come here," he said, pulling her into his arms. She came stiffly, and when she would have pulled away he tightened his hold. "It's only things, Evie. I know this sucks but we can replace all those things."

"No we can't," she whispered. "You had Maya's things in there, you can't get them back."

She burst into tears and tore herself out of his hold, making a run for the bathroom. He caught her wrist before she could lock herself away and yanked her forward until she was flush against him. "Is that why you've been so quiet? Because you're worrying about that?"

"You love her," she cried, her tear-drenched eyes looking up at him through thick lashes. "And she's gone, all you have left are the things in your house, and now they're gone because of me. Because you and your team are helping me. It's not fair."

Anger surged through him, and Evie felt it and tried to pull away, but his hands clasped around her biceps holding her in place, then he leaned down so he was looking her directly in the eye. "Stop that right now," he said fiercely. "Yes, I loved Maya, and yes there were some of her things in my house that are gone now, but no one can ever take away my memories of her or my love for her. *That's* what keeps her alive, not things. It is not your fault that the cartel is after you, and it is not your fault that they set fire to my house, so stop blaming yourself. You have done nothing wrong. I don't blame you for what happened, I'm *worried* about you and how you're handling this. Talk to me, Evie. What's going on inside your head? What are you trying to hide from me?" He knew how Evie worked, knew she had spent a lifetime keeping her feelings to herself because she thought no one cared.

But he cared.

"I … I'm … I'm just *tired*," she murmured as she sagged forward.

Fox caught her and scooped her up, carrying her over to the bed. Evie needed to take a shower and eat something, but more than that she needed sleep. He balanced her in his arms while he pulled back the covers then laid her down and tucked her in. Because he couldn't help himself, he ran his fingertips down her cheek, his thumb brushing across her bottom lip. She looked up at him with blue eyes that were so sad he ached inside.

"Sleep, sweetheart, things will look better once you've had some rest."

He turned to go and turn off the lights, but Evie's hand caught his. "I know it's a bad idea, but ... could you ... umm ... lie down with me? I'm ... scared to be alone."

"Oh, honey." Fox couldn't even put into words how much he hated the fact that she was looking at him with such doubt, like she believed he might turn his back on her and deny her comfort and security when she needed it most. "Of course I can."

Fox kicked off his shoes, turned off the lights, made sure his gun was on the nightstand where he could reach it if he needed it, then he stretched out on top of the covers next to Evie and curled an arm around her shoulders, settling her against him. She rested her cheek against his chest and snuggled against his side, relaxing against him.

He kissed her forehead then stroked her back, hoping to calm her enough that she could get the sleep she needed. "Sleep, sweetheart, I won't let anything happen to you."

A shudder rippled through her but then she pressed closer until she was plastered half across his body. "I know," she said, then he felt her let go of her guilt, pain, fear, and vigilance and allow herself to drift away, secure in the knowledge that he was watching over her.

Her faith in him buoyed his hope that he could get her back, and content, Fox allowed himself to doze while he soaked up the feel of having Evie back in his arms where she belonged.

* * *

11:36 A.M.

· · ·

As she came awake, the first thing Evie registered was that she was warm and cozy and had slept way better than she thought she would have.

Sleepily, she blinked open her eyes to see Owen's hard chest beneath her. She used to love waking up that way, draped across him, deliciously warm. She was a cold sleeper, but Owen was a hot sleeper, and he always kept her nice and toasty. In Owen's arms was the only place she had ever felt like she truly belonged and now she had to remind herself that that hadn't been real.

Already she was falling under his spell again, and she knew the more time she spent with him, the deeper she would get. It would do her well to keep reminding herself that, she could get along with him, they could be pleasant to one another, maybe even pretend that they were friends, and she had to admit it was easier to do now that she knew Owen didn't blame her for the fire at his house. Yesterday she'd thought he did, he'd been distant and cold, but now she thought about it maybe that was her projecting her own guilt onto him.

"Feeling better?" Owen asked.

Evie lifted her head to look up at him and offered up a smile. "Yeah. I think I needed some sleep. I know nothing is fixed, my house is still gone, and there's still a cartel after me, but I'm alive, and in one piece, and I have a lot of people who will help me stay that way, so I should be grateful and not complaining."

"You amaze me, you know that? I can't get over how resilient you are. After everything you've been through, and I don't just mean the last few days, you can still wake up in the morning with a smile on your face looking for the positives."

The look on his face confirmed his words, and she felt herself blush. This man put his life on the line to rescue strangers, take out terrorists, protect the country he loved and the people who lived in it, being able to smile after a bad day was nothing compared to that.

"I'm so proud of you. You keep pulling it together after you keep getting knocked down, you will get through this, and then you'll fly high like you always do, conquering anything that's thrown up against you." Owen touched his lips to her forehead, and then his gaze met hers and dipped to her lips before rising again. It was a clear question, seeking permission to kiss her, and while she knew she should say no, she was dealing with enough there was no need to torture herself, she couldn't be this close to Owen and deny herself the pleasure of a kiss.

Besides, one little kiss couldn't cause that much damage, right?

Her entire being melted when his lips touched hers. Everything else faded away, her pain at Owen's lies, her doubts about him, the cartel mess, it was just her and the man who owned her heart.

Evie probably would have thrown caution to the wind, lived in the moment and dealt with the disappointment later, and done a whole lot more than just kiss Owen, but he drew back. "As much as I don't want to, we better get up. We're traveling out to a cabin, a safe house owned by Prey, and I want to get you there and settled before tonight."

She didn't much want to get up right now either, but Owen was right, they had more important things to worry about right now than making out. "Do I have time for a shower?"

"Yep, go take your shower, and I'll jump in once you're done. I don't want to draw any attention to us so we won't order room service, but we can stop for drive-through somewhere on the way to the cabin."

Evie nodded, resisted suggesting he shower with her, and climbed out of bed, rifling through the suitcase of clothes

Lavender had bought for them and hurried to take her shower.

Thirty minutes later, they were climbing into Owen's SUV packed and ready to go. As he started driving, she could see his attention was focused on making sure no one was following them so she settled into her seat and stared out the window.

The miles ticked over and the further away from the hotel they got, the more self-conscious Evie found herself getting. Gone was the easiness she'd felt when she'd woken in bed next to Owen, now she was back to feeling awkward. She'd fallen asleep yesterday when he and his team were talking with Eagle about the long-term plan for her safety, and now she wished she hadn't. She should have been paying attention, asking questions, making sure she was informed because after all it was her life they were talking about.

Maybe it was the fact that she knew soon Owen would be gone, and strangers would be responsible for her protection.

It was going to be weird having people she didn't know watching her every move.

Creepy even.

She was sure that they were good at what they did, and she would trust them to keep her alive, she'd talked with Eagle a little, and knew all about his company, they were the best in the business, but she didn't know them. If she didn't know that Owen and his team could get called out at any second so he physically couldn't be in charge of her security long term, she might even swallow her pride, accept the fact that she'd end up hurt, and ask Owen to stay with her.

"What do you feel like eating?" Owen asked.

"I'm easy, whatever you want," she said, turning to study his profile. It would be a whole lot easier to pretend like she was over him if he wasn't so sexy.

"Burgers?"

"Sounds fine."

Owen pulled in and ordered them both burgers and fries. Their fingers brushed as he passed her her food and she felt like a teenager again, excited about the tingle that fluttered through her body at the simple contact. They ate in silence, just the sound of the radio filling the car, and Evie found herself sneaking looks at Owen. He didn't seem to notice, so she took the opportunity to study him surreptitiously. He had a strong jaw, and his eyes could go from a light sunny brown to a brown so dark it appeared black, she loved his smile, but she also loved his fierce expression. He was a warrior through and through and he had fought alongside Maya as she battled cancer, and alongside her after she was raped.

Too bad he didn't love her.

"You want me to pull over and pose for you, sweetheart," Owen asked with a grin.

Her cheeks heated and she averted her gaze. "Ego," she muttered but couldn't not smile as she resumed staring out the window.

They left the city behind, and the constant blurring of the passing trees lulled her off to sleep, and the next thing she knew the squeal of tires and a loud bang jerked her awake.

"Owen?" she asked, looking from him to the back window.

"Someone is shooting at us," he said tightly. "You prac-ticed your shooting recently?"

"N-no," she said as another bullet flew past the car. She could shoot a gun, Owen had taught her, but she wasn't good enough to shoot a moving car while in a moving car.

"Okay, you grab the wheel, just keep it steady." Owen was already twisting in his seat while pressing down on the gas.

A bullet hit the back window, shattering it, and Evie

screamed even as she unbuckled her seatbelt so she could lean across the center console to reach the steering wheel.

"Stay down." Owen's hand on her back shoved her down flat, the console digging into her stomach painfully, but no way was she moving even an inch, she didn't want to get shot.

Owen fired off a shot at the car pursuing them, but then he cursed, and a moment later, she found she couldn't keep the car going in a straight line.

Panicked, she tilted her head up to look at Owen. "I can't control the car."

"They shot out our tires. Get back in your seat, get your seatbelt back on." Owen shoved her roughly toward her seat as he quickly sat down and buckled himself in.

Her shaking hands could hardly find the seatbelt let alone pull it across her and snap the buckle in place. She screamed as the car lurched, and she assumed their attackers had taken out another tire.

"Hold on," Owen said, battling with the car as it swerved across the road.

They were heading off the road, right toward the trees that lined the quiet street, they were going to hit. There was no way to avoid it because with at least two, maybe three or even four, tires taken out, Owen could no longer really control where the car was going.

Even though she was prepared for it, the collision slammed her against the dash and then against the window. Owen said something, but she didn't hear what it was. Pain shot through her and then blackness descended upon her rendering her helpless.

* * *

2:21 P.M.

. . .

Pain sliced through his arm as the car hit the tree, but Fox didn't have time to worry about it. With practiced ease, he shoved it away to deal with later. Right now, he had to make sure that the shooters didn't get to them. At least he hadn't lost consciousness in the crash, although he couldn't say the same about Evie, her scream had been cut off abruptly, and she hadn't said anything since.

Fox could hear the approaching vehicle so he ripped off his seatbelt and shoved open his door, closing it again as he took his weapon and ran into the trees. It killed him to leave Evie behind, especially unconscious and so very vulnerable, but he needed the element of surprise on his side, otherwise the men sent to kill them would just shoot on sight. If he distracted them, he could take them out first.

He had just tucked himself into a position that allowed him a good view of the car when he saw two men approaching. He'd managed to wing one while they were driving and he could see blood streaking the man's shoulder. The two approached cautiously, weapons drawn, as though they were expecting bullets to come flying from the inside of the car.

Bullets would be coming but not from where they expected.

He could see the exact moment they noticed there was no one in the driver's seat. Fox didn't hesitate, he fired twice and took out both men. As much as he would have loved to be able to interrogate them, find out exactly what the cartel knew about Evie, and him and his team, they were over an hour from the city, it would take too long for his team to get to them, and the cartel could have someone else after them by then.

Hurrying back to the car, Fox ignored the bodies and wrenched Evie's door open, reaching for her. There was blood streaking the side of her face, and she was deathly pale in the overcast afternoon.

"Evie, honey, wake up," he urged. He could carry her out of here if he had to, but there was a pain in his arm he hadn't had a chance to address yet, plus the cops could show up here any moment, and he didn't want to hang around and explain to them what had happened. Fleeing the scene of the crime meant he could be throwing himself into a world of legal troubles, but he was banking on the fact that the tires on his car were all shot out, as was his back window, plus there was the fact that there was a known threat hanging over Evie's head to work in his favor.

Besides, he would gladly take a murder rap if it meant Evie stayed alive.

Since she hadn't stirred, he touched his fingers to her neck and was reassured by the weak thumping of her pulse that she was still alive. "Come on, sweetheart, wake up for me."

She still didn't stir so he unbuckled her seatbelt and reached for her, sliding an arm under her knees and his other behind her back, he grunted as his injured arm took her weight, but he was still able to easily maneuver her slight weight out of the car.

Fox was about to set her down to grab everything they'd need from the car when Evie began to stir. One second she was out, the next she was awake and fighting him. Obviously, she thought he was one of their assailants, and she screamed and began to thrash in his hold, managing to get a swipe in at his injured arm, he was really going to have to do something about that arm, but first they had to get out of here.

"It's okay, fairy, it's me, it's Owen, they're dead, they can't hurt you," he soothed.

"Owen?" she said, going completely still.

"Yeah, honey, right here."

She looked up at him with fear and pain clouding her big blue eyes. "They're dead?"

"Yeah, babe, they're dead."

"How?"

"I killed them."

Evie threw her arms around his neck. "Thank you. You saved my life again."

"I think we've been over that before. You don't have to thank me for that, sweetheart. I have to put you down for a moment so I can get what we need from the car then we're going to have to make it the rest of the way to the cabin on foot."

"We're not waiting for the cops and an ambulance?" she asked as he carefully set her down on the ground a few yards from his wrecked car.

"You want to risk one of the cops showing up being on Perez's payroll?" he asked.

Evie gasped and shook her head, wincing at the movement.

"Rest for a moment," he said, cupping the side of her face that wasn't covered in blood and caressing her cheek with his fingers. He needed to assess how badly she was hurt, but they had to put some distance between themselves and the wreck before anyone stumbled across it and called it in.

While Evie sank down and closed her eyes, Fox went and grabbed his emergency pack from the car. It had MREs and bottled water, a first aid kit, flashlights, something to make a fire with, and mylar blankets. They had a lot of ground to cover to get to the safe house and with both of them injured it was going to be slow going. He could push through the injury, he'd done it dozens of times before, but Evie had a head injury, and she'd never had to do anything like this before. He was worried about her.

Fire burned through his arm as he put the pack on his

back and went back to Evie who was lying still. "Evie, honey," he said, shaking her gently.

She winced but opened her eyes and pushed up so she was sitting. She looked dazed and she was obviously in pain, but her eyes widened when she saw blood on him. "Owen, your arm."

"It's fine," he said shortly. He could use it and it had feeling, therefore it was good enough not to be any immediate threat to him.

"It doesn't look fine. Let me see it, I'm an ER nurse, I know what I'm doing."

"We don't have time, we need to move now, the longer we stay here, the more danger we're in. You can look at it later," he said. He was sure he could tend to it himself, but it would give Evie something to do that she was confident in and could help to calm her. "Hold onto me and get up slowly, you're going to be dizzy, and I wish I could give you some time to regroup but we have to get out of here. Tell me if you can't make it on your own and I'll carry you."

"I can make it," she said fiercely. Evie allowed him to put an arm around her waist and help her to her feet. He could tell she was unsteady by the way she gripped his arm tight enough that he winced, but after a minute she pushed him away. "I'm okay, I can do it. You don't need to worry about me slowing you down."

"I'm not worried about that." Yes he could out hike her in his sleep, but he knew Evie was tough enough to pull her own weight. Before they set out, Fox took a moment to let his gaze travel Evie's body and be grateful that she was alive. It had been close. If he'd been knocked unconscious too then they both would be dead right now, or if Evie hadn't been able to get her seatbelt back on she would have been thrown from the car when it hit the tree.

But they had survived, and now it was his job to keep her alive.

Slipping his good arm around her waist, he pulled her closer and pressed a quick kiss to her lips, then he took her hand, knowing she was going to need help keeping her balance, and guided her off into the woods.

They had around twenty miles to go to make it to the cabin, and he was loathe to stop anywhere along the way because he didn't trust anyone anymore. Somehow Perez had been able to track him and Evie even though they hadn't been followed and he'd checked his car for bugs, the man had a far reach and the only place he'd feel safe was at Prey's safe house. He could easily cover a mile in minutes, but most people would take fifteen to twenty minutes, and that was at full capacity. Evie was far from full capacity, and it would probably take them closer to thirty minutes to cover a mile, meaning it would take them close to ten hours to get to the cabin, and that wasn't accounting for the fact that Evie was going to need regular breaks to rest and regain some strength. They'd have to hike for as long as they could and then spend the night out here somewhere. That was far from ideal, but it was unavoidable.

He'd get Evie to that cabin, and he'd make sure the cartel wasn't able to get to her, and then he'd make her his again. He wanted to shower her with love, with affection, make it so she never doubted her worth again. He would build her up rather than contributing to tearing her down. Right now though, all he could do was hold her hand, keep her on her feet, and lead her to safety.

* * *

10:33 P.M.

. . .

Evie was on autopilot.

One foot in front of the other.

She repeated that like a mantra in her head, and she was pretty sure it was the only thing that was keeping her on her feet.

She was way beyond exhausted, had passed that goalpost hours ago, now she existed in some sort of weird zone where she moved only because of willpower.

No way was she letting Owen die out here because of her mess.

So she had to keep walking.

Pain throbbed in her head with each step she took, and residual dizziness meant she had to keep shooting out a hand to grab onto the nearest tree so she didn't fall flat on her face. If she did, she knew Owen wouldn't hesitate to scoop her up and carry her the rest of the way, but he was injured, she was pretty sure worse than he had let on, and she didn't want to cause him extra pain or work.

Her stomach was still churning, and she'd refused to eat anything the last couple of times Owen had stopped for a short break. Evie knew her body needed fuel, but she was also a nurse and she knew that eating and throwing it right back up was going to put her in a worse position than if she just didn't eat. So she was forcing herself to drink some water, just enough to keep hydrated, but not too much to overload her sensitive stomach.

Owen was setting a grueling pace, although she knew that he was still making concessions for her. If he was on his own, he would have made much better time, even injured he'd probably already be at the cabin. She was slowing him down and she hated that. This was her mess, her problem, he was doing her a favor, and he'd lost his house, been shot at, and was now traipsing injured through the woods to get her to safety.

She still wasn't quite sure why he would go to all this effort.

Was it because he hadn't been able to save Maya so he wasn't going to accept defeat with her?

That made the most sense, and it was what her head said had to be the reason, but her heart … her heart hoped that there was another reason. A more personal reason. Like maybe this had nothing to do with Maya, and he was here just for her.

But that was probably wishful thinking.

Still daydreaming about it helped to pass the time.

Evie stumbled over a root, her feet barely able to lift off the ground any longer. She flung out a hand, her palm made contact with the tree trunk, but her elbow buckled and she fell into the tree, holding back a grunt of pain as her bruised and battered body took a hit it didn't need.

She didn't know how, but she managed to straighten and keep walking, but it was getting harder and harder to keep her feet going.

Annoyed at her body's weakness, Evie pressed on, she couldn't give up now, she had no idea how much distance they'd put between themselves and the wrecked car but it probably didn't matter anyway, it was like the cartel could find her no matter where she was.

That was a depressing thought.

Evie stumbled again, this time there was nothing to use to break her fall, and she went down hard on her knees.

"You need a break," Owen said, crouching beside her.

"No, I can keep going," she said breathlessly, shoving away his hands and somehow managing to stagger back to her feet. She wasn't going to get Owen killed even if it meant finding strength she wasn't sure she had to keep moving.

"Evie, you've done amazing so far, but you're done in." Owen stood and pulled her against him, taking her weight.

"If we stop now I'm afraid I won't be able to get going again," she admitted.

"If you keep going and push yourself too hard you're going to wind up passing out, and I'll have to carry you the rest of the way to the cabin," Owen countered. "Is that what you want?"

"No. But you're in this mess because of me. If you were on your own you'd already be at the cabin. You've had to go slow for my benefit, and I hate it." Evie turned around in Owen's embrace so she could rest her cheek against his chest and wrap her arms around his waist. He was so big, so strong, a perfect wall of muscle that would keep her safe from any threat. She didn't want to let him go, now or ever. He'd said and done a few things over the last couple of days that suggested he wanted a second chance with her, but she wasn't sure if that was just wishful thinking on her part. Either way, she was exceedingly glad to have him here with her right now.

"You have a concussion, and you've walked for over eight hours through the woods. You've kept the pace I set, and you haven't complained once, you've more than pulled your weight. Now it's time to rest. I'll make us a camp, find us a safe place to hide away for the night in case the cartel tries to track us, then after we've both gotten a few hours sleep we'll start walking again."

"How close are we to the cabin?" she asked, not at all sure she wanted to know the answer.

"We're about three-quarters of the way there."

"So another five miles to go." That didn't sound like a lot. Most days it would be a pleasant couple of hours walk, but through the woods, injured, it felt like forever.

"It's just about eleven, we sleep for a couple of hours, then start walking again, and we should make it to the cabin by sunrise," Owen encouraged her. "Once you get there you can take a long, hot shower, relax all those tired aching muscles. Then you can lie down in a nice, soft, comfortable bed, close your eyes, and sleep."

"That does sound amazing," she murmured. Sleepy now that her body didn't have to focus on trudging along after Owen, Evie felt her eyes grow heavy and probably could have fallen asleep on her feet if Owen hadn't gently eased her away from him.

"You wait here, and I'll scout around and find us somewhere to hide out."

"No," she said quickly, glancing around the dark forest, she did not want to sit alone out here with nothing but her imagination for company. "I'll go with you."

In the pale glow of the moonlight, Owen's forehead creased in a frown and he looked like he was going to order her to stay, but then he nodded and reached for her hand. "We'll go together."

His words had a finality to them that made her think that he didn't just mean looking for a place to sleep, but then he was walking and pulling her along with him, and she didn't have the mental energy to think about anything else other than remaining upright.

She stumbled clumsily along, if it wasn't for Owen's hand tightly holding hers, she would be flat on her face. But his hand was there, a steady anchor through the dark, and the pain, and the constant swirling in her head. He kept her grounded, kept her fear at bay, and made her feel like there would be a way out of this, an ending, that she wasn't going to be stuck in this nightmare forever.

Evie was practically a zombie by the time Owen stopped walking. "Here we go, honey, crawl in here for me." He guided her down and toward a hollowed-out tree trunk. Evie didn't question, didn't worry about the creepy crawlies that were no doubt living in there, just crawled in and sagged against the tree. "I'm going to set up a few measures to let us know if anyone gets too close then I'll be right back."

"Hmm," she murmured, already half asleep.

It felt like just a second later that she was being shaken awake.

"Honey, you need to drink some water for me," a soft voice commanded.

"Too tired."

"I know, sweetheart, but I need you to drink or you'll get dehydrated and end up in worse shape than you already are." A firm arm circled her shoulders and sat her up, then a water bottle was held to her lips.

Evie obediently sipped at the water and tried to clear the fog from her mind. "Owen."

"Yeah, honey, I'm right here, ready to tuck us in for the night."

"No, your arm, I need to take a look at it," she said as she roused herself. He'd already rebuffed her every time they'd stopped for a break, even though he had done a brief assessment of her injuries, but she really needed to check it out.

"My arm is fine, and you need rest," he said as he spread a blanket over them then tugged her over so she was snuggled against his side, his arm curled around her shoulders, the blanket tucked around them both. "Sleep now, sweetheart."

Owen kissed her forehead, and a brief smile touched her lips before she stopped fighting the urge to sleep that had plagued her since their car was run off the road and drifted away.

# CHAPTER 9

April 6ᵗʰ

2:07 A.M.

*Pitter-patter, pitter-patter, pitter-patter.*

The sound stirred Fox out of sleep, and as soon as his mind snapped to attention he realized what it was.

Rain.

Obviously, it had clouded up and started raining in the couple of hours since they'd crawled into the hollowed-out tree and gone to sleep. It wasn't himself he was worried about, walking in the rain didn't bother him, but at the very least Evie had a concussion, the last thing she needed was to be hiking while drenched. Plus it caused visibility issues. The moonlight had been enough that he hadn't required to use a torch. Still, without that light, he would have to choose between waving around a beacon alerting anyone in the vicinity to their position, or risk Evie falling in the dark and potentially injuring herself further.

He was adding night vision goggles to the emergency pack he kept in his car.

Since he wanted to get Evie to the cabin before the sun rose and they still had several hours of hiking left to get there, Fox gave her a gentle shake. She was still curled up against him, right where she'd been since she fell asleep, she'd been so exhausted she'd just crashed. Fox hated having to wake her, she needed rest to recuperate, but they weren't safe out here.

"Wake up, Evie," he said softly, giving her another shake.

"Hmm," she moaned and burrowed closer.

"Come on, honey, the sooner we get to the cabin the sooner you can rest for real," he said, shaking her harder this time.

"Owen?" she said in that sleepy morning voice of hers he'd always found irresistible.

Leaning down, he pressed a quick kiss to her lips. "Rise and shine, fairy."

"What time is it?" Evie asked, slowly sitting up and wincing as her obviously stiff body protested.

"A little after two. If we get going now, we'll be at the cabin before the sun is up."

"Okay." She went to crawl out of their hidey-hole, but he stopped her with a hand on her shoulder.

"I'll go first, just in case there's anyone out there."

Evie nodded and sunk back down resting heavily against the tree, and he could see the exhaustion in her posture. Fox wasn't sure she could make it the rest of the way. Carrying her would leave them both vulnerable since it would make it harder for him to protect her, but it was doable.

Leaving Evie to rest for a few more moments, he removed the branches he'd used to cover up their hiding spot, crept out, and pulled his pack out behind him, then secured the area and removed the traps he'd set last night. He didn't want anyone innocent to stumble into them.

"You can come out, Evie," he called softly when he returned to the tree.

"It's raining." She sounded surprised, she'd obviously been too zoned out to hear it.

"Which means visibility is going to be bad. I don't have any NVGs so we're going to have to use a torch."

"Someone might see us," Evie protested, sounding worried.

"Better than you falling and getting hurt."

"I won't fall," she promised.

"Evie, it's wet and slippery, and from the way you're clutching the side of the tree you're still dizzy."

"I won't fall," she repeated firmly. "I won't let you down, Owen."

"Oh, baby, I'm not worried about that. If you get hurt and we have to go to the hospital, the cartel will be able to track us there."

"I'll hold onto your pack, you'll be able to see better than I can where we're going," she said through chattering teeth.

She was already cold, and he didn't want to waste time debating it. "Fine. For now, you hold onto me. First drink a little water, and the same rules apply as yesterday. If you can't keep walking, you tell me and I'll carry you."

From the stubborn tilt of her chin, he knew she wasn't going to admit if she needed help. They both drank a little water, then Fox took her elbow and helped her stand, but when she went to hold onto his pack, he grabbed her hand instead.

Since Evie needed to conserve her strength, they didn't talk as they started walking. The couple of hours sleep hadn't helped Evie regain much strength. Barely fifteen minutes into what would be at least two hours of walking, probably closer to three, she began to stumble.

The rain made it even more miserable trekking through the woods, and despite the pace he set, Evie's teeth continued to chatter, and he could feel tremors rippling through her. As much as he wanted to slow down and give her more breaks, she really needed to get out of the rain and the cold. The pain in his arm had long since dulled, he'd need to tend to it at some point, but his priority was Evie.

He kept breaks to a minimum, just a few minutes to drink some water. Although he tried to get her to eat something, Evie said her stomach was still too nauseous to try eating, and since his goal was to get her to the cabin as quickly as possible he didn't argue, just made her drink, took her hand again, and got them walking.

Ever so slowly they got closer to the remote beachfront cabin. They were about a mile out when Evie's legs gave out, and even with his supportive hand she hit the ground. A small moan escaped her lips, and she shook badly.

"I got you." Fox scooped her up and settled her soaked body against his chest, hoping to give her whatever heat his own cold body could muster.

"I can walk," she murmured weakly, but she made no attempt to move.

"It's not far to go, just rest."

Her weight didn't slow him down, if anything, now that he didn't have to match Evie's much slower pace he was able to move much faster. Fox stopped just short of the cabin and set Evie down behind a large tree.

"Stay here, I'm going to check the cabin is secure then I'll come back for you." Pausing only long enough to kiss her softly on the lips, Fox headed for the cabin.

It took only a quick check of the security system to see that no one had breached it. Leaving his pack on the table inside, he ran back out into the rain to collect Evie. Her eyes were closed, but when he picked her up she opened them and looked up at him.

"Is it safe?"

"It's safe," he assured her.

Inside, he set Evie on her feet and immediately stripped off her wet clothes. For two years he'd dreamed of getting her naked but not like this. Her skin was pure white and cold to the touch, and once he had her in just her bra and panties, he grabbed all the blankets from the bed and wrapped them around her then carried her to an armchair, put her down, and dragged it over so it was directly in front of the fireplace. He quickly built a fire before stripping off his wet clothes and digging some dry ones from his backpack.

Hot drinks were next, and he prepared them both a cup of steaming coffee, carrying Evie's over to her so she didn't need to get up.

"Sorry, it's not the fancy stuff you like," he teased.

She offered up a weak smile. "As long as it's hot that's all I care about right now."

Sipping his coffee, he gave Evie a visual once over. Her color still wasn't good, and the rain had washed away what was left of the blood he hadn't cleaned off when they'd first stopped after the crash. Since she'd been able to walk for hours, he didn't think she had any life-threatening injuries, but he still needed to check her out.

"How's your head?"

"Sore."

"Still dizzy? Nauseous?"

"A little, it's mostly gone, now it's just a headache."

"Anything else hurt?"

"Everything," she said with a groan, sinking further into the chair and her bundle of blankets.

"Let me see." He set his mug on the fireplace mantle and stood expectantly in front of her chair.

"I'm okay, Owen."

"I'll be the judge of that. Evie, please," he whispered when she looked like she was going to argue. "I promised you I'd keep you safe and you were shot at, in a car accident, and had to hike to safety. I just need to make sure you're okay."

When she gave a small nod, he parted the blanket and ran his hands up and down each limb searching for injuries. There were blisters on her feet from the walk, and bruises on her chest and stomach from the seatbelt. There were also bruises on her right shoulder where she'd probably hit the window, and the cut on her head probably needed stitches, but he might be able to get away with gluing it or using butterfly bandages.

"So, did I pass inspection?"

Smiling at her arched brow and barely concealed grin, he nodded. "Barely. I'll take care of the blisters and the head wound then you can go and take a shower."

"I need to look at your arm too," she said with that stubborn glint in her eye.

"After I patch you up."

She obviously caught that he was brushing her off because she rolled her eyes at him before another shiver rolled through her.

"You're still hypothermic. Drink your coffee, and I'll go find the first aid kit." Fox found it in the bathroom and brought it back, kneeling in front of Evie's chair and grasping one of her ankles. He cleaned each of the blisters carefully before turning his attention to her head. "There's glue in here so I can stick this back together for you," he told her with a grin.

Evie didn't smile back, there was a thoughtful expression on her face as she watched him. He was leaning in close, her breath puffed warmly against his chilled skin, and when she turned her gaze to his lips it took every bit of his restraint not to kiss her. The only reason he did restrain was because he wasn't sure he could keep the kiss gentle and not ravish her like he'd wanted to do ever since she walked back into his life five days ago, and he was pretty sure Evie wasn't ready for that level of intimacy yet.

Instead, he grabbed the glue and carefully applied it to the gash on her forehead. "There we go, all done. There are waterproof bandages in here so put one on when you take your shower."

"I'll take a shower after I look at your arm," Evie said stubbornly. Her face was set in that don't mess with me look he remembered so well, and since he knew she wasn't going to relent he did.

"Fine." He set the first aid kit beside her and shoved up the sleeve of his t-shirt to reveal the gash on his bicep.

"Doesn't look too deep, it won't need stitches," Evie said. With practiced hands she cleaned and bandaged the wound, then looked up at him with those pretty baby blues. "All done."

"Thank you. You okay for a moment if I go call my team, let them know what happened?"

"I'm not going to fall apart, Owen. I'm scared, and I'm sore, and I'm definitely exhausted, but I'll be okay."

"I never doubted that for a single second." Giving her a quick kiss, he left her to rest and warm-up, and went into the small kitchen to make his call. Once he was out of sight his legs gave way, and he sat down hard in a chair, the reality of what could have happened settling in now he wasn't focused on getting Evie to safety.

He could have lost her.

Really lost her.

Never getting her back lost her.

There Evie was, holding it together better than he was and he was trained to deal with all sorts of danger. But what kind of training prepared you for bullets flying toward the woman you loved?

For two years he'd been putting off attempting a reconciliation with Evie because he'd been scared she'd turn him down flat. Scared. Him. That fear had almost cost him his chance permanently. As awful as it was, this issue with the cartel had forced his hand, and there was no way he wasn't taking this opportunity to win her back.

\* \* \*

5:50 A.M.

Now that she was alone, Evie found the shakes setting in.

Only this shaking had nothing to do with the cold.

Safe here in the cabin, warming up, no longer worrying about having to hike and keep pace with a Navy SEAL, no longer worrying about the cartel tracking them down, the shock of what could have happened—what very nearly *had* happened—was setting in and hitting her hard.

Bullets.

Shattering glass.

The impact of the car hitting the tree.

Blood.

Pain.

Shooting.

It all flashed through her mind in a rush, making her stomach churn worse than from her concussion.

Tears welled up, but she refused to let them fall. She didn't want Owen to see her crying and think she was weak. He seemed to be under the impression she was strong, but she wasn't. It took effort to let go of hurtful words or deeds, to see the best in the world and the people in it, and right now, she just didn't have enough strength left to put in the effort.

Because she knew her ability to hold in her tears was limited, she quickly finished the rest of her coffee, then keeping the blankets tucked around her, she went to the kitchen where she found Owen still on the phone.

"I'm going to go take a shower," she whispered.

"Hold on a second," he said to whichever teammate he was talking to. "Call out if you need anything. I mean it, Evie, no tough-girling it out, if you get dizzy, or you think you're going to pass out, or you're in pain and you need me, just call out and I'll be right there."

His concern over her wasn't helping her no crying in front of him plan, so she quickly nodded her assent and hurried through the bedroom and into the bathroom. It was much nicer than she had expected. There was a huge tiled shower at one end of the bathroom, a jacuzzi tub at the other. The tiles were a light gray color and matched the marble counter.

Dropping the blankets, Evie headed for the shower and turned the water on. While she waited for it to heat, she pulled off her damp underwear, pulled her curls out of the ponytail, and taped a waterproof bandage over her head by feel. She avoided looking at herself in the mirror and stepped into the shower, closing the glass door behind her.

Heat immediately enveloped her, and she sighed in bliss as the hot water poured down upon her overworked muscles. It was so much nicer than the cold, hard rain.

She stood there for a long time just letting the water work its magic, not thinking of anything but how nice it felt to be safe and warm. She didn't notice the ache in her tired muscles, the pounding in her head receded, and the sting of the water hitting her blisters faded away.

Evie wanted to stay in this little bubble, not let any of what was happening in her life seep in.

But it did.

Fear seemed to mix with the steam and curl around her, and she felt like she was back in the car, someone shooting at them, Owen shoving her back into her seat, telling her to buckle up.

Her legs trembled and she sunk to the warm tiles. Curling her legs to her chest, she buried her face against her knees and stopped trying to hold in her tears. She could have lost Owen, one of those bullets could have hit him, or the accident could have killed him, or those two men who had come after them, thinking they were helpless and trapped in the car could have shot them.

Owen had killed to protect her.

She knew he was a SEAL and knew he had killed a lot of people in his career, but this was different. He'd killed those two people for her.

For *her*.

Evie tried to keep her sobs quiet so the shower would drown them out, but all of a sudden, someone was sitting beside her, and then she was maneuvered to sit between bent knees, propped against a hard chest. Hands smoothed down her spine and stroked her hair, and lips kissed her temple and tear-streaked cheeks.

"I'm sorry," she said, crying harder now that Owen was here to witness her meltdown.

"For what? Crying?"

She nodded, his image was blurry through the tears in her eyes, and she pressed her face against his neck, inhaling the scent she knew so well, the scent that usually calmed her but today only made her sob more.

"Why are you sorry for crying, baby?"

"You think I'm strong? I don't want to let you down."

"Let me down? Evie, if you weren't shaken up by everything you've been through these last few days, I'd be concerned."

Evie lifted her head to look at him. Was he just saying that to be nice? She didn't see Owen falling apart, couldn't imagine anything making him lose control, except maybe when his wife had died. "Really?"

"Absolutely. You're hurt." One of his fingers traced around the lump on her forehead. "You're exhausted." His finger trailed down her cheek and along her jaw down to her chin. "And you're scared. Any normal person would be experiencing a crash right about now, that doesn't mean you aren't strong. Did you complain while we were hiking here?"

"No."

"Did you pull your weight and walk yourself even though you had a head injury?"

"Yes."

"Did you try to help me with the car when they were shooting at us?"

"Yes."

"Did you do all of that while terrified for your life?"

"Yes, well, but I was scared for your life too."

Owen smiled at her. It was a tender smile, the kind he used to give her when they were married, and he didn't think she was looking at him. "Then that means you're strong. Crying doesn't change that."

"You're always so strong though, you never break down."

"Oh, honey, that's not true. When I left you to go into the kitchen to call my team I barely made it there before my legs gave out. There are only a few times in my life I have been truly terrified. When I realized Maya was dying and I couldn't save her. When you walked out of my life, and I realized I might have to live without you. And when I had to climb out of that car knowing whoever the Perez cartel sent after us might shoot you before they realized I wasn't in there with you."

What Owen had just said was both sweet and reassuring, but her mind was stuck on one little word. He'd said that he'd realized he *might* have to live without her. Why was there any doubt? When she'd left she'd told him it was over, and as far as she'd been concerned it was. Did he think differently?

"*Might* have to live without me?" she couldn't help asking.

"I hope I don't, Evie, I never wanted to live without you." His eyes met hers directly as he said those words and he held her gaze letting her see he was serious.

He *was* serious, wasn't he?

He sounded serious.

Problem was, she didn't trust him anymore.

Actually, that wasn't the real problem.

The real problem was she didn't trust *herself* anymore. Her judgment left a lot to be desired and she no longer felt like she made good choices. She saw what she *wanted* to see, not always what was really there.

When his eyes dipped to her lips, there was one thing she was sure of.

She couldn't turn down an opportunity to kiss Owen. Even if it was a bad idea, she'd do it time and time again and deal with the consequences later.

Like it always did, when Owen's mouth captured hers the rest of the world disappeared, they may as well have been the only two people left after the apocalypse. His hands tangled in her hair as he tilted her head to get a better angle, and Evie hummed her appreciation as her own hands slid up to hold his shoulders as she shifted closer until she was all but plastered against him.

"You taste so good," Owen murmured against her lips.

"Then why did you stop?" Greedily she crushed her mouth to Owen's, she needed more of him. Evie had no idea what the future held for her or for them. Owen said all the right things, but she didn't know if she could believe them or not. And while he made her feel all the right things, she wasn't making any more decisions based on her feelings. All that did was get her into trouble.

This could be the only time she got to do this, the last time she would ever kiss Owen, and if it was then she was going to make sure she got enough of him to last her a lifetime.

Just in case.

* * *

3:03 P.M.

He could watch her sleep for hours.

Okay, Fox acknowledged that was a little creepy, but Evie looked so sweet when she was asleep. Her long lashes fanned out across cheeks that finally had some color back in them, her hands were folded together and pillowed under one cheek, and her mouth formed a small o. But the rise and fall of her chest was what kept catching his attention.

It wasn't because she was naked.

Well, it was *partly* because she was naked and he was a guy, a guy who loved breasts, Evie's in particular, but mostly it was because it reassured him that she was alive. He hadn't failed her—yet, anyway. Since she was still in a whole world of danger it remained to be seen whether or not he could keep her alive.

Fox had an arm curled around her shoulders, she was

lying across his chest, and he had his hand positioned so it rested loosely around one of her wrists, his fingertips resting above her pulse because just like the rise and fall of her chest, the steady beating of her pulse also reassured him.

After that amazing kissing session in the shower they'd dried off, and both exhausted, tumbled into bed and fallen asleep in each other's arms. This was the second time in the last few days he'd had the pleasure of sleeping while holding Evie close, and he wasn't sure how he was going to be able to go back to sleep without her little body hogging the bed if he couldn't convince her that he loved her. She wasn't convinced, he could see it in her eyes, and he wasn't sure what he had to say or do to prove it to her.

Evie stirred, and he knew he was expecting too much from her when she was preoccupied with staying alive. Believing him when she'd spent two years thinking she knew he didn't really love her wasn't high on her priority list right now.

"Morning, beautiful. Well, afternoon actually."

"What time is it?" Evie asked sleepily as she pushed up into a sitting position and rubbed at her eyes. She had a real thing about knowing the time, yet frustratingly she never wore a watch, so unless her phone was in easy reach, she always used to ask him what time it was.

"Just after three. You hungry?" He'd originally gone into the bathroom earlier to ask her what she wanted to eat, but then he'd heard her crying. At first he'd decided to just sneak away, let her cry the tears she clearly hadn't wanted him to hear, but then he'd realized that was stupid. Evie was hurting, and he wanted to be there for her so he'd stripped off his clothes—but left on his boxers so he didn't freak her out—with the intention of just holding her and comforting her, but they'd ended up making out.

"Actually, yeah, I am …" Evie trailed off, her eyes going

wide as she apparently realized she was naked. Her hands flew to cover her breasts and she scrambled off the bed, her wild gaze scanning the room in search of something to cover herself with but there was only the blankets tangled around him on the bed.

"I've seen you naked before, Evie," he said, amused by her sudden bout of shyness.

"I know," she huffed, one arm wrapped across her chest, her other hand covered the apex of her thighs.

"I even saw you naked this morning when we were in the shower together, you know kissing and touching each other like a couple of teenagers." He knew it wasn't fair to tease her when she was clearly embarrassed, but she was so darn cute with her cheeks pink and her brow creased.

"I know that," she ground out.

"And I saw you naked when we tumbled into bed together, limbs all tangled, sleeping in each other's arms."

Evie's cheeks turned bright red, and her gaze moved to the middle of the bed, right where his crotch was, and he knew his tumble into bed comment had sparked thoughts of the two of them having sex. Fox couldn't help but laugh. She was adorably naïve sometimes, he hated that her sweet, inno-cent view of sex had been marred by the man who raped her.

"Well ... umm ... I'm aware that we were ... not wearing clothes when we ... fell asleep, but that was then and ..."

He grew serious. "And what, honey?" They hadn't had a chance to talk about them yet, about the future, about what she wanted, about what he wanted. Now that they were safe here the talk he wanted to have with her had jumped to the top of his to-do list.

"And we're ... you know ... not together now ... and it's ... I don't know ... awkward. Are you done torturing me yet?"

"Teasing," he corrected with a grin. "And yeah. I threw your clothes in the drier earlier so they should be dry by now, or Eagle said there would be clothes here you were free to use since what we packed is still in the car. Why don't you get dressed and meet me in the kitchen and we can have something to eat."

"Okay, sure," she agreed, eyeing the bathroom like she wanted to move toward it but didn't have any more hands left to cover her backside.

Taking pity on her, Fox got up, feeling her eyes traveling his naked torso as he crossed the room to the door. There was only one bedroom so all the clothes were in here, but he'd give her some space to get herself together, get unflustered, and then he'd get dressed.

"Oh, Evie?" he said as he paused at the door.

"Yeah?"

"It's not together *yet*, not, not together *now*," he corrected, then left before she had a chance to respond.

While he scoped out the kitchen to see what they had to work with, he heard the shower turn on. He listened carefully for any signs that Evie was crying again, but the water ran for about ten minutes, and five minutes after that, Evie appeared in the kitchen doorway with a pair of jeans and a sweatshirt in her hands.

"I brought you clothes," she said with a pointed look at his mostly naked body.

"You used to love it when I walked around the house naked." He couldn't resist another rib as he took the clothes from her outstretched hand.

Of course her cheeks went that cute shade of red again, and she quickly fixed her gaze on the wall behind his shoulder. "I'm not getting sucked into this game again, Owen."

"Aww, that's no fun, I love teasing you."

"Yeah, you always did," she muttered, but a smile tugged at the corners of her mouth and he knew she had taken all his teasing as he had intended it, good-naturedly.

"Because you're so adorable when you're flustered," he couldn't resist adding as he pulled on the jeans.

"Hey! Adorable?" she demanded, swatting at him hard enough to unbalance him right when he was putting his second leg into the jeans, and he landed right on his backside on the kitchen floor. Evie squealed with laughter, tears rolling down her cheeks as she clutched at her stomach.

"Oh, you think that was funny, huh?" he asked, choking down his own laugh as he pushed to his feet and reached for Evie.

She squealed again and darted out of reach, running through to the bedroom. "You can't catch me, Fox." She giggled.

"That's what you think, fairy," he shot back, reaching the bedroom just as she ran into the bathroom. "Tactical error, sweetheart, you just went into a room with no other exits. You're mine, and when I get you, I'm going to tickle you." Evie was ridiculously ticklish, just the lightest of touches down her ribs or across her stomach had her practically convulsing with laughter.

"Cockiness gets you every time," Evie singsonged as he threw open the door and choked on a mouthful of water. She stood there, smug as can be, the handheld showerhead in her hands and aimed directly at the door, she'd been ready to get him as soon as he stepped through it.

"Anybody ever tell you you're an evil genius, fairy?" Fox asked with a laugh as he put his hands in front of his face to block the water then snagged a hold of Evie's wrist, jerking her forward and spinning her around so he had her back pressed against his chest. "But you know I'm taller than you, I'm bigger than you, I'm stronger than you, and I'm faster than you, that means I always get to win." With a twist of her hands, he had the water squirting her instead. She wriggled in his hold and giggled with a freedom he hadn't heard in a long time.

"Well, we're both wet again and basically back in the shower again," Evie said through her giggles.

"You know what that means, right?"

"What?" She twisted her head around to look up at him over her shoulder.

"It means I get to do this again." Shutting off the water, he turned Evie so she was facing him, and hooked a finger under her chin to tilt her face up, then he leaned down and claimed her mouth.

# CHAPTER 10

April 7th

7:25 A.M.

Evie pulled up the covers and smoothed them out, then fluffed the pillows and set them neatly at the top of the bed. She felt a little bad that Owen had let her have the cabin's only bed while he slept on the couch, but it had been so good to spend the whole night sleeping in an actual bed in a place she felt safe that her remorse was fleeting.

She'd already showered and dressed, so there was nothing else to keep her in the bedroom. If she didn't go out to have breakfast now, she would have to admit that she was hiding.

And she wasn't.

Definitely wasn't.

Yesterday with Owen had been fun even, but she was cautious about allowing herself to get used to it. This was now, and she could enjoy his company, even make out a little, but she would not let herself accept that it would last past the next couple of days. Eagle's men would be moving in soon to take over, and Owen would go back to the city where he'd go back to work and back to his life.

When that happened, she'd be on her own in this.

She was used to that, and in a lot of ways, it didn't bother her, she trusted Eagle because Owen did, and this was her fight, but she'd miss Owen more than she cared to admit.

Yanking her unruly mop of curls into a ponytail, Evie fortified herself and then swung open the bedroom door and walked into the main room pretending she wasn't as nervous to see Owen as if it was their first date.

"Morning," he said, looking up from the book he was reading to smile at her. He was wearing nothing but a pair of sweatpants. The pillow and blanket he'd slept with were neatly folded and sitting on one of the two armchairs while he sprawled on the couch. His dark hair was a mess but it just made him look so adorably handsome that she could hardly think of anything but running her fingers through it.

"Morning. Sleep okay?" See, she could do this. Casual conversation wasn't as hard as she'd thought it would be. So long as she didn't look at his bare chest that was. If she did, she'd be throwing herself at him and they'd do nothing but make out all day.

"Evie."

"Hmm?" she asked, finding it very difficult not to stare at his chest. Why exactly was doing nothing but making out with a sexy SEAL a problem? In this second, Evie couldn't think of a single reason why it would be.

Owen laughed. "I said I slept fine, but from the way you're staring like that maybe you didn't sleep well."

The amused lilt to his voice told her he was teasing her again, but still she blushed at having been caught ogling him.

"Umm, no, actually I slept fine. Thanks for letting me have the bed."

He looked offended that that was even in question, but nodded in acknowledgment. "You hungry?"

"Yes, I don't know how after we polished off all that food we cooked yesterday, but I'm starving." Yesterday after they'd made out for the second time in the shower they'd spent a couple of hours cooking up a storm, eaten, then hung out for a bit before she'd crashed.

"You haven't been eating a lot the last few days because of stress, you needed to catch up on that as well as sleep. There's a stack of pancakes for you, you can reheat them in the frying pan if you want, but I know you like them cold."

She grimaced at the quirk, she actually often enjoyed food more when it was cold than hot, something which she had been told over and over again was weird. "Thanks. You've been up for a while?"

"Couple of hours."

No surprise there, Owen was always up before the sun. He followed her into the kitchen and took a seat at the table while she grabbed the plate of pancakes he'd left for her and found some maple syrup in the pantry, bringing both with her to the table. It wasn't until she'd taken a couple of bites that she realized he was staring at her with an inscrutable expression.

"What?" she asked.

"We need to talk."

Her hand froze halfway to her mouth. "Is there a problem?"

"No, but I want you to know what to do if there is one. We didn't get outside yesterday, and we came in from the back when we arrived, but this cabin is right on the beach. If anything happens, you're to run straight down to the water. There's a dock with a boat, it's got a tracker which Eagle and my team will be able to access, you're to get in it and get away."

"And what will you be doing?" Evie didn't like the idea of running away and leaving Owen to fight her battles. She knew he was a SEAL and he could take care of himself, but it still felt like being a coward to tuck tail and run.

"I'm going to be making sure you get away."

"I don't want you to get hurt for me, Owen," she said as she set the fork down, no longer hungry.

"Tough."

"Tough?"

"You don't get to make that decision for me."

"We're not together, you don't have to risk your life for me." Evie hesitated but then decided she may as well just say it. "I know you didn't get to save Maya, but that doesn't mean you have to risk your life to try to save me instead."

"Is that what you think I'm doing?" His voice was calm, and he was watching her as though he was interested in her answer.

Evie shrugged. "Well, yeah, I guess. I know that I was Maya's replacement, so it would make sense that since there was nothing you could do to help her beat cancer that you would go all out to save me instead."

"I hate that you think that."

"What?"

"That you are Maya's replacement. You're *no* replacement, Evie."

"But ..."

"I know it's my fault that you think it. I'm the one who decided not to tell you about Maya, and you were right about the reasons. I *did* doubt at first that I really loved you. I knew that I cared a lot about you, but I wondered the same thing you did, was it just because you look so much like Maya."

"I don't think I want to talk to you anymore." Humiliation

burned brightly inside her as she shoved away from the table. For her, being married to Owen had been the best time of her life, she'd finally felt special to someone, but for him their marriage had been about being as close to his dead wife as he could get. She'd suspected that but hearing him admit it was too much.

She was at the door when his hand closed around her wrist, stopping her with a firm but gentle hold. "Evie, I said that I had worried that you were right, not that you were. At first, yeah, I wondered if what I felt was real, but I quickly realized that what I felt for you was as real as it gets. I loved you, Evie, I'm *in love* with you. I love, Maya, always will, but I love you every bit as much. My love for you is different because you're different, we're different, but it's not less than my love for her, it's equal. I'm in love with you, Evie."

"No, you're not," she countered sadly. "If you loved me you would have fought for me. I wasn't playing games," she added quickly, "when I found out about Maya, I knew I had to leave, but maybe … maybe I hoped you loved me enough to come after me, ask me to stay, prove to me that you loved me. But you didn't, Owen, you let me go so easily."

"A mistake. I thought you wanted space and I didn't know how to convince you that I was in love with you."

"Then what makes you think you can convince me of it now?"

"Because the alternative is more years without you. I've missed you, Evie. I hate coming home from a mission and not having your sweet face waving at me through the window as soon as I pull into the driveway. I hate not having you there to brighten my world and make me laugh when I'm trying to banish from my mind the horrors I've seen. I miss every single thing about you, even the ones that drove me crazy when we were married. What I feel for you is a separate thing from Maya. It has nothing at all to do with her.

Yeah, I had doubts at first, and I knew I should have told you, but I was worried telling you would mean losing you. I was afraid that you would feel like you were a substitute, but, Evie." His hands moved to grip her shoulders, and he bent his knees so he could look her directly in the eye. "You are not second in anything to me. You're an amazing, sweet, funny, compassionate woman who sees the world in a way most people can't, and I always felt honored to have your love."

"Why are you telling me all of this?"

"I thought I'd been pretty clear over the few days we've spent together but if you need me to spell it out for you then I will. I'm telling you this because I want you back. I never wanted to let you go in the first place, but you were hurting, and I didn't know how to hold onto you then without hurting you more. I won't let you go again without fighting for you. You're mine, you were from the second I laid eyes on you, and I'm yours. I can't live the rest of my life without you, I don't want to, I don't want to miss you anymore."

Evie didn't know what to say to that.

It was everything she'd ever wanted to hear Owen say, and he didn't look or sound like he was lying, which meant she had a lot of thinking to do. Could she let go of her insecurities about always coming in second?

\* \* \*

8:10 A.M.

Fox watched Evie carefully to gauge her reaction to his words.

Evie was an open book, she couldn't hide what she was thinking for anything, and he saw hope splash across her features before she reined it in. That hope was replaced by caution that told him as clearly as words that she wanted to believe him but wasn't convinced yet.

That was okay, at least she was starting to hear him, he could work with that.

"You still have doubts," he said, a statement not a question, but she nodded.

"I'm sorry, you seem sincere, and you're saying everything I always wanted you to say, but I don't know if you're saying it now out of fear because there's a ruthless cartel after me. I always believe in people, *always*, but most of the time it ends up biting me. When I walked away from you, I promised myself that I wouldn't ever do that again. That I would start listening to my head more and my heart less."

"So, are you saying I don't have a chance with you?" Fox wasn't sure he could take no for an answer, especially given that Evie had just told him that it had hurt her that he hadn't fought for her last time.

A slow smile lit her face. "No, I don't think I could ever say that. I love you, and I don't know what the future holds. For now, I think we have enough to worry about without putting pressure on whether or not there is an us. How about we just take this time to get to know each other again, hang out, have fun, and see where things go."

That was actually better than he'd been hoping she would say. "Does hanging out together also mean making out?" he teased, well half-teased because he certainly wasn't going to say no to making out.

Evie relaxed and giggled. "Well, we kind of already have been making out."

Fox stepped closer, sliding a hand across her hips and settled it on her bottom, pulling her closer until she was right up against him, right where she should be. His free hand curled around the back of her neck as he lowered his mouth and slowly kissed her. He deliberately kept it soft and gentle, wooing her with his lips and his tongue, wanting to show her that she was important to him, that she was special, but he also wanted to leave her wanting more.

She sighed softly when he finally released her, and Fox knew he'd achieved his goal. His good mood dimmed when Evie started to walk back to the table, and he noticed her limping.

"Hey, what's wrong?" he asked.

"What?"

"You're limping."

"Oh, the back of my ankle is a little sore, just from the blisters."

"Let me see."

When he walked toward her, she rolled her eyes at him and plopped down into her chair at the table. "It's fine, you don't need to fuss."

Rather than argue, he simply planted his hands on either side of her waist and picked her up, carrying her to the counter and setting her down. Evie was shaking her head at him, but she was smiling, and he knew that she understood his concerns when it came to her being injured. He'd lost his wife, had to stand by and watch Maya waste away unable to stop it from happening. When he'd been with Evie, he'd worried over any little bump or bruise, or any time she got sick. She'd put up with it good-naturedly even though she hadn't got it then, she did now though, and he knew she'd let him check her out to put his mind at ease.

His hand circled her foot, and he lifted it, bending her knee so he could see what was making her wince. Blisters were painful, but they shouldn't be affecting her walking to that extent.

When he saw the back of her left ankle he knew exactly why she was in pain.

"This is infected." It came out a little accusatorial, and Evie arched a brow.

"You say that like it's my fault," she said.

"Sorry, I'm just concerned. If this gets bad we'll have to risk a trip to the hospital."

Fear coated her eyes, and he wished that she hadn't been thrown into this nightmare. "Do you think I need antibiotics?"

"Yes," he said without hesitation as he probed the weeping, red, puffy skin. "Eagle has a well-stocked first aid kit, and I saw antibiotics in there when I was tending to your wounds when we first got here. Come on."

Scooping her into his arms, he carried her through to the bathroom. Evie's arms slipped easily around his shoulders, and with a content sigh she snuggled into him, tucking her face against the crook of his neck. Fox touched his lips to her forehead, telling himself he was doing it to check to see if she had a fever, but really it was just because she was irresistible. How was he supposed to hold her but not kiss her?

In the bathroom, he set her on the vanity, then grabbed the kit from under the sink. Carefully, he cleaned away the crusty puss that had oozed out, slathered it in antibiotic cream, applied a Band-Aid, then added a bandage, wrapping it around her foot and ankle.

"Okay, pull your pants down so I can give you a shot," he said as he prepared the syringe.

Evie laughed. "That's the least romantic reason for taking my pants off I can think of."

Fox shot her a grin. "Agreed." When Evie lifted her bottom enough to tug her jeans down to reveal her thigh, he swabbed it with an alcohol wipe, then injected the antibiotics. "Hopefully that should clear it up, if it doesn't, we can get Eagle's on-call doctor to write you a prescription and have it sent here."

"Sounds like a plan," Evie agreed as she slid down to the floor and buttoned her jeans.

"I wanted to run more self-defense drills with you today, but that will have to wait until we get that infection under control."

"It's only my ankle, we can still do that."

"No, I want you to rest and keep off your feet. If that infection gets into your bloodstream we're in trouble. I don't want to have to decide between trying to deal with a life-threatening infection here or risking your life by taking you to a hospital."

"I'm not going to die, Owen." Evie placed her hands on his arms and stood on tiptoe to kiss his cheek. "I know you worry, but it will be okay. I believe that. I trust you, and I trust your friend Eagle. I don't care how many resources this Luis Perez has there's no way he is going to come out on top."

Her trust in him went a long way to calming the anxious ball of worry that had settled in his gut, especially since he had damaged that trust in the worst possible way. Now he had a chance to undo some of that damage, maybe help Evie go back to living based on her heart and not her head, it was what made her ... her.

"You don't know how much you trusting me means," he told her, burrowing his face in her thick curls. "I want to make it better. I want to erase the hurt I caused you. I wish I could do it over and tell you about Maya right away so you never ever doubted that when I was with you I was one hundred percent with *you*."

"We can't go back though, Owen," she said, pulling back so she could look up at him. "But maybe a future for us isn't as impossible as I thought it would be. I don't know, Owen, I want to tell you what you want to hear because I don't want you to hurt, but I can't just jump in with my eyes closed and my fingers crossed and hope that it all works out."

"I wouldn't ask you to, sweetheart. All I'm asking is that when you do jump in, you know without a shadow of a doubt that I am there with my arms open, ready to catch you." He meant that, but he knew Evie had to accept it before she was ready to commit to anything. Fox would rather cut off his own arm than ever make her doubt herself and her worth ever again. They had a few days here where it would just be the two of them, and he intended to make the most of them.

"Okay, I'll work on believing that," she promised.

"I know you will." Reaching out to take one of her curls, he twirled it around his finger. "Since self-defense training is out for today I have something else that you can do to occupy yourself."

"Yeah?"

"Eagle mentioned that this place has some art supplies, so once you finish breakfast, you can do some drawing or painting."

"Oh, that's perfect," she said, clapping her hands, her blue eyes sparkling with delight. As she went off, practically skipping her way into the kitchen, Fox couldn't help but smile, nothing and no one, himself included, was ever going to dull Evie's bright light if he had anything to say about it.

* * *

6:42 P.M.

"Finished," Evie announced with a satisfied smile. She'd been working on this painting for most of the day, and while she could have done a better job if she had her own paints and brushes, she was pretty happy with the end result.

"Let me see," Owen said from the table in the kitchen where he'd been working on his own painting. He'd asked her for a few tips when they'd got the art supplies out after breakfast, but had otherwise been pretty secretive about whatever he was working on.

"I'll show you mine if you show me yours," she countered, snatching up her work as he entered the living room and holding it facing her chest so he couldn't see it.

"You drive a hard bargain, fairy," Owen said, but his cheeks brightened despite his easy tone.

Her eyes widened when she realized he was actually nervous to show her what he'd painted. Her Owen was *never* nervous. "You scared to show me?" she asked, amused.

"Hey, I'm not an artist like you," he shot back defensively.

"Who cares? I think it's cute that you spent the day painting with me."

Owen made a face that screamed appalled. "SEALs aren't cute."

"Whatever," she said, trying to hide a smile. "Then I guess you don't want to see what I painted. It's for you," she added.

Curious now, he crossed the room to plop down onto the couch. "Fine. But you go first."

Evie smiled hopefully as she turned the painting around, nervous now and hoping that this hadn't been a mistake. Owen looked surprised when he saw what she'd drawn, but he didn't look angry or unhappy in any way. "You said you liked it, and you kept it, I felt bad that your house got burned down because of me and my mess, so I thought the least I could do was paint you another one. I mean, it's not quite as good as the first one, I have better quality brushes and paints, plus I was painting on a canvas and not paper like this, but it's better than nothing ..."

Owen touched a finger to her lip to stop her babbling. "I love it, thank you. To be honest, I'm a little surprised that you painted me at Maya's grave again. I get why you did it the first time, you were hurt and angry and working out your emotions, but now …"

"Now you said you loved me, that what you felt for me was equal to what you felt for Maya just different because I'm different, and I'm trying to believe you. I would never have asked you to pretend Maya didn't exist, I just wanted you to look at me the same way you looked at her grave," she explained.

Instead of speaking, Owen just turned around his own picture to show her, and she couldn't stop tears from misting her vision when she saw what he'd spent the last few hours working on. It was him looking at her, and the expression on his face echoed the one in the painting she'd just redone. Sure the dimensions were off a little, and it was lacking some of the details that her painting had. The brush strokes were a little messy, but it was without a doubt the most beautiful picture she had ever seen in her life because etched into every line was Owen's heart.

"Umm, it would be good if you said something now," Owen said nervously.

"I love it, it's beautiful, you're really good for a beginner, and is it for me?"

"Who else would it be for?" Owen laughed at her.

Evie set her painting down and threw herself into Owen's arms. He caught her and set his painting down so he could wrap both his arms around her and hold her close. She cuddled against him, pressing one hand to his chest, above his heart. "Tell me something about Maya, something that she taught you."

He was quiet for a moment, just long enough that she thought he wasn't going to answer her, but then he spoke. "I know you won't believe this because you never met that version of me, but before Maya, particularly before she got sick, I wasn't the most tender, caring guy. I didn't want to talk about emotions, didn't know how to, I mean, I was raised by a single dad, former Special Forces, we didn't chat about how we were feeling. But then she got sick and she'd be throwing up for hours, or huddled under the covers shivering, and she needed me to take care of her, not just physically but emotionally. So I learned how to be soft, tender. When she got the terminal diagnosis, alpha male toughness suddenly didn't seem important. I started cuddling her more, I'd brush her hair when she was too weak to do it, and learned how to do all sorts of fancy braids to make her feel pretty. I'd put her makeup on for her and paint her nails because she loved those things, especially after she lost her hair. I'd do the laundry, and the cleaning, and the cooking, and feed her. I'd bathe her and dress her, and we'd talk, about anything and everything, including our feelings and emotions, and after a while I realized it wasn't so bad if it brought me closer to the woman I loved."

Evie felt her heart melt a little. She could imagine Owen sitting painting his wife's nails and doing her hair, he was such a softie underneath the alpha SEAL persona. "That's so sweet. Maya was really lucky to have you."

"Want to know what I learned from you?"

She smiled and began to stroke his chest. "Sure."

"You taught me that there can be light even in the darkness. When I met you I was grieving the loss of Maya, my father's health was going down, and most of my time was spent ridding the world of those who wanted to destroy it. There wasn't any light. Then there you were, you'd been raped and he might have killed you, and yet you still found things to laugh about. You still fought so hard to be positive, you focused on those positives instead of the negatives, and you made me want to do the same."

Tears misted her eyes again. "I really did that?"

Lips pressed to her temple and stayed there for a long moment. "Yeah, you did."

They snuggled together on the couch for a while, Evie allowing the protective wall she'd built around her heart to crack a little. She wanted to hope for a happy ending for her and Owen, but she was going to do her best to remain objective, rein in her natural inclination to believe that everything would be okay because there were no guarantees. Even if she and Owen could rebuild their relationship it didn't change the fact that a cartel wanted her dead. And trusting Owen, his team, and Eagle and his company didn't mean that all of them weren't just men. Men who could fail even if they did their best.

"Want to go swimming?" she asked, abruptly straightening.

"It's already mostly dark out."

"So the tough SEAL can't go swimming because it's dark? You're a *SEAL*."

Owen laughed and ran his hands up and down her arms. "Okay, sure, if you want to go swimming we'll go for a swim."

"Really? You're agreeing already? I had a whole list of other reasons ready to go to convince you. I was going to tell you the saltwater would be good for my infected blister, and that I'd be able to see the boat you want me to escape in if the cartel finds us. You're losing your touch, Mr. overthinks everything."

"Haha, very funny," Owen said, but she could tell he was fighting a grin.

"Want to go skinny dipping?" Evie asked, struggling not to laugh.

Owen's jaw went slack, and his eyes wide. "Tell me you're

joking," he said in a strangled voice. "Because I can't look at you naked and not throw you down on the sand and make love to you."

Evie burst out laughing, and it felt so good to laugh like this with Owen again. "I'm joking."

"You're a regular comedian tonight." Owen lifted her up and set her on her feet. "Go see if Eagle has bathing suits. Preferably a one-piece that covers everything," he added with a mutter and a swat on her bottom.

Giggling happily, Evie went to the bedroom in search of a swimsuit. There were several in different sizes in one of the dresser drawers, and she chose a blue bikini she knew would match the blue of her eyes. No way was she going to go with a modest one-piece. She wasn't quite ready to sleep with Owen, and yet she wanted to want to make love to her. It was silly, but she wanted to feel desirable, she was called cute because of her small size more often than she was beautiful, and sometimes it messed with her self-confidence. Changing quickly she went back out to the living room.

Owen took one look at her and made a strangled sound, and she knew she'd gotten what she wanted. He was dressed in just a pair of boxers, and her plan to make him want her fled from her mind as she took in his chiseled chest.

Now all *she* wanted to do was make out.

Who cared about swimming when you could make out with someone that good-looking?

Stalking across the room, Owen grasped her hand and pulled her through the cabin and out the back door. "You keep looking at me like that and we won't end up getting any swimming done."

"Is that a problem?"

Owen snorted. "No, not a problem, but I have a feeling you're not ready for more yet, so we're sticking to just kissing, and that's going to be hard to do when you look at me with that hungry expression."

Evie laughed again and some of the sexual tension dissipated. Owen was right, she wasn't ready for more than kissing yet, and she really did want to work out some of her anxiety by swimming.

Tugging her hand free from his grip, she went running across the soft sand and threw herself into the water. The cold stole her breath for a moment, and she shivered but didn't stop walking through the waves until she was deep enough to dive down and start swimming.

Almost immediately, Owen was beside her, a barrier between her and any threats that might approach from the beach as they swam parallel to the sand. For once it wasn't the smooth strokes that settled her it was the large man keeping her company.

# CHAPTER 11

April 8<sup>th</sup>

1:33 A.M.

The moon glittered on the water, and Fox stood on the cabin's back porch and watched the waves rolling across the sand, picturing Evie standing in them, the moonlight glistening off her blonde curls as water streamed down her. She'd looked so sweetly sexy that he hadn't been able to resist hauling her into his arms and kissing her until they were both rethinking the not ready for sex thing.

Swimming beside her in the ocean, knowing she was wearing nothing but a teeny tiny bikini, then having to walk back into the cabin and watch her go off to shower and go to bed with nothing more than a goodnight kiss had him painfully hard. He'd thought about fixing that problem himself, but somehow, he couldn't bring himself to do it. The only way he wanted to get off was with Evie. Besides, watching her start to relax around him, laugh with him, touch him and kiss him, was enough for now.

More than enough.

He was lucky she was allowing him to be in the same room as her, let alone actually be willing to give him a second chance.

The door to the cabin opened and he spun around, already knowing it wasn't a threat. It was Evie, and any thought he'd had that maybe she'd changed her mind about the two of them falling into bed fled when he saw her face. She was wrapped in a blanket that she was clutching tightly around her shoulders, her eyes were red-rimmed, and she was worrying her bottom lip with her teeth.

Immediately he set his drink down on the small table on the porch and went to her, pulling her against his chest. It had been a couple of hours since they'd come back from their swim, long enough for her to have slept and been woken by nightmares. "Bad dreams?"

"Yeah." The word came out as a shuddered breath and then she sunk against him, pressing close and he could feel shivers wracking her small body. "Owen, do you think … would you mind …"

"What, honey?" he prompted.

"I know we're not really together, and it's a lot to ask, so it's totally okay if you want to say no."

"Would you just say whatever you want to say?" he said, amused by her sudden bout of nerves.

"Could you maybe sleep in the bed with me? Just sleep," she added quickly. "I know you, uh, will probably be uncomfortable," she said, shifting slightly against where his hard length was pressed against her body. "So it's okay if you don't want to. It's just I'm … scared. And you make me feel safe."

Fox tightened his hold on her, he didn't care how uncomfortable things were for him. If Evie needed him, he would be there for her. "Course I can."

"Really?" She pulled back and tilted her head up to look at him, eyes wide with surprise like she had actually thought he would say no. It served to remind him that although they were making progress, he still had a long way to go in earning her trust back.

"Always there for you, fairy."

When he scooped her up to carry her back to bed, Evie immediately protested. "You don't have to carry me I can walk."

"Well, you do have legs, so yeah you can walk, and run, and jump, and skip, and hop."

"Owen." His name was said with exasperation, and she rolled her eyes, but some of the fear bled from her face, and he smiled down at her. It was a testament to how much he'd missed her, and his recognition of how badly he'd let her down when even helping her to relax a little made him feel like he'd actually done something worthwhile.

In the bedroom he set Evie on her feet, unwrapped the blanket from around her, trying really hard not to notice that all she was wearing was a t-shirt that clung to her like a second skin, and a pair of sleep shorts that barely covered anything. He spread the blanket back out on the bed, then picked Evie up and lay her down, stretching out beside her then tucking them both in.

Evie didn't hesitate to snuggle up at his side, her head pillowed on his chest, and her fingers absently curled against his abs. Absently Fox began to stroke her mass of curls, they'd dried after their swim and were now soft as silk around his fingers.

"Want to talk about your dream?" he asked.

She shuddered and shook her head. "No. I want to

pretend for just a little while that there isn't a cartel after me that will rape and torture me before they kill me if they manage to catch me."

He could go without thinking about that too. He'd already lost one woman he loved, and no way was he allowing a cartel to get their hands on the other one. "Okay, well close your eyes and try to get some more sleep, I'll be right here holding you the whole time."

Her head nodded against his chest, but her fingers continued to move against his skin, tracing lazy circles in a pattern, small ones then getting bigger. When her fingers dipped too close to his still rock-hard length, he grimaced and caught her hand, holding it loosely in his own.

"Uh, you keep that up, honey, and we won't be getting any sleep," he said, struggling to calm his heart that had started thumping in his chest as he couldn't not picture how much he longed to make love to her again.

Evie didn't say anything, but as soon as he released his hold on her hand her fingers resumed swirling circles, and she made no attempt at keeping them in a PG location.

"Evie," he warned, voice strained. She'd made it clear she wasn't ready to commit to anything yet, that she wanted to go slow, and he respected that, respected her, but if she kept that up despite his best attempts at self-control, his body would eventually hit the point of no return.

"Hmm?" she murmured, the picture of innocence.

"You should stop doing that." He sucked in a breath as she brushed right above the part of him that was already pulsing with excitement as though it expected this to have a happy ending.

"Maybe I don't want to stop," she said, propping herself up on an elbow to look at him. There was something different in her eyes, a determination that said she would get what she wanted, but he didn't want the first time they had sex again to be because she was scared and in need of a distraction. He didn't want it to be something she regretted in the morning.

"Evie," he started.

"Don't," she said, leaning down to silence him with a kiss. "It's not the nightmare that changed my mind it was the ocean. When we were swimming, you put yourself between me and the beach to protect me, my strong, hunky, wall of protection. Part of me still wonders if you're doing it out of guilt or because you couldn't save Maya, but even if that's part of the reason I still know that you care deeply about me. I want this, Owen, I want *you*. It's been so long, and I don't want to wait. I want to feel you inside me, I want to make love to you. This isn't going to be something I wish I could take back later."

That was all he needed to hear.

Fox snapped into action. He rolled over so Evie was beneath him and his mouth immediately claimed hers. Balancing his weight on one arm, his other hand swept up under the t-shirt Evie wore to caress her breasts. She moaned into his mouth when he palmed one and began to knead it.

Touching her wasn't enough, he needed to taste every inch of her tempting body.

"Owen, no, don't stop," she pleaded, her hands grabbing his shoulders when he tore his lips from hers and began to trail a line of kisses down her neck.

"Don't worry, fairy, I'm not going to leave you hanging," he promised.

Licking and nipping his way across one collarbone, he lifted his mouth and covered one of her nipples through the thin material of her t-shirt.

"More," Evie begged, her eyes falling closed. Eager to please, he shoved her t-shirt up, baring her beautiful breasts, and sucked one nipple into his mouth, teasing it with the tip of his tongue.

Evie began to pant, shifting restlessly beneath him, her hips coming off the mattress as she silently begged for where she wanted his mouth. Happy to oblige, Owen moved down her body, tossing the blankets aside and grabbing her shorts, pulling them down with him until he had her mostly naked beneath him.

For two long years, he'd dreamed about this, having the woman he loved in his bed, waiting for him to touch her.

Settling between her legs, he pressed light kisses first to the inside of her left thigh, then her right, then he pressed the gentlest of kisses to her center, and her entire body trembled.

"Owen, please," she begged.

Ignoring his own thrumming need, he ran his tongue along her before drawing her little bundle of nerves between his lips and sucking hard. Her hips came off the bed again, and her fingers curled into the blankets. Slipping a finger inside her tight heat, he stroked deep before adding a second finger, stretching her, preparing her to take him.

"Oh, yeah, please, more," she panted.

Curling his fingers around so they hit that spot inside her, he sucked hard against her bud. "Come for me, baby," he whispered against her.

And she did.

Beneath him she flew apart, her breathing going ragged, pleasure rippling through her muscles as they trembled beneath him.

As she rode the wave of ecstasy, Fox thrust inside her, burying himself fully as the last of the orgasm had her internal muscles clamping around him. Holding back his pleasure, his fingers touched her where their bodies joined and he began to thrust.

"Come again, sweetheart."

He kissed her and increased the pressure with his hands, and Evie's fingernails clawed at him as a second orgasm hit her, and she shook, and panted, and pulled him closer. Fox thrust one more time into her heat, and then he allowed himself his own release, joining her in indescribable pleasure as they shared the most intimate of journeys.

Barely remembering to keep his weight off her so he didn't crush her, Fox rested his forehead against hers.

"Was it always that good?" Evie asked sleepily.

"Hey." He swatted at her hip as he withdrew from inside her. "You know it was."

"I didn't think it was possible that it was as good as I remembered, but you just proved me wrong." She opened her eyes to give him a tired smile.

Touching a feather-light kiss to her lips, he climbed out of bed and went to the bathroom. It wasn't until he was running a cloth under warm water that he realized they hadn't used a condom. A mistake, yes, but if Evie wound up pregnant he certainly wouldn't be complaining.

"Evie?" he said as he approached the bed.

"Yeah?"

"We didn't use a condom."

"Oh." Her eyes widened, and he knew she hadn't realized it either. "I'm still on the pill."

Even though he knew the timing wasn't right, he was a little disappointed that there was no chance they had just made a baby. Gently, he cleaned her, then put the washcloth in the hamper, and went out to the living room to lock the doors and set the alarm.

"Think you can sleep without nightmares now, sweetheart?" Owen asked as he slipped back into bed and spooned Evie against him.

"Mmm, yeah," she murmured, snuggled backward to get closer. "I always sleep better when I'm wrapped up in your arms."

Fox smiled at the stroke to his ego, but the truth was he always slept better when he was wrapped up in her arms too. Evie's light kept away his demons, and tonight he would be her light and keep hers at bay.

\* \* \*

10:28 A.M.

"Hit," Owen said with a grimace.

"Yay," Evie squealed as she popped a red peg on the square she'd just called. After breakfast, they'd gone through the shelves in the cabin's living room, which were stocked with games and books, as well as the art supplies they'd used the day before. As soon as Owen had spotted the game Battleship he had pounced on it, no surprise there given that he was in the Navy and loved anything even vaguely related. "That's your last ship I just found, all I have to do is hit the rest of it and then I win. Again," she couldn't help but add.

"I could still make a comeback," Owen said, frowning as he put his own red peg on the now hit submarine.

Evie made a scoffing sound. "You still have two of my ships left to find. How exactly do you think you stand a chance at beating me?"

"It could take you a while to find which direction the submarine is facing," he grumbled.

She giggled at that. "The submarine is only three spaces

long, and A 1 is in the corner which means it can only go horizontal or vertical, that's only four possible squares. Once I find which direction it's in, there are only three possible squares, and if I guess right the first time, it's only two possible squares."

"Since when did you get to be such a fan of math?" Owen asked, his expression amused as he looked at her across the table.

"We aren't all as smart as you, Mr. Genius, but if it means beating you in a game then I'm all for numbers." She poked her tongue out at him. Owen was smart, so much smarter than she was, although he'd never made her feel like she was stupid, and she knew that she wasn't, she was intelligent enough, just not a genius like he was. Most of the time when they played games he beat her. Unless the game was completely one of chance, he always seemed to manage to find a way to get an edge, in fact she was surprised that so far today she had managed to beat him five out of the six games of Battleship they'd played. His expression had turned tender, and suspicion sparked inside her. "Have you been letting me win?"

"Who? Me?" Owen asked, dark eyes wide with exaggerated innocence. "Does that sound like something I would do?"

"Normally, I'd say no, you're very competitive and you have been known to sulk when you lose in that sports betting pool thing you and your team used to do, but today, with me, I wouldn't put it past you. So have you been letting me win?"

Owen's head tilted to the side as though he were trying to figure out which answer he should give if he didn't want her to be mad at him. "I might possibly have not tried my hardest, you were so excited when you got a hit with your very first guess, and I can't get enough of seeing that smile on your face. You're so pretty, but when you smile … you transform into something so beautiful it's like you're from another world. I'd do anything just to see it, including letting you win at Battleship."

Her cheeks flushed but with joy not any sort of embarrassment. "I wish I could thank Maya for all the work she did turning you into such a softie. Who would guess that under all those muscles, and that smoldering gaze, and that alpha attitude you have going on, that there was such a sweetie."

"Well, let's not let anyone else know, kay?" he teased.

The game forgotten, Evie pushed away from the table and rounded it to Owen's side, sitting down straddling his lap. Hands on his shoulders, she melded her lips to his. Kissing Owen was an almost magical experience, it made her entire body go hyper-sensitive. The feel of his hands on her hips was enough to make her feel like the two of them were fused together. And in a way they were. Maybe not their bodies, but there was a connection between them that not even time had been able to dull.

When she'd walked away she'd been so certain that it was completely over, that she was nothing but a second class replacement for the woman he truly loved. When he hadn't fought for her and had kept his distance for two years, she'd been further convinced that what she'd thought was between them was completely one-sided.

Now she was starting to believe that she was wrong.

It was scary letting herself believe that what he was saying was true. All her life she'd gone with her heart, let it guide her through this crazy world, but losing Owen had made her rethink everything about herself including her philosophy on life. Now the prospect of doing what had come naturally for so long filled her with a strange sense of uncertainty.

Owen was saying and doing all the right things, he wasn't pushing her to do anything that made her uncomfortable, he was risking his life to keep her safe, and she was ninety percent sure she believed him, but there was that niggling little bit of doubt in her head. Her parents' voices in her mind, berating her for being so naïve, for allowing people to use her, for not being good enough, smart enough, beautiful enough, and while it used to be easy to shove it aside, lately it had been much harder.

She'd only ever been in love once, with Owen, and that had given him the power to nearly destroy her. These last few days with him, while wonderful, had made her realize that he'd hurt her more than she had realized. He'd made her lose faith in herself, people, and the world, and she wasn't quite sure how to get back to the woman she'd been before.

"What are you thinking about?" Owen asked, pulling back so he could look at her.

Evie shrugged, not wanting to say that she'd gone from melting into a toe-curling kiss to rethinking her entire existence.

"I don't have all of you yet, do I?" He didn't sound angry or annoyed. He didn't say it like he was trying to guilt her or remind her that he was working hard to gain her trust back.

"I'm trying," she promised.

"I know you are, and I know the two of us here together has sped things up, maybe we shouldn't have slept together last night."

"No," she said firmly. "I wanted what we did last night. And I like spending time with you. The last few days have been great, I've been so busy reconnecting with you that I've hardly had time to worry over Luis Perez and his cartel. I want this." She waved her hand between them. "I want to be able to move forward, and I want to believe you, and I want to see if maybe we can be together again."

"But you don't trust me."

"Not you," she said sadly. "I don't trust me. I'm kind of battling with myself right now. I made myself start making more logical decisions, but it feels so foreign. My heart keeps trying to take over again, but then my head reminds it that I don't always do so well when I listen to my heart. Then the two kind of have a back and forth, and in the end, I feel like I'm no closer to knowing the right thing to do than when I started trying to make a decision."

"You're putting too much pressure on yourself, and you aren't giving yourself enough credit. You use your head, you're smart, and just because you look for the best in people, and just because sometimes people have taken advantage of that, doesn't mean that you have to change anything about you. I happen to think you're pretty perfect just the way you are. Stop trying to change, just be you, you can be more logical without having to give up looking for the best in everything. I'm sorry if I'm making you feel pressured, you don't have to make any decisions about your future right now, or once this mess with the cartel is sorted out, or in any time frame except what makes you feel comfortable."

"Thank you for understanding." A small amount of the pressure she was putting on herself eased. He was right, she didn't have to work everything out right now. She knew that she had to be smarter, but it didn't have to be a big deal. Right now, her heart said to give Owen the chance to prove to her that he loved her and she was going to let that be enough.

Owen took her face between his large hands and kissed her forehead. "I understand that I'm the one who hurt you, I'm the one who made you doubt yourself. I understand that you being willing to give me a chance is more than I deserve, and I understand that I'm the luckiest man in the world to have you sitting on my lap right now."

Evie smiled and snuggled against him. "Right now, I feel pretty lucky too. You made a mistake, I know you'd take it back if you could, I do believe that."

"I'm glad you know that because I would. Hurting you was the last thing I ever wanted to do, but I was selfish. Going forward, that's what I'm promising you, I will never be selfish when it comes to you again. You are always going to come first to me. Always. Now, are you ready to beat me again in Battleship?"

She laughed and pressed a quick kiss to his lips before returning to her chair. "No more letting me win, I want to beat you for real."

"No chance of that, darlin'," Owen teased.

Evie narrowed her eyes at him. "That sounds like a challenge, and you should know, Owen LeGrand, that I always rise to meet a challenge."

* * *

5:54 P.M.

"I heard that," Fox teased Evie as her stomach grumbled loudly.

She giggled and swatted at him good-naturedly. "It's been hours since we had lunch, no wonder I'm hungry."

"After how much you ate I'm surprised you can fit any more in that tiny body of yours today," he joked.

"Hey!" They'd been sitting on the couch reading, Evie was sitting sideways with her feet in his lap, but now she scrambled up to swat at him. "It's hardly my fault that you make such delicious sandwiches."

That made him laugh. "They were just toasted cheese sandwiches."

"But you do something to them, I don't know what, but somehow yours are better than any others I've ever tasted," Evie explained.

There was a peace in her eyes that hadn't been there earlier. She'd done amazing these last few days, dealt with the stresses of being hunted without complaining about her life being tossed upside down, and she was actually willing to give him a second chance. But there had still been shadows lurking in her gaze, she'd been battling with herself trying to decide whether she listened to her head or her heart, but his words earlier, telling her she could do both, and that she didn't have to make any decisions right now seemed to have eased her burden.

He was pleased he'd been able to help her, and they'd had a nice day, playing games, then sitting together reading. It was quiet and relaxing and reminded him of when the two of them used to hang out together back when they'd just met. Fox hoped there were a lot more afternoons like this in their future.

"What do you want for dinner?" he asked, tugging Evie onto his lap, enjoying the feel of her slight weight against his thighs.

"Know what I really want?"

"What?"

"Homemade vegetable pies," she said dreamily. Evie had an obsession with anything that was made of pastry. "But we don't have any fresh vegetables, and we don't have a car so we can't go and buy any."

"We don't need one," he told her.

"There's a vegetable garden hidden around here somewhere?"

"No," he said with a laugh, kissing her quickly on the lips. "But there is a freezer. I know frozen vegetables aren't as nice but they're better than nothing."

"Yeah, they are," Evie said enthusiastically, already sliding off his lap and hurrying through to the kitchen.

Fox followed her a little more slowly, propping his shoulder against the doorjamb as he watched her rifle through the freezer and the pantry, setting out boxes and bags, and pots and pans. She was humming to herself and she was so happy that he actually felt a burning behind his eyes. This was what he wanted his future to look like, he was an idiot for messing up what he'd shared with Evie, and he vowed that he would never do that again. If she took him back, he'd make sure she never regretted it.

As much as he wanted to put his focus on Evie and their relationship, he had to keep his head in the game. The danger hovering over Evie hadn't dissipated. Yeah, they'd made it to the cabin in one piece, and things had been quiet ever since. He'd spoken to his team, he knew the car had been found, and the cops knew that Prey Security was protecting Evie, but at some point they were still going to have to present her to them because she was their only witness tying Miguel Perez to a murder.

His instincts screamed at him to keep her here with him where she was safe, Prey would be moving in soon to take over her security, and despite the wonderful day they'd spent together, Fox couldn't shake this feeling in his gut that something bad was about to happen.

"You going to stand there all day or are you actually going to do something useful, like help me?" Evie demanded, hands on hips.

He grinned and shoved away the uneasiness swirling in his gut. "I made lunch, I thought it was your turn to cook."

Her eyes narrowed. "You better be joking, mister."

"I'm joking," he said with a laugh at her sassy attitude. "Tell me what you want me to do."

"You can make the filling or the pastry, your choice."

JANE BLYTHE

"We have to make the pastry by hand?" he asked.

"Yes." Now it was Evie's turn to laugh. "I can't believe you're a Navy SEAL who will go anywhere and do anything. Hike through jungles, trek through deserts, swim through oceans or rivers, and yet you won't get your hands dirty in the kitchen."

"Hey, I hate when stuff gets under my nails," he said with a shudder.

Evie threw her head back and laughed. "You're too funny. Come on, you can make the filling, that should be nice and clean."

Pausing to put his hands on Evie's hips and nuzzle her neck, Fox picked up the bags of frozen vegetables she'd pulled from the freezer. "You want me to throw in some of all of these?"

"Sure, the more the merrier," Evie replied, adding cups of all-purpose flour and self-raising flour into a large glass bowl.

"Want me to add some spices?"

"You can look and see what there is, but don't put in too much, I want to taste the vegetables and the pastry." She licked her lips, and her eyes got that half-hooded look of desire, and all thoughts of food and cooking flew from his mind. He wanted Evie, naked and on her back beneath him, that same look of desire on her face as she watched him go down on her.

"Hmm, sure," he said, clearing his throat and tearing his gaze away from her.

Evie didn't seem to notice, and resumed humming as she added butter to the flours and mixed it with her fingertips. Before he could start picturing those pretty little fingers touching a certain body appendage he possessed, he focused on thawing the vegetables in hot water and added a couple of spices.

By the time he had prepared the filling, Evie was rolling out pastry and fitting it into a pie pan. "Oh, you know what we should do?" she squealed, sounding like a kid on Christmas morning.

"What, fairy?" he asked, amused by her innocent enthusiasm for life.

"We should find some cookie cutters, make the top of the pie look really special." Without waiting for him to comment, she started going through drawers and cupboards searching for cookie cutters. "Ooh, look, hearts," she announced a moment later, holding up a round tin with a clear lid containing five hearts in varying sizes.

"You are a romantic through and through," he said tenderly. He might have physically saved Evie's life, but she had saved him from the darkness that could have—*would* have—claimed him by shining light into his world.

"That I am." She shot him a grin before opening up the container and using the shapes to cut hearts in the pastry she'd already rolled out. "You put the filling in, and I'll add the hearts as I cut them."

They worked together, and ten minutes later, they had an adorable looking pie with a large heart in the center and a circle of smaller ones around it, ready to go into the preheated oven.

"So, what do you want to do while we wait for dinner?" Evie asked as she set the timer.

In answer, Fox wagged his eyebrows at her.

Evie rolled her eyes. "Really? You're such a guy. We only have twenty minutes till the pie will be ready, and I seem to remember someone bragging that his woman always came at least five times in any bedroom encounter, I don't think we have time for you to complete such lofty goals."

"How about I give you a massage, that way I can still get

my hands on you," he said, shooting her his most winning smile.

Expression suspicious, she nodded slowly. "Okay. Yeah, I guess that would be nice."

"Nice?" He faked indignation. "You used to love my massages."

"Only they never ended up being just massages," Evie countered.

"You really going to turn down these magic hands?" he asked, holding his hands up and twinkling his fingers.

"You're so silly," she said, but headed out of the kitchen toward the couch.

"Uh uh, on the bed, and take off that sweatshirt." He placed his hand on the small of her back and altered her trajectory toward the bedroom.

"If my beautiful pie gets burned I'll be blaming you, Owen LeGrand," she warned, but complied and shrugged out of her shirt and lay down on her stomach on top of the covers.

"Duly noted." Fox already knew they would be eating the pie reheated in the microwave—or in Evie's case probably cold—later, when the timer went off he'd take Evie's pie out of the oven, and then he was returning to the bedroom to ravish every inch of her delectable body.

Climbing onto the bed, he straddled her hips and placed his hands on her shoulders and began to knead her muscles.

"Owen," Evie said, attempting to turn around when she felt evidence of his arousal pressing against her back. "You said my pie wouldn't get burned."

"And it won't," he promised, adjusting the pressure so Evie moaned in delight and sunk back against the pillows.

"Better not," she mumbled.

"Relax, sweetheart, let me make you feel good."

"You're incorrigible," she muttered but made no further attempt to move.

"And you love me for it."

"Yeah, I do," she agreed as her body turned to putty beneath him. Fox hoped she wasn't too hungry because he wasn't letting her out of this bed for a long time.

# CHAPTER 12

April 9th

9:06 A.M.

"So, what are we going to do today?" Evie asked as she walked out onto the cabin's back deck and wrapped her arms around Owen's waist. She pressed her face to his back and inhaled his scent, letting it settle her nerves. Yesterday they'd had so much fun together, and Owen's words that she didn't have to choose between listening to her heart or listening to her brain, that she could actually do both, had lifted a weight off her shoulders.

And yet, she was tense this morning because it was clear Owen was tense.

It had started yesterday afternoon, a sense that Owen wasn't as relaxed as he was trying to make her think he was. He'd distracted her with making dinner and the massage that had turned into hours in the bedroom before eating her pie at close to midnight, but through it all, she'd known. Even though they had been apart for years, her ability to feel what he was feeling hadn't dimmed.

Owen turned so he was facing her, his eyes flaring when he saw that she was wearing one of his t-shirts over her jeans and a long-sleeve t-shirt. "You really have to ask? Is there anything else I'm going to want to do when I see you in my clothes besides rip them off you and take you to bed?"

She laughed, some of her anxiety fading away. She'd known that wearing anything of Owen's was a surefire way to get him to make out with her, and she couldn't seem to get enough of that. "What are you waiting for then?"

With a hungry growl, Owen lifted her off the floor, and she wrapped her legs around his waist and kissed him as he carried her inside. The effortless way he carried her made her feel safe in a way that nothing else could. She knew that nothing and no one could get to her so long as she was with Owen.

A knock at the door had them both freezing.

Just like that, she snapped from turned on and happy, to afraid.

"Is that Eagle's men?" she asked as Owen set her on her feet.

"No, he would have texted to tell me they were here."

"The cartel?" Evie shook even as she said the word. It had been days since they had arrived at the cabin and with no signs of the cartel that had run them off the road and shot at them, she'd allowed herself to believe that she was truly safe here.

"Don't think they'd knock, sweetheart," Owen said with a quick smile. His gun materialized seemingly out of thin air, and he nudged her toward the bedroom. "Go lock yourself in there and don't come out until I tell you to."

Uneasy leaving Owen to face whoever had arrived at this secluded cabin alone, Evie did so only because she knew that she couldn't offer any real assistance anyway. Owen was the SEAL, she was an ER nurse, he was infinitely more qualified for this than she was.

Trusting him to keep her safe, Evie was just closing the bedroom door when she heard a voice yell out. "Police."

Police?

Were they here to arrest them because of the two men Owen had killed to save them both from the cartel?

Hovering where she was, she watched Owen cautiously open the door. Detective Coughlan stood there, his hand hovering above his weapon, as he eyed them carefully.

"Detective," Owen said, not putting away his own weapon. "What are you doing here?"

How did he even know they were here? That was the real question as far as Evie was concerned.

The detective caught sight of her, and Owen frowned when he turned and saw that she hadn't locked herself in the bedroom.

"Ms. Walter." The cop nodded at her. "Glad to see you're alive and in one piece, we weren't sure after we found the car. And the bodies," he added, turning his gaze back to Owen.

"What are you doing here?" Owen repeated his question.

"I'm here to get Ms. Walter and bring her in. She's being placed in protective custody."

"We have Evie's protection under control," Owen said.

Detective Coughlan merely nodded. "I'm still going to need to bring her in. The decision was made. I'm just here to collect her."

"How did you know we were here?" Owen asked.

The detective shrugged. "This was the address I was given."

"Where's your partner?" Owen asked.

"Working on finding Miguel Perez, didn't think it would take both of us to come and collect Ms. Walter." The cop moved his hand closer to his weapon. "Should I have brought my partner along?"

The implied threat against Owen was enough to make Evie hurry across the room to Owen's side. "No, of course not. But I don't trust the cops, I feel safer here with Owen."

"You're free to discuss that with my Commander when we get back, but I don't think it will make a difference. I'm to bring you in, and you're going to be placed in protective custody."

It sounded like she wasn't going to get any say in the decision and she looked helplessly up at Owen. The cops couldn't be trusted, they knew that already, someone had leaked her name and address to the cartel. Going back there was basically offering herself up to Luis Perez on a platter.

Owen took her hand and laced their fingers together. "I'll come with you."

"No."

They both looked to the cop who was all but glowering at them. "I don't want Evie going on her own," Owen said.

"My orders are to bring her in. Her, not you."

"I don't care about your orders, my only interest is keeping Evie alive." Owen took a threatening step forward, and the detective immediately pulled out his weapon.

"Do I need to arrest you?" Detective Coughlan demanded.

Evie knew exactly how Owen's mind worked. He would gladly get himself arrested if it meant the detective had to take both of them back to the station. But getting himself arrested would most likely get him kicked out of the SEALs, and there was no way she was letting him throw away his job over this.

Moving so she was in between the two men, who looked

more like two lions about to fight for dominance, she ignored Owen's glower. "It's fine, Owen's just worried. You don't need to arrest him, I'll go back with you." Turning, she looked at Owen over her shoulder. "You can meet me there, right?"

"Of course," he said, and although she could see he hated this, he also knew there wasn't any other option.

Almost like he was disappointed to have to do so Detective Coughlan put away his weapon and made a hurry-up motion with his hand.

Although this was the last thing she wanted to do, Evie hugged Owen hard, trying not to cling. "I'll be okay," she said, trying to reassure both of them but knowing she failed on both counts.

"I don't like this." Owen's grip on her was almost crushing, and because she was worried he would do something stupid to get himself arrested she quickly pulled out of his embrace.

Evie could feel Owen's eyes on her as she grabbed her purse and followed the cop out to the car. She had to force her feet to keep moving so she didn't turn and flee back to the safety of Owen's arms.

Detective Coughlan guided her into the back of the police car, and she watched Owen, standing in the cabin's front door until they turned a corner. Then she sagged against the seat and stared out the window.

The cop didn't talk and the next couple of hours passed in silence. When they reached the city, she straightened and shoved away her fears and borderline panic, it was time to pull it together. She didn't know if she would be allowed to see Owen when they got to the station, or if she would immediately be whisked away, but she had to prepare herself for the possibility that she was on her own from here on out. That meant she had to be strong.

"Will I be able to see Owen again before I go wherever I'm being placed?" she asked, meeting detective Coughlan's eyes in the rear vision mirror.

A slow smirk slid across his face. "You won't be seeing your SEAL boyfriend again."

"What do you mean?"

"I mean, you won't be seeing *anyone* again, not where you're going."

Realization hit her like a ton of bricks.

Detective Coughlan was the mole in the police department, the one working for the cartel, who had leaked her name and address, and he wasn't taking her to the station to be put in protective custody. He was taking her straight to the cartel.

Her gaze flew to the door but there were no interior handles. Why hadn't she noticed that when she'd gotten into the car? If she had, she could have screamed to Owen that it was a setup and he would have saved her.

Now there was no one to save her but herself.

Shoving her hand inside her purse she opened the phone's voice memo app and started recording. She had no way to know if this recording would ever be found, but she would act on the assumption that she would get out of this alive.

She had to.

Believing anything else right now would have her falling apart.

"It's you. You're the one working for Perez," she said flatly, faking a resignation that was pretty close to how she was feeling.

"We came to an arrangement a while back that benefitted us both," Detective Coughlan confirmed.

"Why? Don't people become cops because they want to save people, because they believe in justice?"

"When justice for the people who matter most to you burns you then you start looking elsewhere."

She arched a brow at him, wondering what had happened that had turned him from cop to cartel informant.

"My ex-partner and my wife were having an affair. What I thought was my kid turned out to be theirs, I didn't find that out until after the three of them had been murdered. I was working overtime one day while my partner and my family took a family fun day. They were caught up in a convenience store robbery and killed. It wasn't until I nearly drowned myself in the bottle, and almost lost my job trying to get the kid who killed them during an initiation into the Perez cartel locked up for life, that I found out the truth. The kid got off on some technicality so I decided to aim higher up the pecking order. Found myself kidnapped and in a meeting with Luis himself, he told me the truth about my wife and partner, that my kid wasn't mine, then offered me a deal; work for him and make more money than I ever dreamed of. Money is a whole lot less messy than love." He met her gaze again and shrugged. "Once I hand you off to the cartel I'm disappearing. Too risky to keep going now since your SEAL will tell everyone that I was the one who picked you up, and when you don't turn up they'll know that I lied."

No way was she disappearing, being murdered by the cartel or sold to some monster with money.

Going out the door wasn't an option, but she could try to get out through the trunk. Most sedans had part of the back-seat that collapsed so she could get through it, find the hatch to open the lid, then jump.

"What are you doing?" Detective Coughlan demanded when she turned in her seat and began to pull at it.

"Getting out of here," she said.

The cop cursed, and the car swerved as he pulled it over. Oh well, if he wanted to come and open the door to try to stop her, she'd certainly take that escape route over throwing herself from a moving car.

Tensed, her muscles coiled and ready to spring, Evie put her feet against the door and kicked just as Coughlan was opening it, causing him to stumble a little. Knowing she had to take advantage of this very tiny window of opportunity, she shot out of the car.

She didn't get far before the cop grabbed her and yanked her up against his body. She was too short to try head-butting him, so she stomped as hard as she could on his foot, then rammed her elbow back into his groin. She must have connected well enough to cause pain because he howled and released her, doubling over as his hands cradled his aching manhood.

Evie turned to flee, but another police car pulled in behind Coughlan's and a pair of cops got out.

"Grab her," Coughlan yelled through clenched teeth.

Before she could do anything else, Evie found herself being shoved roughly down onto the pavement, her arms pulled behind her back and secured with handcuffs.

"He's trying to kill me," she said, thrashing in the cop's grip, no idea whether he was just an officer who thought he was helping out a colleague who had just been assaulted or another of Perez's men.

"She high?" the cop asked Coughlan, clearly not believing her.

"Please, he's a dirty cop," she begged as she was dragged to her feet.

"Yeah, sure." The cop holding onto her rolled his eyes and shoved her into the back of the other police car as she was read her rights.

"Wait, please, my purse," she said when he went to close the door. If she could get her purse then she'd have the recording proving that Coughlan was dirty. She might not trust these cops, but when they took her to the station she'd use her one phone call to call Owen, and when he came she'd give the recording to him.

When the cop nodded and retrieved her bag from Coughlan's car, Evie breathed a sigh of relief. So long as these two cops weren't dirty too then she had just been saved from certain death. Being cuffed and arrested was a small price to pay for her life.

* * *

2:18 P.M.

"Where are they?" Fox demanded, pacing outside the police station. "They should have been here hours ago. It only takes three hours tops to make it from the cabin to here, and it's been five since she left with the detective."

"Maybe they're not letting anyone see her," King suggested, not batting an eye when Fox threw a glare in his direction.

"Something is wrong, I can feel it. I knew it, all day yesterday I had this gut feeling that something bad was going to happen. How did the cops find out about the cabin? It's supposed to be one of Prey's safehouses. There is no way they should have known where to find us. And the Commander knew we were bringing in Prey to protect Evie because he said he didn't have the resources or manpower to do it. Why would he send Coughlan out there but not contact Prey first?"

Although he hadn't really been expecting any of his team to offer an answer, Eagle came storming toward them. When Evie had left with Coughlan, Fox had immediately called his team to tell them what was going on. King and Shark had driven out to pick him up, and by the time they got to the city a very unhappy Eagle had been there to greet them.

"We have a mole at Prey," Eagle announced, storm clouds practically hovering around him. "It's the only explanation. I'm so sorry, Fox."

That made sense, and as much as part of him wanted to go off on Eagle for not knowing he had a mole in his midst, given what had happened with Spider's wife Abby, he and his team were hardly in a position to be throwing stones. Instead, he just nodded once and said, "Find him."

"Oh, I will," Eagle said, his expression making it clear that when he identified the mole the man or woman would wish they had never been born.

"A mole inside the police force is one thing, but getting a mole inside Prey, that's next level," Chaos said, straightening from where he had been lounging against the wall of the precinct. "Prey is the best, and Eagle is not a man I'd want to get on the wrong side of, Falcon even less so, that's a lot of risk to take just to be an informant for Perez."

"Perez is a powerful guy," King said.

"Sure," Chaos agreed, "but in a choice between getting on Perez's bad side or Falcon and Prey's, I'd be picking Perez every time."

"Agreed, this would have to go beyond money. Whoever the informant is, Perez has something on him, something that would make him or her risk working for me knowing what would happen if they got caught," Eagle said thought-fully. "Raven is on it. If anyone can find out who the traitor is it's her."

Fox had to agree with that. There was no one better when it came to all things computer than Raven Oswald. Right now, however, he cared more about finding Evie than he did figuring out who the mole at Prey was.

"Shawn says to come in and meet him," Shark announced,

shoving his phone into his back pocket. "He also said to tell you not to lose it when we meet him."

His eyes narrowed. Why was Shark's brother worried about him losing it? Had something happened to Evie? Had the car been in an accident on the drive back here? Had they been ambushed by the cartel? Prey had been compromised so there was a chance that the cartel had known all along where Evie was staying and had been merely waiting for the perfect opportunity to take her out.

Unable to wait another second, Fox stormed inside the police station where Detective Shawn Kirk was waiting for them. He knew Shark's brother well enough. The man was happily married with two little girls and a baby boy, and would sometimes come over when the team had a barbecue or were hanging out together. Today the look on the man's face had his blood running cold.

"What's going on?" he demanded.

Shawn merely turned and motioned them to follow him as they walked through the precinct. They'd turned a corner into a corridor he knew was lined with interview rooms when he saw Evie.

Her hands were cuffed behind her back, her clothes were streaked with dirt, and there was a graze on her chin.

Fox lost it.

"What. Is. Going. On?" he bellowed, attempting to shove past the cop to get to Evie, who was being guided into a room.

"Owen," her sobbing voice echoed down the hall, and he pushed at Shawn who had shoved him up against the wall.

"Get the hell off me. Evie was arrested? For what?" He had to get to her, she needed him, whatever had happened to her had happened because he had ignored his instincts and allowed her out of his sight. The rest of his team looked no happier than he was and crowded around Shawn in a manner that could only be defined as threatening.

"What's going on, Shawn?" Shark demanded, pulling his brother off Fox.

"She was arrested for assaulting Detective Coughlan," Shawn explained.

Fox swore. "Dammit, he's the mole."

Shawn nodded. "I agree," he soothed, hands held up placatingly. "When I heard that she was being brought in and that she was claiming she hadn't assaulted an officer but been trying to escape a dirty cop who was intending to hand her over to the cartel, I knew that Coughlan was the mole we'd been looking for."

"So why is she still in cuffs being treated like a criminal?" Fox demanded. Never in his life had murder seemed so appealing. If Shawn didn't start explaining in the next three seconds, Fox would be sitting right beside Evie in handcuffs.

"Because there's someone else," Shawn said quietly. "I had to play along to see if I could draw whoever it was out into the open. I kept her safe, man, she didn't go to booking, and she wasn't sent to jail. I had her put in an interview room and left there. She's okay, she's scared and confused but she's okay, I had someone I trust outside her room the entire time."

"I'm going in there, and you're going to remove those cuffs right now," he seethed, storming down the hall.

"I intended to," Shawn said mildly, following behind him.

"Owen," Evie sobbed again when she saw him, eyeing the cop standing by the door as though she wanted to run into his arms but was afraid the cop would stop her if she tried.

He had no such concerns, he merely strode across the room and pulled her into his arms. "It's okay, sweetheart, I'm here now. I'm so sorry, I should never have let you go."

"It's Coughlan, he's the dirty cop, I have proof, but they

don't believe me. They arrested me, they cuffed me, they wouldn't listen to anything I had to say, just left me in a room for hours," she cried into his shirt as she pressed her face against his chest.

"I believe you, Ms. Walter," Shawn said as he moved behind Evie and removed the handcuffs.

As soon as she was free, Evie wrapped her arms around him and clung to him while she cried. "He was taking me to Perez," she said, voice muffled as her face stayed firmly pressed to his chest.

"It's all right, honey, he won't get near you again. Where is Coughlan?" he demanded as he sat and pulled Evie into his lap, one arm holding her securely against him while his other hand gently massaged her bruised wrists.

"In the wind, but there's a BOLO out on him, we'll find him," Shawn replied.

"He said he was going to disappear after he handed me over," Evie said, lifting her tear-stained face.

"Now he'll be too worried trying to evade the cops and the cartel," Shawn said with a smile of satisfaction.

"You really believe me?" Evie asked the detective.

"Yes. Coughlan is the mole, but I'd love whatever evidence you have against him," Shawn told her.

"I recorded him with my phone, but I don't have my purse anymore. They took it when they brought me here," Evie explained.

"I'm sorry I had to make it look like you were actually going to be booked and charged," Shawn said, pulling the other chair over so he was sitting directly in front of them. "But there's another mole. Coughlan was already being investigated before this, IA has had their eye on him for a while now, ever since he went off the deep end after his wife and son's murders, then one day returned to work as though nothing had happened. He's made a lot of calls to the same number from a burner phone we found hidden in his desk here at the precinct. We believe that person is another cop, possibly the one who went after Evie that first night and who set the fires."

"It's your job to find your second traitor, my job—our job," Fox amended, looking at his team, "is to keep Evie alive. With the department compromised and Prey compromised, I'm not handing her over to anyone else."

"Prey is compromised?" Evie asked.

"I'll explain later," he told her. "Right now, I'm taking you out of here. I assume she's free to go?" The look he gave Shawn said there was only one acceptable answer.

"Of course, and I'm going to be shouting it from the rooftops. If there is another cop involved then he's going to want to make a play for Evie to find out if Coughlan sold him out," Shawn told him. "I'm assuming you'll all be checking into a hotel?"

While the idea of Evie being used as bait went against every single one of his protective urges, Fox knew it was the easiest and quickest way to eliminate at least one of the threats hanging over her head. "We will be," he confirmed.

"You're not leaving me, are you?" Evie asked, sounding panicked by the idea.

"No. Never," he vowed.

If Evie was bothered by that vow she didn't show it, quite the contrary, all she did was curl her hands into his shirt and burrowed closer against him, giving a small content sigh when he tightened his hold on her. That gave him hope for their future, but before they could have that future, the Perez cartel needed to be taken down along with the dirty cops and Prey's mole.

# CHAPTER 13

April 10<sup>th</sup>

1:34 A.M.

"We don't have to do this if you don't want to," Owen told her as they walked hand in hand down the hotel corridor.

"I know," Evie said, smiling tiredly at Owen's protectiveness. It felt nice to know how much he cared. "We've been over it all a million times already and I'm okay with it. We're at the hotel, we don't try to hide we're here, and we hope that the second dirty cop will come after us. Well me. And then Shawn and your team will come riding in on your white horses to rescue me and arrest that guy ... or girl ... whoever, then maybe we can use them to turn the tables on Perez."

"I will be the only one doing the rescuing," Owen said fiercely.

"Is that so?"

"Yes."

"And why is that Mr. Macho Alpha SEAL?"

"Because you're mine." Owen grabbed her shoulders and pressed her up against the wall as his mouth hungrily claimed hers in a kiss that could only be described as a promise. "You got a problem with that?"

Evie tried to focus through the heat humming through her veins. How could Owen kiss her like that then expect her to form coherent thoughts or sentences? "No. No problem," she murmured, and it was true. In the hours she'd spent cold and terrified, handcuffed and in an interview room, she'd had plenty of time to think. Facing what she'd thought was either imprisonment on felony charges of assaulting a police officer, or death at the hands of the Perez cartel, one thing had been crystal clear to her.

She loved Owen.

That love didn't magically erase the pain she'd felt at learning he'd kept such a massive secret from her, nor did it automatically restore the trust that had been damaged, but it was enough. Enough for them to have their second chance, a chance to do it right this time. Now if people would just stop trying to kill her, they could get down to fixing what had been broken.

"You're good with being mine?" Owen asked, apparently surprised that she was no longer trying to figure out her feelings and what she wanted.

"Yes, because if I'm yours that makes you mine."

"Damn straight," he said with a satisfied nod. Then he sighed and leaned down so his forehead rested against hers. "I wish I could take you inside and spend the night making love to you then hold you as you sleep."

"I do too, but the dirty cop has to think I'm alone and vulnerable." As much as she was putting on a brave front so Owen didn't worry, she was terrified of going into her room alone knowing that someone would likely come after her. She was physically and emotionally exhausted after the day she'd had, and nothing would be better than making love to her man then falling asleep wrapped in his arms. She just had to be strong a little longer and then she could have that.

"All right, let's get this over with." He took her hand and they walked the rest of the way down to her room. Owen opened the door for her and led her inside where a very tall, very muscled, very intimidating man stood waiting for them. She would have been terrified of him, but she knew this had to be Eagle.

"Ms. Walter." He nodded at her, and despite his impassive face, she saw the anger and regret in his deep blue eyes. "I wanted to apologize in person for someone from my company leaking the address of the safehouse to the cartel."

Since it was clear he was truly regretful and determined to find the mole, Evie offered him a warm smile. "It's Evie, and it's okay, it's not your fault."

Eagle eyed her for a long moment, then gave a half-smile as he looked at Owen. "She's a keeper, Fox."

"That she is," Owen agreed, slinging an arm around her shoulders in a sideways hug.

"I will find the mole," Eagle vowed. "Raven is already working on it, and if anyone can find him, she can."

"Raven?" Evie asked.

"My sister."

"Oh … *oh*," she said again as she realized something. "I thought Eagle was your call-sign like Owen is Fox, but it's not, is it? Your parents actually named you all after birds."

Eagle grimaced. "They thought it would be a cute idea."

Evie laughed at the look on the man's face, it was clear he disagreed. "Thank you so much for everything you did to help me."

The large man brushed off her thanks. "Fox knows to call

if he needs Prey's help, that goes for you as well. You'll find my personal cell number programmed into your new phone." He nodded at a cell phone sitting on the nightstand. She needed a new one since the last had been taken as evidence, but hadn't expected Eagle to provide it.

"Thank you," she said again.

Eagle nodded, then headed for the door. "Come on, Fox, you're in the room to the left of Evie's with me and two of my men. Shark and his brother are in the room across the hall, and rest of your team is in the room to the right of Evie's."

"You sure about this?" Owen asked her.

"Yes, stop asking me that. I just want this over and doing this will make it happen quicker."

"Okay, goodnight then, I'll be right next door, and the room is wired with cameras and microphones, so as soon as he makes his move we'll be here."

"I know, I trust you, and Eagle, and your teams," she assured him.

"Okay," he said, hesitating and she knew the idea of leaving her knowing someone was most likely coming after her just about killed him.

"It will be okay, Owen," she said, offering him the reassurance he needed.

With a last kiss, Owen followed Eagle out of the room, making it clear to anyone watching them that she was now alone and vulnerable. Well, she only appeared vulnerable, but she had a whole team of people who had her back, and that was the only reason she was able to kick off her shoes and head into the bathroom.

After taking a quick shower, she was too nervous to really relax in there but needed to wash off the day's grime and filth, Evie threw on the pajamas they'd picked up on the way from the police station to the hotel, switched off the lights, and then climbed into bed.

As scared as she was lying there waiting for someone to break into her room, exhaustion tugged at her, forcing her eyes closed even as she battled to keep them open.

The next thing she knew a shadowy figure was standing over the bed.

A strangled scream escaped and she shuffled backward on the bed. Their theory was that whoever the other dirty cop was would be working mainly out of self-preservation rather than on Perez's orders, and wouldn't want to do anything to draw attention to themselves. That ruled out—hopefully—guns as a murder weapon but still left way too many options for her liking. Strangulation, knives, and poisons were at the top of her list.

"What did he say?" the man growled.

"Who?" she asked, playing dumb to buy time. Any second now Owen and the others would come bursting in but those seconds currently felt like an eternity.

"Don't play dumb, I don't have time. Did Coughlan mention me?"

"No," she said, scrambling further back and falling off the edge of the bed, landing hard on her backside and sending pain shooting up her spine.

"Good," he muttered, more to himself it seemed than to her. "Then since Coughlan is already dead, taking you out keeps me safe."

That was an interesting titbit, they hadn't known Coughlan was dead. The cartel must have gotten to him and taken him out for failing to deliver her. As soon as the thought flew through her mind, the man was circling the bed to get to her.

Evie scampered back until she was pressed into the

corner. She reached up and grabbed the lamp on the night-stand, swinging it at her attacker as he reached for her.

*Any second now would be good, Owen.*

As though he materialized right out of her thoughts, the hotel room door slammed open and the room flooded with people. Her assailant spun around, startled, and Evie shoved to her feet and crashed the heavy lamp into the back of the man's head.

He dropped at her feet, surprising her.

"Way to go, fairy," Owen's amused voice floated across the room at her.

Actually, everything seemed kind of floaty at the moment.

Woozy, she leaned back against the wall, still clutching the lamp in a death grip.

"It's okay, honey, we got him," Owen soothed as he appeared before her, hands held palms up in a non-threatening manner. "Here, let me take that."

Carefully, he eased the lamp from her fingers, which didn't seem to want to cooperate and let go. Once he had pried it away from her, he gathered her close, picking her up off the floor and cradling her gently.

"I feel odd … floaty …" she murmured, squeezing her eyes closed and pressing her face against his neck.

"You're in shock, honey," Owen told her.

"Oh." Now her body chose to give out on her, she supposed at least it was now and not five minutes ago when that man was standing above her bed.

"Here we go." He sat on the edge of the bed and pulled the blankets free, wrapping them around her now trembling form. "What do you need, baby?"

"This," she said through chattering teeth as she snuggled deeper into Owen's embrace. "This is all I need."

The bustling in the room faded away until all that existed

were Owen's strong arms wrapped around her, his hard body beneath her, his warm breath against her chilled skin, and the feel of his lips pressed against her temple. This was exactly where she wanted to be, where she always wanted to be.

* * *

6:13 A.M.

Miguel thrust in and out of the woman on the bed, his hands curled around her neck as he pounded into her. He came with a grunt as pleasure rippled through him and his hands tightened reflexively.

By the time the bliss-induced haze receded and he glanced down, he saw that the woman's eyes were open and staring sightlessly at the ceiling.

Oops.

It wasn't the first time he'd accidentally killed a woman during sex, sometimes he was a little overly enthusiastic in the bedroom. With a shrug of indifference, he pulled out of the now dead woman and headed for the bathroom to clean up. Once he'd taken a shower, he'd call his father's cleanup crew to dispose of the body for him and make sure there was no trace of her presence in his home.

He took a leisurely shower, then toweled off and threw on jeans and a t-shirt. Usually, he wouldn't bother with clothes, but Antonio was coming over, and they were going to discuss his plans to oust his father from his throne. The idea was a lot more appealing than he'd thought it would be. He'd never really seriously thought before about actually taking out the great and powerful Luis Perez.

Who would?

His father was a wealthy and ruthless cartel boss that had

men hidden in various governments and law enforcement agencies around the globe. With connections everywhere, nobody wanted to risk someone tipping Luis off before they managed to execute him.

But who would expect the hit to come from his own son?

With control over his father's empire, Miguel could hire someone to take care of running all the various operations, and he would be free to spend his days, well, pretty much doing what he was doing now only there would be no nagging presence whining about what a disappointment he was.

With a quick glance at the dead hooker in his bed, Miguel's mind filled with images of all the women he would have access to once he was in control of his father's empire as he headed down to the kitchen. His father's involvement in human trafficking meant that Miguel could have any woman he wanted. Instead of having to be careful not to harm women he picked up in bars—one assault allegation would cause his father to disown him—or paying for prostitutes who he still had to be marginally careful with, a woman who was a human trafficking victim would be completely and helplessly at his mercy.

The idea had him growing almost painfully hard, and he stood in the middle of the kitchen and stroked himself. A woman of his own that he could keep locked up in the house here, that he could play with whenever he wanted, who he didn't have to worry about being careful with, was like a dream come true. It would be like having his very own pet.

Miguel had been fourteen the first time his father had delivered a woman to his bedroom and told him to enjoy himself and learn to be a man. At first he'd been confused, tentative even, but his confidence had quickly grown and he realized that he enjoyed experimenting with what pleasured him.

When he had his pet he could beat her, make her bleed, force her to perform any acts he wanted.

Heaven.

It would be his very own version of heaven.

"Miguel."

He ignored Antonio's voice as he increased the speed of his hand, images flowing through his mind of the perfect woman to keep as his pet. Any ethnicity, any age, he could have a never-ending supply of whatever he wanted.

Pleasure exploded from the base of his spine up through his body, and he came in thick spurts all over the kitchen floor.

Sated and content—for the time being at least—he shoved his semi-hard length back into his jeans and then strolled to the counter. "Susanna," he bellowed.

A moment later a woman appeared in the doorway. Susanna was one of the maids. She was young but had been working for them long enough to learn proper respect and knew to expect and deal with anything in this job. "Yes, sir?" she said, keeping her eyes downcast and her tone respectful.

"Clean up that mess," he said, waving a hand at the white lines on the kitchen tiles.

"Yes, sir." Susanna hurried to complete the task. If she was embarrassed cleaning up semen in the middle of the kitchen she didn't show it.

Turning his attention away from the pretty maid he had been forbidden from bedding, Miguel looked over at his friend. Since Susanna was almost certainly more loyal to his father than she was to him, even if she did work in the home he lived in, Miguel waited to discuss their plan to take over the Perez cartel. "Breakfast?" he asked Antonio.

His friend shrugged. "Sure."

While Antonio slid onto one of the stools at the breakfast

bar, Miguel pulled out pancake mix and a frying pan. "Pancakes?"

"Sure. Whatever."

Antonio wasn't Mr. Talkative today, very unusual for his usually relaxed and cheerful friend, but Miguel was preoccupied with fantasies about all the women he would own in the future and barely spared the man a second thought as he set about cooking breakfast.

The cold press of metal against the base of his neck caught him by surprise, but before he could spin around and rip into Antonio for his childish prank, his friend's tortured voice offered an apology.

"I am sorry, Miguel," Antonio said.

"What?" he demanded, starting to turn.

"No. Don't move," Antonio ordered softly.

A moment later, rough hands grabbed him and dragged him into the middle of the kitchen, where he had been standing just minutes ago as he made himself come. He was shoved into a chair, his wrists and ankles bound to it with plastic zip ties.

"What is this?" he demanded, the first inkling of fear sneaking in when he saw two of his father's enforcers flanking Antonio, who stood with a gun in his hand.

A gun that was aimed at Miguel's head.

"I'm sorry, hermano," Antonio said, and he did look remorseful.

Just like that it clicked.

The reason his best friend since childhood was standing in his kitchen with Luis' men and a weapon.

Antonio had betrayed him.

"You told my father that I was planning on eliminating him," Miguel growled, betrayal a heavy rock in his stomach.

To his credit, Antonio didn't deny it. "He is disappointed with you, said he has given you every opportunity to prove that you are worthy of carrying on his name, and yet you have not. He said you are getting sloppy, the kill in the alley the other night, the fixation on this woman, and that you are risking all our lives by the careless way you treat the women you bring here."

"So he's going to have me killed?" Miguel scoffed at the notion. "Then who will take over his precious cartel when he is gone." When Antonio didn't reply, Miguel's mouth dropped open. "You? He's going to groom you as his heir?"

Antonio's head bobbed in a nod of assent. "He has always been like a second father to me, and he said I have been a loyal and worthy employee. He said I have behaved more like a son than you ever did."

"Just like that, everything that we shared is gone? Over? So you can pretend to be Luis Perez's son?" Miguel spit out the word like it tasted rotten in his mouth.

"I *am* sorry, Miguel, you have always been my brother, but I will not allow your immature behavior and sense of entitlement to ruin all your father has worked to build. You have brought this upon yourself, it didn't have to end this way. You have made yourself a liability, allowing your selfishly motivated murder to be witnessed and then trying to organize a coup? That cannot be allowed to happen, I will not, and your father cannot allow you to bring all of us down with you."

Shock, anger, denial, and fear all rippled through him as he realized his father really had turned his back on him.

Miguel had always believed that blood was thicker than water, that no matter what he did as Luis Perez's only son his father had no choice but to clean up the messes he left behind because he was the only one who could carry on his father's legacy.

Obviously, he had been wrong.

An opportunistic illegitimate son had risen to take his place.

"If my father can turn on me what makes you think he won't turn on you one day?" he sneered at the one man he had thought would always be on his side.

"As long as I please him, there is no reason for him to turn on me," Antonio replied.

Miguel just barked out a laugh. "Are you really that naïve? Luis Perez cannot be pleased. I should know, I wasted enough of my youth attempting to gain his love, his respect, his admiration. He will turn on you, it is not a matter of if, only when. And when that day comes, know that I will be waiting for you in Hell, *brother.*"

"Que dios me perdone. May God forgive me," Antonio muttered, then he lifted the weapon.

Miguel met his death face on, locking his gaze onto Antonio's so the other man had no choice but to look him in the eye as he pulled the trigger.

At least his position as Luis' son earned him a quick and painless death.

The bullet struck him between the eyes and in the next second, Miguel Perez left this planet.

* * *

4:37 P.M.

"How're you doing?" Fox asked as he crossed the hotel suite to where Evie was curled up in a chair. She'd held up amazingly well after the disaster of the previous day and this morning, but no one could go through that and not be struggling at least a little.

Evie lifted her blue eyes from where they'd been staring—

he suspected sightlessly—at the wall to meet his. She offered a tired smile and held out her hand to him. "I'm okay, but I'm better now that you're back, and I'll be even better if you were over here holding me."

When she said things like that it was like his heart was grabbed in a vice. After they'd arrested the man who'd broken into her hotel room to kill her—the police Commander of all people—she'd given her statement and he'd quickly bundled her away into a suite that Prey paid for and tucked her into bed. He'd wanted to be there when she woke up, but there had been a major break in the case, one he hoped meant that the heat was now off Evie.

Still, he should have been here for her when she woke up because it was clear she'd been upset to wake up alone in the hotel room.

"I'm sorry, Evie," he said as he took her hand and squeezed. "I should have been here when you woke up."

Her smile strengthened and she squeezed back. "No, it's okay, I know if you weren't here then it was for a good reason, I just … panicked … a little when I woke up and you weren't here. But then I saw your note, and I was okay."

Every day he was amazed by her resilience. He had no idea how she managed to pull it together after getting beaten down time and time again. "You're really something special." He picked her up and sat down with her on his lap, then hesitated. He knew what he wanted to say to her, he just wasn't sure if she was ready to believe it. Deciding he should take a page out of Evie's book and just trust his heart, he said, "I love you, Evie, and I pray that one day you'll be able to believe that."

She graced him with another smile and slipped her arms around his neck. Her hold on him was vicelike and then she kissed him hard on the mouth. "I believe you, and I love you too, so much."

Fox felt his entire being relax.

Evie loved him.

She accepted that despite the mistakes he'd made he loved her too.

Clutching her tightly to his chest, he couldn't move, could barely breathe, the weight of his emotions nearly crushing him.

He probably would have sat there for hours just holding Evie, but there was a knock on the suite door, and then it opened, and his team, and Eagle, and Shark's brother Shawn all piled into the room. Evie moved as though to get up, but Fox tightened his hold to keep her in place. It wasn't like they had anything to hide, they'd been married, everyone knew he wanted her back, and no one would be surprised that he'd finally made it happen.

"You break the news to her yet?" King asked as he lounged in the other chair.

"Nope, I was waiting for you guys," Fox replied.

"Is it bad news?" Evie asked, searching his face then looking at the others.

"No," he assured her. "It's good news. We hope," he added because they were still going to have to wait and see how things turned out before he was willing to say that she was actually safe and out of the woods.

"Is someone going to put me out of my misery and tell me what the rest of you all already know?" Evie asked.

"So, as you know," Shawn started, "last night it was the police Commander who broke in here to try to kill you, he was the other one on Perez's payroll. He was the one who gave the order to Coughlan to go after you, and the one who originally linked him up with Perez in an attempt to get more men and women on the force who were secretly working for Perez. The Commander was more worried about Luis sending someone after him to take him out than he was about actually getting sent to prison so he started singing like a canary. In exchange for being placed in protective custody, he gave us the address of the house where Miguel Perez has been living."

Evie's eyes grew wide. "So you have Miguel in custody? Does that mean I'll be safe now? You have the two dirty cops and Miguel, so I'm safe. Right?" She looked around hopefully, and Fox knew what they were about to tell her would burst her bubble.

In a good way.

"Actually," Shawn said slowly, shooting her a huge grin, "it's better than that."

"Better?" Evie echoed, her brow creased in confusion.

"When we stormed the house it had been recently vacated, but there was a body in the kitchen. It was Miguel Perez, he'd been tied up and shot once in the head," Shawn told her.

Since she was sitting on his lap, Fox felt the shudder ripple through Evie's body. "So it's over? He's dead, so that means I'm in the clear, right? I mean, his father has no reason to come after me if Miguel is dead. You can't send a dead man to prison so my statement is worthless now."

Although she sounded like she believed what she was saying, he caught the glimmer of doubt hidden deep in her eyes. "Yeah, honey, we believe that now that Miguel is dead the heat on you should die down. I don't think we have to worry about Perez coming after you, especially considering who killed Miguel."

"Oh," Evie said like she hadn't even considered anything to do with who or why the son of one of the most notorious cartel boss' in the world had been murdered. "Who did kill Miguel?"

"His father," Shawn answered.

"His *father*?" Evie said, stunned.

"That's our assumption. Besides the bullet between the eyes, which was what killed him, Miguel was also found with a knife in his stomach. The Perez cartel has a thing about knives, and it's their signature kill, they're ruthless, and a gut wound is a slow and painful way to die."

Evie flinched at Shawn's words, but he could tell she was overwhelmed with relief to know that now she wouldn't have to live looking over her shoulder. "Why would Luis kill his son?" she asked.

"According to the Commander, Miguel was planning on attempting to overthrow his father, only the man he trusted to help him do it told Luis, who took action and decided to take out his son before his son could take him out," Shawn explained.

"And now you're safe," Fox told her, touching a kiss to her temple.

"It's over," Evie said softly, sagging against him.

"It's over," Eagle agreed, "and my team is still looking to take out Luis Perez, as well as find our own mole, so now you can focus on your future." As he said that he gave a pointed look between Evie and Fox.

Fox couldn't agree more.

Their future started right this second.

"Okay, Evie is exhausted, we'll catch up with you guys tomorrow," he announced.

Thankfully, everyone took the hint, and after saying their goodbyes the others all left, and he was alone with the woman he loved.

"Owen?" Evie asked as she rested her head on his shoulder.

"Yeah, sweetheart?"

"I'm sorry I called Shark and not you when I first realized I was in trouble. And I'm sorry I didn't believe you at first when you said that you loved me and not just because I remind you of Maya."

"I don't ever want you to apologize for trying to protect yourself. Us breaking up is on me, I'm just grateful you were willing to give me another chance, and that we're together again now. Because, Evie, we *are* together now."

"I know." The smile she gave him was as bright as sunshine.

"That means you can expect a proposal in the very near future." Seeing Spider married and having his first kid, and Night engaged and expecting a baby had him thinking about family and fatherhood. Only he'd been alone, he couldn't have the woman he wanted and he wasn't interested in anyone else. But now that he had Evie back he wanted it all, he wanted to make her his wife as soon as possible, and he couldn't wait to see her stomach swollen as their baby grew inside her.

"I can't wait," Evie said on a yawn.

As much as he wanted to strip her naked and make love to her for hours, she was exhausted and needed rest. Now that the Perez situation was resolved, she could finally let go and get the deep, healing sleep she needed.

"Come on, let's get you back into bed." Fox stood with Evie in his arms and carried her to the bed.

"Will you lie down with me?"

"Do you really have to ask?"

"Just checking."

Fox stretched out beside her, tugged her onto her side so she was using his chest as a pillow, then tucked them both under the covers. With Evie's warm breath puffing against his skin, and her hair tickling his nose, he closed his eyes, held his woman close, and drifted off to sleep.

# CHAPTER 14

April 11<sup>th</sup>

10:08 A.M.

"Now you can tell us everything," Abby said, looking at her with eager eyes as the three of them sat down on the front porch.

Evie grinned at her friends, it felt so good to be here hanging out with them again like this. While she'd kept in touch with Abigail and Lavender even after she had left Owen, this was the first time she'd hung out with them, Owen, and Owen's team. The guys had offered to be on baby patrol so that the girls could have some time to catch up.

"From that grin, I'm thinking everything between you and Owen is pretty good," Lavender said.

"Perfect," Evie corrected. "It's perfect."

"I'm so glad you two are back together," Abby said. "Owen has been miserable being apart from you."

"If you'd told me that just a couple of weeks ago I would have scoffed at the notion. He lied to me about Maya, and he never made any attempts at contacting me after I left. I just assumed I was right and that he was only with me because it was as close to being with Maya as he could get. Now though, I know that he loves both of us, it's the same but different too. I never thought I would say this, but I'm actually grateful for the Perez cartel because if I hadn't witnessed Miguel killing that man, Owen and I would never have gotten back together." It felt wrong to be grateful for it after everything she'd gone through, but having Owen back meant it was well and truly worth all the fear and pain of the last week.

Abby had paled at the mention of the cartel, but she offered a small smile. "I know what you mean. As awful as what happened to me was, I am grateful that it gave Ryder and I a second—well third really—chance."

"And if I hadn't been held hostage while doing aid work in Afghanistan, then Eric and I would never have become anything more than friends," Lavender added, resting a hand on her stomach where the beginnings of a baby bump was showing. "Now we'll be having a little one in less than six months."

Evie laughed as she realized that all three of them had gotten their happy endings thanks to traumatic events. "We're a funny group, aren't we? It takes being thrown into danger to get the men in our lives to get with the program."

The other two women chuckled along with her. "Our guys are hardwired to respond to danger," Lavender said. "I guess seeing us in it makes them open their eyes to what's right in front of them."

"So have you and Owen …" Abby asked with a waggle of her eyebrows.

Evie felt her cheeks heat, but she nodded. "We made love for the first time while we were hiding out at the cabin, then we did a lot of making out there, it was like being in our own little world. Last night once we'd both gotten some sleep we made love in the bed, and the shower, and the jacuzzi tub, and pretty much christened every inch of the hotel suite."

"Have you two talked about what happens next?" Lavender asked.

"Owen said he's going to be proposing soon. Since both of our houses got burned down thanks to the cartel, we're going to stay at the hotel for a while. Owen said he'll feel better when he gets called out, knowing I'm somewhere secure, and I think Eagle felt really bad that there was a mole in his business that leaked the address of the cabin, so he's footing the bill for the hotel suite for as long as we need to stay there. Once we sort things out with the insurance agencies, I think we're probably going to sell both plots of land and buy a new house. I think both of us are ready for a fresh start."

"So marriage is in the near future for you two?" Abby asked.

"Very near," she corrected. "Last time we didn't go for a big wedding, my family was furious about it, but I didn't care then, and I don't care now. All that mattered to me back then was marrying the man I loved and nothing has changed. I can't wait to be married to Owen again."

"And will there be any little additions to the family soon?" Lavender asked, touching her baby bump again.

"I think Owen and I need a little time to get to know one another again, but we've already lost a lot of time together, so yeah, I think babies are in our near future, probably once we get settled into a new home."

"You'll get plenty of practice with RJ, and then Eric and Lavender's baby," Abby said. "By the time you and Owen are ready, and your own little one comes along, you're going to be an expert."

"Is that a hint for babysitters?" Evie teased.

Stifling a yawn, Abby shot her a grin. "If the first eleven days have been this exhausting, and from what I hear things don't get any less exhausting for a looooong time, then yep it sure is." She snickered. "I can't wait to see Logan babysit, Charlie is a natural with kids, and Grayson is so funny that I know he'll have RJ getting up to all sorts of mischief. My brother will have his own baby soon, and Owen is good at everything so I can't imagine him not managing, but picturing the huge, calm, always stoic Logan "Shark" Kirk dealing with a newborn makes me laugh."

Evie and Lavender joined in the laughter. It was true, the idea of Shark with a baby was amusing.

Lavender stood. "I'll be right back, gotta use the restroom."

"Bring back snacks," Abby said. "And ask Ryder how RJ is, hopefully he'll sleep for another hour or so before he needs a feed, but we don't have him on a schedule yet so we're kind of all over the place."

"Will do," Lavender said as she headed inside.

"So, how are you enjoying motherhood?" Evie asked once they were alone.

"I love it. I know I was hard to live with those last couple of months of my pregnancy because it was so hard being stuck in bed or on the couch all the time, but Ryder was amazing. He was so sweet and understanding, and he took such good care of me. And now RJ is born, even though I'm breastfeeding so there isn't really much he can do to help, he always gets up with me for middle of the night feedings. I'm really lucky to have him, RJ and I both are."

Evie knew that feeling, it was exactly how she felt about Owen. "Maybe we might bump making a baby up on our timeline."

"You getting all ... oh," Abby trailed off, her gaze on the sidewalk outside her and Spider's home. "Are you okay, honey?"

Following Abigail as she hurried down the garden path toward a little girl of maybe five or six, who had fallen off her bike, they both knelt beside the child. "You okay?" Evie asked.

The little girl was crying, but she offered a small nod.

"Where is your mommy or daddy?" Abigail asked, scanning the empty street.

Before the child could offer an answer, a van came hurtling down the street pulling up beside them. Evie assumed it was the girl's parents, maybe she'd gone riding off away from home, and her parents had had to take out their car to go looking for her. Imagining how terrified they must have been had her rethinking the whole have a baby thing. Was she really ready to worry about a child right now when she was still working through what she'd just been through?

The van's side door was flung open, and Evie opened her mouth to ask if they were the girl's parents, but it snapped shut when she saw two men with ski masks covering their faces.

Abigail screamed loudly as one of the men grabbed her and yanked her inside the van. A startled scream was ripped from her own mouth as the other man reached for her. She scrambled to her feet but the man was already on her, snatching her off the street and into the van, which took off, tires screeching.

Abby was fighting against the man restraining her, and Evie fought just as hard, but two other men were back there, and both had prepared syringes. The man holding her immobilized her, her back against his front, an arm clamped around her chest, and one across her stomach, pinning her arms to her side.

The man with the syringe stabbed it into her arm and injected what she assumed was a sedative. Almost immediately, heat flushed through her body, and then a floaty feeling took hold. A glance at Abby showed her friend already sagging, unconscious, in the hold of the man restraining her, and it didn't take long for blackness to seep into her mind.

Although Evie fought against the drug she'd been given, it didn't do any good.

The blackness overtook her, and she joined her friend in unconsciousness, both of them completely vulnerable to whoever had abducted them.

\* \* \*

10:29 A.M.

Watching his friend cradle the tiny baby in his arms, swaddled in a light blue blanket, had Fox immediately picturing himself holding his own child in his arms. He'd love to have a son, someone who might follow in his footsteps one day as he'd followed in his father's footsteps, but having a mini ball of sunshine like Evie would be wonderful too.

They'd talked about the near future, sorting things out with their respective insurance agencies, pooling their money to buy a new house that would be just theirs, staying in the hotel until they found the perfect place, but they hadn't discussed any further than that. When he got Evie alone later today, he would feel her out on the possibility of adding a third member to their little family sooner rather than later.

Then he'd feel her up.

Fox snickered at his own joke as Lavender joined him and his team in the living room.

"I see the little guy is awake," she said, slipping an arm around Night's waist and resting against her fiancé. "Abby was hoping he would sleep a little longer before needing another feed."

"RJ always seems to be hungry, I had no idea how much newborns ate," Spider said, unable to tear his gaze away from his son's sweet little face.

"I'll go grab Abby," Lavender offered, but paused to kiss the baby's cheek, "so you guys can continue to be all goo goo eyes over the baby."

"Goo goo eyes?" Shark echoed, making a face.

"I'm goo goo eyes," King said, "this little guy is adorable, and I've heard that men with babies attract women. It's practically like waving a magnet at them and reeling them in."

Spider made a shocked face then shook his head. "You don't get to babysit him until he's old enough to drive."

"Great, then I'll have a wingman, you guys are all useless." King grinned as though the idea was highly appealing.

"Okay, you don't get to be alone with RJ until he's old and gray," Spider amended.

"That's okay, you don't need the women magnet babysitting, you have me," Chaos said, and from the gleam in his eye it was clear he was already coming up with crazy pranks the two of them could pull.

Spider shot him a dubious frown. "You're going to get my kid arrested, or blown up, or something, aren't you?" Chaos just grinned and Spider groaned, then turned to Shark. "I trust this guy with RJ more than you two."

Shark looked pleased with the compliment but didn't respond, and Lavender laughed then shook her head at all of them. "You're all smitten with the baby, and all jokes aside, Eric and I do trust you to babysit our little one when he or she arrives, and I know Abby and Spider trust you too."

A sharp scream split the air, and just like that all joking and baby gazing ended. Spider thrust RJ into Lavender's arms. "Take him upstairs and lock yourself in the master bedroom," he ordered.

Fox was already heading for the front door. Evie was out there, had something happened to her? They'd assumed the threat was basically over given that Luis Perez had killed his son, and even with the cartel he'd thought she was safe enough sitting on the front porch of her friend's house while he and his team were all inside.

Obviously, he'd been wrong.

His team appeared beside him and cautiously he opened the front door. The porch was empty, and as he scanned the street, he saw a small girl, maybe five years old, on the sidewalk with her bike. It looked like the child had fallen, and even from here he could hear her weeping.

There was no one else about, and no shots were fired as he and his team spilled out of the house. While his men checked for either Evie and Abby, or anyone else hanging around, Fox headed straight for the kid.

"Hey, sweetie," he said, forcing his voice to come out calm and soothing, with no signs of the terror that was swirling inside him. "Can you tell me what happened? Did you see any ladies about? One has lots of blonde curls, and the other one has pretty brown hair just like yours."

The little girl nodded as tears continued to roll down her cheeks.

"Yes, you saw them, or yes, you can tell me what happened?" he asked. The street was empty, but he could see a few front doors opening, people looking out to see what had caused the screams but not wanting to walk into a bad situation.

Walking into bad situations was what they did.

And there wasn't anything he wouldn't walk into if it meant protecting Evie.

There was no way she—or Abby—would have just disappeared. They wouldn't have gone wandering off, especially with Abby's newborn son inside, but they would have come running to help a little girl who'd fallen off her bike.

Had it been a trap?

Had someone used this kid to get Evie and Abby away from the house, making them easier targets to kidnap?

"Honey?" he prompted the little girl. "What's your name?"

"S-Sally," she said through her tears.

"Did you see those women, Sally?"

"Y-yes," she cried.

"What happened to them?"

"It w-was the b-bad men," Sally wept.

"Bad men?"

Sally nodded. "They came to my house."

"Where's your house?"

She pointed down the street.

"What did they do?"

"They hurt my mommy, and they said to ride my bike and pretend to fall over when I got to the house with the ladies on the porch," Sally explained, still crying. "I didn't want to, but they hit my mommy, and she said it was okay. I did hurt my knee." Sally pointed to a red mark on her knee.

"It's okay, honey, I know you didn't want to lie." Looking over his shoulder at Spider who was standing stiffly, and Chaos, he nodded down the street. "Go check on the girl's mother, if we're able to, find out what she knows. Shark, call your brother," he said when the rest of his team joined him. "Honey, what happened to the ladies?"

"They had a big car, like a van, and they took them," Sally replied.

Since he was in the presence of a child, he bit back the vicious string of curses that wanted to burst out.

Evie was gone.

Just when he'd thought it was over and everything was going to be smooth sailing from here on out, she was snatched off the street right under his nose.

A woman who looked like an adult version of Sally came running across the street, Spider and Chaos on her heels. When she reached them, she dropped to the ground and dragged her daughter into her arms. "Are you okay, Sally? Did they hurt you?"

"No, Mommy. But I hurt my knee when I pretended to fall." The little girl showed her mother her knee.

The woman had blood streaking down one side of her head, and there were red marks on her wrists, indicating she'd been restrained. She cradled her daughter, rocking her from side to side as she wept.

Why had the kidnappers picked this woman and her daughter to use?

Was it random or was she somehow connected to the men who had taken Evie and Abby?

"Ma'am, do you know them?" Fox asked.

The woman wouldn't look at him, just clutched her daughter and rocked.

Spider squatted beside her and took her chin, forcing her to look at them. "Tell us who they are or go down as accomplices. They took my wife. My ten-day-old son is inside my house waiting for his mother to come and feed him, only she can't because you helped someone kidnap her."

Since Evie had been snatched right along with Abigail, Fox wasn't in a particularly charitable mood. The woman knew something, and it was clear she was hesitant to tell them what it was.

That was unacceptable.

"Who are they?" he demanded.

Fearful dark eyes met his. "I don't know them, I swear, but my ex-husband, he had a drug problem, he's in prison, but he got mixed up with the Perez cartel. I swear, I've never done drugs, and I kicked him out when I found out. I filed for divorce and got custody of Sally. The men said that Derek had made a deal with them for my safety, to keep them away from us. They said if I wanted that deal to continue I had to help them. They wanted your wife," the woman's eyes moved to Spider, "and another woman. I'm sorry, I didn't want to do it, but they would come after Sally if I didn't. I couldn't let that happen."

Unfortunately, he understood that.

Spider stood and began to pace, raking his hands through his hair.

Fox felt about ready to rip his hair out, anything to alleviate the fear building inside him. The Perez cartel had Evie and Abigail, and he had no idea how they would get the women back.

*  *  *

12:36 P.M.

The swim to consciousness seemed to take forever.

Evie struggled through it, some innate instinct telling her that it was very important that she wakes up.

Finally, she reached the surface and blinked open eyes that felt like they had been glued shut.

The first thing she registered was the gentle rocking.

Was she in a hammock?

No.

That made absolutely no sense.

The ceiling above her head was smooth and white, but when she turned her head she saw a window, through the window was water.

The ocean.

They were on a boat.

Struggling to sit up, Evie scanned the rest of the room, her gaze immediately falling on Abigail who was sprawled on a bed next to her.

Still woozy from whatever drug she'd been injected with, Evie swayed as she shoved off her bed and teetered the couple of steps between the two beds.

"Abby?" She touched her fingertips to her friend's neck and was relieved to find a strong pulse.

There was no answer, and helplessness washed over her.

Evie pressed her hands to her eyes, determined not to cry. She had to stay strong. Hold it together. Owen and the rest of the guys would have heard their screams. When they came outside and couldn't find them, they would know they'd been taken. No way would Abigail walk away from her ten-day-old son, and the guys would *have* to know they hadn't left on purpose. They'd have to.

So long as she kept telling herself that then maybe she could keep it together.

Maybe.

She'd done okay in the car with Coughlan, she's managed to hold it together and even save herself, and she'd escaped the man who had gone to her house to kill her that first night after she'd witnessed Miguel committing murder. She could do this. All she needed to do was gather as much information as she could. The more she knew, the better she could protect herself and Abigail.

The room they'd been left in was nice but small, it didn't take long to search it and the tiny attached bathroom. Besides the window next to the bed she'd been left on, there was only one other exit. A door that was of course locked.

A groan tore her attention back to her friend, and when she saw Abigail's lashes fluttering on her pale cheeks she hurried over to the bed.

"Abby?"

"Evie?" came the weak reply.

"It's me. Can you open your eyes?"

"Where are we?" Abigail asked as her unusual eyes—one a silvery gray the other a golden brown—opened slowly and she winced as she looked around.

"Do you remember what happened?"

"Unfortunately, I do." Abby grimaced and allowed Evie to help her sit up.

"They took us to a boat." Evie gestured out the window.

"A boat?"

She shrugged. "I guess they want to take us somewhere."

"But where? And who are they?"

"I wish we could have gotten a look at their faces," Evie said. It was so much easier to fight an enemy when you knew who they were and what they wanted.

"Yeah, me too. But we screamed, and the guys will have heard us, they'll know we're missing, and they'll be looking for us. Let's just hope they find us quickly," Abigail said softly.

Evie prayed they did.

Abigail had been missing for fourteen months, and when she was found almost a year ago it was a fluke. Owen and his team had been sent in to rescue three abducted little girls, and Spider had stumbled across Abby, locked in a cage and close to death.

Is that what was going to happen to them?

"They'll find us," she said, sitting beside her friend and putting an arm around Abigail's shoulders.

Abby hugged her back, a fierce determination in her eyes. "Yeah, they will, and in the meantime, we're going to find a way to save ourselves."

The same determination slowly seeped into her.

Abigail was right. They weren't helpless, and they weren't alone, they had each other, and between the two of them they would do everything they could to find a way to escape.

"We'll figure something out," she said confidently. Okay, so she wasn't actually confident in their ability to find an escape route, but she did know that they would do their best to make it happen.

The door to their room suddenly flung open, and a well-manicured man dressed in a smart black suit strolled in. He had jet black hair streaked with gray that was neatly combed, there were a few wrinkles around his dark brown eyes, and his nose was slightly crooked like it might have been broken at some point.

He looked familiar, but she couldn't place him.

On either side of him were two men, dressed all in black, both well-armed with handguns in holsters on their hips, and machine guns in their hands.

Beside her, Abby gasped and everyone's attention—including her own—snapped in her direction. Abigail had shuffled further back on the bed, adding a couple of feet distance between herself and the three men, she had also gone deathly pale and started to shake.

Evie's gaze bounced between her friend and the men, and realization dawned. "You know who he is."

"I'm pleased to hear that, Ms. McNamara, or is it Flynn now? I did hear that you were married," the man in the suit said.

"Have you been watching me?" Abigail asked, looking horrified by the possibility.

How did she know this man?

And why was he so familiar?

"I like to keep apprised of what people I am interested in are doing," suit man replied.

"Interested in?" If it was possible, Abby seemed to pale further.

"I enjoyed watching you." This time when the suit man spoke, hunger glittered in his dark eyes, and he took a step toward the bed.

Had he watched Abigail?

When?

Where?

Evie gasped as she realized why the man looked familiar and how he'd had cause to watch Abigail. "You're Luis Perez."

Luis' attention swung in her direction, the hunger in his eyes replaced by anger. "I am sure the police showed you my picture when you were speaking with them about my son."

It was clear that even though he had been willing to kill Miguel to keep him from attempting a coup, he was still angry that she had been the catalyst for the situation by telling the cops what she'd seen in that alley.

"Why did you kidnap us?" Abigail asked.

"Ms. Walter messed with my family. Even though Miguel is gone now that doesn't mean she gets off scot-free. I think with those curls and those big blue eyes she'll fetch me a great price when I sell her. But you, Ms. Flynn, are here for a more personal reason." Luis nodded at one of his men who stalked toward them. Knocking Evie out of the way, he grabbed Abigail and dragged her across the room.

"Let go of me," Abigail screamed as she struggled to get out of the man's grip.

Evie moved automatically to help her friend, Luis words about selling her had not yet sunk in, but the other man aimed his weapon at her, and she froze.

"You, Ms. Flynn, are going to be mine. Your friend will be

trained and sold, but I'm keeping you for myself. I have been enchanted with you ever since you spent time on my property. Those eyes of yours, I have never seen anything like them. I watched Alex with you, watched him touch you, watched him take you." Luis reached out to stroke Abigail's face. She struggled and tried to move away but couldn't get far because of the man holding her.

"Don't touch her," Evie yelled.

"Oh, I'm going to touch her, she belongs to me now, and I will do with her whatever I choose." Luis reached out and grasped one of Abigail's breasts, from the way she winced, Evie knew he hadn't been gentle. "You, on the other hand, are merely a business transaction, you are expendable, so I'd watch your mouth if I was you." Luis nodded at the man holding Abigail, and he released her, then moved back to stand beside his boss. "We will soon be in Mexican waters, and not long after that we will arrive at my home."

"You won't get away with this," Abigail screamed at him as the three men left the room. "When my husband finds us he'll kill you."

Alone again the two women ran to each other, holding each other tightly. Right now, Evie didn't see how they were going to get out of this. They were in the middle of the ocean, soon they would be out of US waters, heading toward a cartel's compound. Even if Owen, and Spider, and the others figured out the cartel was after them it didn't mean they would get to them in time.

At least not in time to save her.

While Luis Perez was obsessed with Abigail and intended to keep her, Evie was going to be trained as a sex slave and sold.

She'd thought the danger surrounding her was gone, that she and Owen were free to finally get back to their lives together, but now she might never see him again.

\* \* \*

1:14 P.M.

Time was ticking by too quickly.

Evie and Abigail had been gone now for almost three hours. That was long enough for the cartel to have whisked the two women away someplace they would never be found.

Fox was struggling to focus. All he could picture was Evie's head on his chest as they lay in bed together last night. If he blocked everything else out, he could still feel her warm breath puffing against his skin, still feel her blonde curls tickling his nose, still feel her slight weight lying across him.

Now she was gone.

Possibly forever.

"We need to figure out if Abby or Evie was the target," Matthew "Wolf" Steel said, sounding as frustrated and fearful of this situation as Fox himself felt. They'd called in another team to help them find the women, and since Wolf and his team had been involved in Abigail's rescue almost a year ago, and he and all of his men were close with her, they had seemed like the best choice. Now, the two teams were gathered in a room on the base, trying to figure out a plan to get Evie and Abigail back alive. While this was personal for him, Spider, and Night, and by extension the rest of his team, Wolf and his men had all had their women live through dangerous ordeals, and there was no one better to help them now.

"It could be either of them," Spider said, glancing at his phone where he had the app linked to the baby monitor in RJ's crib open. Lavender was looking after the baby, but Fox knew that Spider felt torn between looking after his son and looking for his kidnapped wife. "Perez allowed Alex to keep

215

Abby on his compound for fourteen months so there's a chance he wants her for some reason. And Evie was willing to testify against Luis' son, even if he did eliminate his son as a threat, there's a chance he still wants revenge."

Fox agreed, either woman could be the target.

Right now, though, he didn't much care about which one of them had been targeted, he just wanted to find out where they were and bring them home.

"You reach out to Eagle?" Christopher "Abe" Powers asked. "Heard that he was planning an op to take out Perez."

"I'd love to be in on that," Hunter "Cookie" Knox muttered. Cookie had rescued a woman from human traffickers in Mexico. The woman had been hooked on drugs by her abductors and was now Cookie's wife. Fiona was also a close friend of Abigail's, the two had bonded over their experiences. It was no wonder that Cookie wanted in on taking down a well-known drug trafficker.

"Eagle is sending us everything he has on Perez and the cartel, including any planes or boats that he owns," Fox explained. "Perez's men have two kidnap victims, and they want to get back to Mexico as quickly as they can. Chances are they won't risk driving, they'll take a private jet or a boat of some sort."

"That makes the most sense," Night agreed. Abby was Night's sister so he was every bit as afraid for the women's safety as he and Spider were.

"So what's the plan?" Sam "Mozart" Reed asked.

"We hope that Eagle has a complete list of any boats or planes Perez owns, and then as soon as we get it we start checking to see if he filed any flight plans or if anything flew out of the smaller airports. We check out the closest harbor to see if any boats matching descriptions of anything Perez owns recently left," King replied.

"It's still bothering me that we don't know Perez's

motives," Faulkner "Dude" Cooper said, tapping the end of a pen on the table.

"What if he went after both of them?" Kason "Benny" Sawyer suggested.

"Like a two for one," Chaos said, nodding like he agreed with that idea.

"You think they were both the targets?" Mozart asked.

"Abby has been home for almost a year now. Why would he wait all this time to go after her?" Spider demanded, clearly not liking the idea that Perez wanted to get his hands on Abigail specifically.

"What was your original reasoning for why Abby had been kept so long?" Wolf asked. Although it was clearly a rhetorical question, Spider answered anyway.

"That the cartel intended to sell her or keep her for themselves." Spider looked sick at the thought of either of those possibilities.

"So he took Abby because she's gorgeous and knows that with those eyes of hers he'll get a lot of money for her, or he's obsessed with her. Did he take Evie for the same reason?" Abe asked.

"Yes." The word felt like it wanted to strangle him, but Fox forced it out. "If he didn't, if all he wanted was to teach her a lesson for agreeing to testify against Miguel, and to send a message about what will happen to anyone who stands up against the cartel, then he would have shot her, or stabbed her in the gut and left her to bleed out."

A hand closed over his shoulder, and he looked at Spider, took comfort in their solidarity, and their shared determination to scour the globe if that was what it took to find the women who owned their hearts.

"That makes sense," Wolf agreed. "If he wanted her dead you would have found her body next to the kid."

"Or he dumped her somewhere so she could bleed out

slowly," King suggested, wincing as he said the words and shooting Fox an apologetic frown.

"No reports of any bodies matching Evie's description found," Chaos added.

"Evie is a beautiful woman. He probably thought he could teach her a lesson and make some money off her," Benny suggested. "He took them both for the same reason, he's either keeping one or both of them for himself or he intends to sell them. Pretty, young Caucasian women, especially one with Abby's eyes, and a pretty little blue-eyed blonde, he'll get a lot of money for them."

"All right, so we have motive," Dude said, "now we need to figure out the where."

"Chances are he'd go to his compound," Mozart said.

"We've breached it before, we can do it again," Shark said with calm determination. If you didn't know the man, you'd think he was completely uncaring of the fact that two of his team members' women had been abducted, one of whom was a new mother leaving behind her ten-day-old son, but Fox knew that Shark cared. Sometimes he thought Shark cared too much and the only way he didn't self-destruct from the strength of his emotions was to shut them down, lock them up so tightly that Fox wasn't even sure Shark knew how to let them back out.

"If we work with Eagle and Prey then maybe we can actually take down the cartel once and for all," Wolf said thoughtfully.

The room rumbled with agreement. Luis Perez needed to be taken down. Of course, another cartel would rise in its place, but Perez dominated gun, drug, and human trade, had contacts everywhere, in almost every country across the globe. The world would be a better place—even if only marginally—if Luis Perez was no longer in it.

"We also need a list from Eagle of all properties Perez

SAVING OWEN (SPECIAL FORCES: OPERATION ALPHA)

owns or might have access to in case he decides he's brought enough heat down on himself for the time being and thinks he better not head home just yet," Dude said.

"Even if he does head back to the compound, it's not going to be as easy to breach as it was when we've done it before," Abe cautioned. "This time he's going to be expecting us to come after Abby and Evie. He has to know that Evie is involved with a SEAL because you've been all over the situation, making sure she was kept safe, and if he's been watching Abby then he knows she's married to a SEAL. He'll be expecting us, Prey too, because the dirty cops knew of their involvement. Perez would know Prey's reputation, and he'd be expecting a joint Prey and SEAL assault. He's going to have his security beefed up to the max, he's going to be prepared for us. Getting in and out will be difficult."

"But not impossible," Wolf countered. "Not for us anyway."

"Definitely not for us," Spider echoed.

"And with Prey on board, Perez doesn't stand a chance no matter how many men he has and how many weapons he has access to. We know Perez's men are bloodthirsty but not well trained, they're no match for us," Fox said confidently. Especially not when they would be there on such an important mission.

This wasn't just saving someone they knew, it was saving the woman he loved, and the woman Spider loved. His entire team—Wolf's too—loved both Abby and Evie like little sisters, they would go all out, failure wasn't an option. If he didn't get Evie back he'd have lost another woman he loved. He would have to accept that she'd been taken from right underneath his nose. Whatever happened to her was on his head, and he wasn't going to spend the rest of his life knowing that she had lost hers because of his failures.

All the phones in the room dinged simultaneously announcing incoming emails.

When he looked down at his phone, he saw Eagle's name on the screen, he prayed his old friend had come through for them with the information they needed.

\* \* \*

8:22 P.M.

"It's dark," Evie said, peering out the window, then looking over her shoulder at Abigail who was on a virtual scavenger hunt for anything that could even vaguely be considered a weapon.

Luis Perez hadn't returned to their room, but he'd had food delivered to them along with a message for each of them. Evie had been told to enjoy the food and comfort of a bed while it lasted because this would be the last time she would ever be given a nice meal and sleep in a bed, and have access to a bathroom, once she was in the compound that would end. Abby had been told to make things easy on herself. If she submitted to Luis willingly, then she would be treated like a queen.

Evie already knew from the look on her face that Abigail had no intention of ever submitting to a man like that. She would fight him at every turn until he either got tired of her and killed her, or she was rescued.

Evie hoped she had the strength to fight, she didn't want to give up. If she was going to die then she wanted to do so making Owen proud.

"Now is the time to make our move," Abby said, gathering everything she had been able to find and joining Evie at the window.

"What exactly is our move?" Evie asked.

Although they'd been here for hours, they hadn't been able to come up with an exact plan. They knew they wanted off this boat, they just didn't know exactly how to make it happen. Although they'd only seen Luis and two of his men, there had been at least five involved in their kidnapping— four in the back of the van with them plus someone driving —so there was a minimum of five armed men on the boat. More than the two of them could hope to take down, especially with virtually no weapons. Without weapons, they couldn't really hope to attempt to take over the boat and drive it back to shore, which really only left them with jumping off and trying to swim out of this mess.

"Well, get out of this room is the first step," Abby said. "Then I guess we'll go looking for the life raft, or at least life-jackets."

"I wish there was another way." Evie was a good swimmer but swimming for her life, in the middle of the ocean, in the dark, with a cartel hunting them, was not your usual swim.

"Me too. Even if we get into the water there's no guar-antee we can get away, but at least we stand a chance. I want to go home to Ryder and RJ." Abby's voice wobbled, and she absently touched a hand to one of her breasts, no doubt subconsciously thinking about how much her newborn needed her.

"A chance is better than sitting here," Evie agreed. "Owen and Spider will be looking for us, if they find out the cartel has us they'll know to go to Perez's compound, but I'd still rather take my chances in the ocean than waiting here and praying the guys know about the cartel taking us."

"Same. We got this," Abby said firmly.

"Yeah, we do."

"Okay, let's see about getting through this window."

While Abby had been finding anything in the room that

could be used as a weapon, Evie had been working on the window. It was rectangular and definitely large enough for both of them to fit through, but the part that was supposed to open had been screwed closed. Abby had given Evie her engagement ring, and she'd been able to use it to unscrew it, now they just had to see if it would open or if Perez had done anything else to it.

"Here you go." She handed Abigail the ring, then put her hands on the window and eased it sideways.

"It worked," Abby said, her sigh of relief echoing Evie's own.

"Now, let's get out of here."

"Here, take these first, the best I could do." Abby handed her the fork from their meal and a couple of pieces of wire she'd managed to nab from the beds' mattresses. "Not a lot but better than nothing."

It definitely was, and Evie slid each of her little weapons into a different pocket, just in case she might not be able to get to one of them at least she'd have options.

Putting her hands on the now open window ledge, Evie peeked cautiously out to see if anyone was about. The boat was empty. Wherever Luis' men were they obviously didn't think that she and Abby would be getting out because he hadn't bothered to post anyone out here.

Thanking their lucky stars, Evie carefully lifted one knee and propped herself on the window ledge, then climbed through. Abby quickly joined her, and they took a moment to check out the vessel they were on. It was larger than Evie had thought it was, she didn't know much about boats, but this one was huge and looked luxurious, not that she'd expect anything else considering it belonged to Luis Perez. Since she didn't know much about boats, she wasn't sure where the controls were, or where the men were likely to be. She also didn't know what kind of layout boats had and if the men could easily spot them.

Still, it wasn't like they could just stand here. "Where do you think lifejackets or the life raft would be?"

"No idea, my guess would be either inside, which means we're not able to get to them, or somewhere down there." Abby pointed down to the end of the boat where it seemed to open up to an outside area.

That was as good a spot to search as any, so inch by terrifyingly slow inch, she and Abigail made their way down the side of the boat.

Never in her life had she been so scared.

One wrong move, one wrong footstep, one bump against the windows lining the side of the boat, and that was it.

Luis and his men would spot them. They'd be dragged back inside, and might be beaten or maybe even raped. That was a very real possibility given who Luis was, what he did, and his reasons for taking them.

Somehow they managed to make it to the back of the boat and immediately started searching.

"Evie, I think I found something," Abby whispered.

Turning to see what her friend had found, movement in her peripheral vision caught her attention. "Abby, someone's coming."

Panicked eyes looked up at her, and Abby nodded and gestured that they should try to go back the way they'd come.

"We're going to have to jump in and hope for the best," Abby whispered.

"We don't know how far we are from shore. We could drown or freeze before we get there," Evie said.

"It's our only choice," Abby reminded her, already hooking one leg over the side of the boat. "If we swim fast we can get far enough away before they realize we're gone. They're going to search for us, but they won't know which direction we went in, and the fact that it's dark will work in our favor."

"Okay, okay," she murmured, knowing that Abby was right. This was their only choice, and they already knew they might have to swim this without the help of a lifejacket or raft.

Abby dropped down into the water with a splash, and Evie moved to follow her, but suddenly hands wrapped around her and she was yanked back.

"Got them," the man yelled. Then looked around. "Where's your friend?" he asked, shaking her hard.

No way was she telling him that Abby was already in the water. Her friend had a new baby, she had to get home to RJ. If Evie had to pay the price for Abigail's freedom then she would do it.

"She jump in the water?" the man asked, continuing to shake her as he spoke.

Evie clamped her lips together.

"The boss isn't going to like that." The man raised his weapon and began to fire it into the water where Abigail had just landed.

Had her friend been hit?

Fear for Abby made it hard to worry about herself and what her punishment for nearly escaping was going to be. If Abigail had been hit, there was no way she could survive out there in the ocean. There was no land in sight, and blood loss and shock would mean hypothermia would come for her quickly, sapping her strength and making it virtually impossible for her to swim very far. And there was the very real possibility her blood could attract sharks.

As she was pulled down the side of the boat, away from the only chance at escape that she was going to get, Evie prayed that somehow, someway Abby would make it, and if by some chance they weren't all out of miracles for today that maybe she would make it home too.

* * *

9:01 P.M.

Eagle had come through for them.

Luis Perez owned four boats, one of which he had recently used to travel to the US, mooring it in San Diego.

That same boat had left just hours ago.

No doubt with Evie and Abigail on board.

As soon as they found out about the boat, his team and Wolf's had headed out. They were now going on eleven hours since the women had been taken. Each minute that ticked by his fear ratcheted up another notch. Almost eleven hours was a long time to spend in the presence of one of the world's most wanted men.

Was Evie hurt?

Fox knew she wasn't okay, at the very least she'd been abducted and held prisoner. She was still alive, he was almost certain of it. Perez wouldn't have gone to all this trouble only to have killed her already. There were still a million ways Evie could have been hurt that wouldn't end her life but would make her suffer.

He stared out of the helicopter, watching the inky night sky and the twinkling stars. Was Evie looking up at those same stars praying that he was coming for her?

"Time to jump."

The voice came through his comms, and Fox focused his mind. He dragged in several deep breaths, forced down his fear for Evie, it was time to go get his girl and bring her home.

Since Perez had several hours head start following him by boat wouldn't get them there quickly enough, so they'd taken a helo. He and his team had headed straight to follow Perez's boat while Wolf and his team had flown into Mexico then boarded zodiacs to meet them in the water.

They'd been able to track Perez's boat because Raven Oswald had hacked into its GPS so they knew where Evie and Abigail were. However, they couldn't take the helo too close or Perez would know they were there and was likely to do something rash like kill Evie and Abigail just out of spite even if he knew he couldn't get away.

They'd be swimming the rest of the way to the yacht, which had stopped moving almost thirty minutes ago. He had no idea why, but it had given them the in they needed. They could jump, then swim in, and board, take down Perez and his men, and rescue the women.

When his turn came, Fox jumped, adrenalin flooding his system, giving him the edge he needed to keep his worry over Evie under control long enough to rescue her. But when he did get her back home she'd be lucky if he ever let her out of his sight again. And first thing he was doing once a medic checked her out and he got her alone in their hotel room, was stripping her naked and worshipping every inch of her body. Second thing he was doing was putting a ring on her finger and making her his wife.

He hit the water and allowed his body to go down before he started swimming. As they approached Perez's yacht, he and his team spread out, they needed to approach from every angle.

Fox hadn't gone far when he caught sight of something floating in the water not far from his position.

A person.

A small person.

Not Perez or one of his men.

But as he got closer, he saw it wasn't Evie either.

It was Abby.

"I found Abby in the water," he said into his comms.

"Dead or alive?" Spider's panicked voice asked.

"Don't know. I'm about to reach her. I'll swim her to the surface, call Wolf and his team, we need those zodiacs now."

Reaching Abby, he shoved a regulator into her mouth, then hooked an arm across her chest and quickly swam them both to the surface. The yacht lights weren't far away. If Wolf and his team came in with the zodiacs here, Perez and his men would hear them, putting Evie in greater danger.

Keeping his hold on a limp Abigail, he started swimming further away from the yacht. It felt wrong doing so, Evie was on that yacht and she needed him, but right now he had his friend's—his brother's—unconscious woman in his arms, and there was no way he was abandoning Abigail even if it did kill him to move in the opposite direction from Evie.

Just as he'd reached a distance safe enough from the yacht for the zodiacs to come in, one appeared beside him. Fox hoisted Abby up, and Wolf and Cookie grabbed her, pulling her up and into the craft, then he climbed in behind her.

"How is she?" he asked as he removed his regulator.

"Hypothermic," Cookie replied, already working to strip Abby out of her jeans and sweater.

"Alive?"

"Yeah, she's alive," Wolf replied. Positioned near Abby's head, he had one hand curled under her jaw, his fingers on her neck, his cheek above her mouth.

"Spider, you hear that? She's alive," he said into his comms.

"I heard," came Spider's tight reply. "Five minutes out."

"Injuries?" he asked. Kneeling beside Abby, he took the thermal blanket Abe passed him and spread it over her once Cookie had her out of her wet clothes. She was shaking which he took to be a good sign. If her body temperature had dropped too low then her body wouldn't be trying to warm itself.

"Bullet wound in left bicep," Wolf replied, running his hands over Abby's body in search of injuries. "Can't find anything else."

"She was shot?" Fox had no idea what would have prompted Perez to shoot Abigail, but it didn't bode well for Evie. Was she out in the water somewhere too? Had they been wrong in thinking Perez had taken the women to keep for himself or sell? Maybe he'd simply brought them out here to make their bodies harder to find.

"R-Ryder," Abby murmured as her teeth started to chatter and her eyelashes fluttered against her white cheeks. She began coughing up the water she had swallowed, she'd need to be watched for secondary drowning once she was taken to the hospital.

"He's coming, honey, it's me, Owen. Can you tell me what happened?" he asked as he stroked her hair, allowing Wolf to tend to the gunshot wound. He needed to know if Evie was still alive and if she was on the boat or if they needed to start searching the waters for her.

"O-Owen?" Her eyes opened slowly and she blinked, looking around unfocused before her gaze settled on him.

"Yeah, sweetheart, I'm here, you're safe now," he soothed. "I know you're cold, and I know you're hurting, but I need to know what happened."

"Luis w-wanted m-me," she said through chattering teeth. "He w-was going t-to s-sell Evie. We e-escaped from th-the r-room he h-had us i-in. We w-were going t-to jump, b-but one of L-Luis' m-men found us. I w-was already i-in the w-water, E-Evie w-wasn't. H-he sh-shot at me. I-I'm sorry, O-Owen, I m-must have bl-blacked out f-for a m-moment, and th-then I w-was so c-cold, and m-my arm h-hurt so badly. I sh-should have g-gone b-back for h-her. I-I'm s-sorry."

Wolf had finished wrapping her arm so Fox carefully pulled her shaking body into his arms. "Shh, honey, it's not your fault, I'm glad you're alive and you're safe, and I will get Evie back, okay?"

Her head nodded against his shoulder, and he held her tightly, stroking her hair as he kept her tucked closely against his chest. Then Spider was there, and Fox passed Abigail over to him.

"Abby?" Spider demanded.

"I-I'm o-okay," she murmured, sounding sleepy now.

"Stay awake, Abs," Fox ordered. "She was shot in the arm and she's hypothermic, she also took in some water," he told Spider.

"You guys should take one of the zodiacs, take Abby in, she needs medical attention," Wolf said. "My team will go after Evie and Perez."

"I'm going with you," Fox said firmly. "Spider and the others can go back in the zodiacs with Abby, get the helo to pick them up when they land, get her to the hospital as quickly as possible. I'll go with your team to get my girl and end Luis Perez once and for all."

"You sure?" Spider asked, clutching Abigail tightly like he half expected her to vanish into thin air.

"Yes."

"I can take her back alone."

"We don't know if Perez has other men with him and you can't hold her and drive at the same time. With Wolf's team there are seven of us, enough to take Perez. You guys need to take care of Abby right now. Abs, you know how many men are on the yacht?"

"We g-guessed a-at least f-five plus P-Perez, b-but don't

know f-for s-sure. S-so tired," she murmured and drooped against Spider as she went limp.

"Abby?" Spider said, shaking her gently. "She's out."

"You guys need to go. Wolf, you and your guys ready?" he asked the other team leader.

"Ready."

"Then let's go get my girl."

* * *

9:10 P.M.

"She's gone," the man dragging her along the side of the boat told Luis Perez who seemed to have appeared out of thin air.

"What do you mean, she's gone?" Luis roared.

Evie kept her head down not wanting to draw any extra attention to herself. This was going to be bad. She was just here as punishment for daring to speak out against the cartel, but Luis was obsessed with Abigail. He'd been keeping tabs on her for almost a year, and now that he knew she was gone, possibly dead, he was going to lose it.

"She jumped off the side of the boat," the man holding her explained.

"Well, go in after her and find her," Luis ordered. "How far can she have swum?"

"I'm not going in there," the man balked at the notion. "I don't know how to swim and what if there are sharks in there?"

"Why would sharks be circling the boat?" Luis demanded.

The man shrugged, and since he was standing so close, Evie could feel his unease as he realized it had been a mistake to shoot at Abby.

Apparently, Luis sensed this because he took a menacing step closer. "What did you do, Diego?"

Diego shifted uncomfortably but seemed to know that not offering an answer was worse than whatever answer he would give. "I shot at her. Don't know if I hit her or not," he added quickly.

"You shot at her?" Luis' voice had gone deadly quiet.

"She was trying to escape," Diego tried to explain.

"Then you jump in after her and drag her back onto the boat, it wasn't like she could get far out here." He waved his arms to indicate the expanse of ocean surrounding them. Then he nodded to a young man beside him. "Antonio, take care of our friend Diego here."

With a single nod, Antonio stepped forward, pulled her out of Diego's grasp, and shoved her in the direction of another large man. Then he pulled out a weapon and aimed it at Diego, who was sweating profusely and squirming as though he knew what was coming next.

Evie didn't know, but she did know that she didn't want to know.

She really, *really*, didn't want to know.

"Down on your knees, Diego," Antonio said in a voice that was flat and emotionless. It was like this man didn't have a conscience, a soul, like he was a robot hiding in a human body.

Diego hesitated all of a millisecond, but that was all it took.

Antonio fired his weapon, blood bloomed on Diego's left knee, and he howled in pain as he dropped to the floor.

The sound of Diego's screams was unlike anything she had ever heard before.

It was almost inhuman.

Her stomach revolted and she only just managed to turn to the side before she threw up.

Her vomiting caught Luis' attention and he turned to her with what could only be described as a devil smile. Her body physically chilled and she started to tremble.

"Return our little escape artist to her room, Jose. Antonio, I am sure you can finish off our little problem here while I spend some time with our guest. Organize the rest of the men to search for Abigail, she can't have gone far, I want her found. If she is not, you will all pay the price for Diego's sins."

Jose obediently dragged her through the boat and back into the room she and Abby had escaped from not even half an hour ago. Evie prayed that Abby was either far enough way that Luis' men wouldn't find her or that she was already dead. She felt so bad wishing for her friend's death, but in the end it would be more merciful than whatever Luis planned to do with Abigail.

In the room, Jose held onto her while another man—she didn't know his name—brought a chair into the room.

This couldn't be good.

Briefly, Evie thought about trying to fight her way past the men. She still had the weapons Abby had gathered, but what would be the point? She wasn't getting off this boat on her own, that one chance had come and gone, and making any attempt to do so would only wind up with them hurting her worse.

Screams continued to echo through the boat, and she cringed as she wondered what they were doing to Diego. He was a monster, and he'd tried to kill her friend, would have tried to kill her too if she'd been in the water when he found them, but nobody deserved to be tortured like that.

Why couldn't they just kill him and be done with it?

Jose pushed her into the chair and held her in place while the other man tied her wrists and ankles to the chair arms and legs with pieces of rope.

Tears threatened to pour out, but she bit her tongue and

held them back. She didn't want to show any weakness in front of these men. They were wicked, evil men who would take pleasure in her pain, and since she couldn't stop them from hurting her, she could at least take away some of that satisfaction.

The seconds seemed to stretch until they were moving impossibly slowly, terror unlike anything she had ever experienced before clawed inside her. At least before she hadn't been alone, Abby's presence had been comforting and reassuring, and together it had seemed like they at least stood a chance.

Now it was just her against half a dozen or more trained killers.

Despite her vow to hold it together, her breath began to saw in and out of her chest. What were they going to do with her? Where was Owen right now? He'd be looking for her but was he even close to finding her?

"Ms. Walter, I'm sure you can understand why I'm so frustrated," Luis said as he joined them in the room. Although his tone was now conversational, his dark eyes were like twin black holes of doom. "I have waited a long time to make Abigail mine, and now you've helped her escape. I am sure you know that I cannot allow that to go unpunished."

His tone was falsely apologetic, Evie knew he didn't care one way or the other about punishing her. After all, he intended to sell her, and she was just a piece of merchandise. Her value rested only in her remaining alive, other than that she doubted he cared about what condition she was in.

Evie didn't bother commenting on what Luis had said. Anything she would say would only serve to give him further reason to hurt her.

"Jose has always had a soft spot for blondes, especially

those with curls, I am sure he would be happy to be the one to teach you your first lesson. Resistance is futile."

When his boss nodded his head at him, Jose stepped closer. The smile on his face made her stomach churn, and Evie couldn't stop a whimper from escaping. Jose lifted a large hand and ran it through her curls, she shied away from him, but tied to the chair she couldn't get far.

"Nowhere to go, princesa," Jose said. He held her head with his other hand while continuing to play with her curls. He moved closer, his putrid, hot breath adding to her nausea, then his tongue came out and he trailed the tip of it along her cheek.

Evie scrunched her eyes closed, her entire body quaked as she focused on trying to breathe through the smothering fear.

*Don't fight back.*

*Don't fight back.*

*Don't fight back*, she chanted to herself.

Fighting back would only make it worse.

When his lips pressed against hers in a bruising kiss, all logic fled her mind and she thrashed wildly against her bonds and sunk her teeth into the lips punishing hers.

Jose reeled back. "La perra," he swore and backhanded her, causing her head to snap to the side and her eyes pop open.

Blood dribbled down his chin, and a sense of satisfaction smoothed away the rough edges of her terror. She'd done that. She had. She may be at the mercy of Luis and his men, but she wasn't completely helpless.

The plan she and Abby had come up with hadn't changed.

Stay alive.

Escape if possible.

If not stay strong, Owen and his team *would* be looking for her.

Determination mixed with her fear and she felt a renewal of strength. She could do this. It wasn't like she had a choice, this was happening, she was here, and she would have to suffer whatever punishment Luis and Jose dished out, but she could make sure it didn't break her.

The fist flying into the side of her head somehow managed to catch her by surprise.

Pain bloomed inside her, but she barely had time to process it before the second blow came. There was another and another, and Evie thought she might be screaming, begging him to stop, apparently it was harder to stay strong while being beaten than she had thought.

The blows continued to rain down on her, and when blackness ebbed at the edges of her consciousness, she grabbed hold of it and let it wash her away.

* * *

9:28 P.M.

The yacht was huge, much bigger than he had been anticipating. Fox and Wolf's team had no problem scaling the side, gaining access to the craft. Although his heart wanted him to go running through the boat, searching every room to find Evie, his head kept his feet still as he and the others spread out.

If he wasn't mistaken—and he was a bit of a yacht enthusiast, his dream was to own a luxury yacht one day—Luis Perez owned a Mirgab VI, one Fox himself had looked at when he daydreamed about what he'd buy if he won the lottery. This yacht could accommodate up to twelve guests as well as house a crew of up to ten. Although Abby said Luis was traveling with at least five of his men, chances were there were at least a dozen more on board.

There were five decks, they were currently standing on the main deck, and they split up to search for both Evie and Luis. As much as he was here to make sure his woman made it through this alive, he also intended to make sure Luis didn't. The man had caused enough pain and suffering to the people he cared about, not just Evie, but allowing Abby to be kept prisoner on his estate for over a year, then abducting her and planning to keep her as his personal sex slave.

The man deserved to die.

Actually, he deserved a whole lot more than death.

The yacht was lit up like a Christmas tree, but there was nobody about, no one out patrolling, and while that worked to their benefit something didn't feel right. Luis had no reason to know that his yacht had been boarded, but for a man worth as much as he was, for a man with as many enemies, and wanted by as many governments as Luis was, Fox would have thought him to be more careful. Even out in the middle of the ocean.

Still, Fox had seen more than one man brought to his knees by cockiness, maybe Luis would be the next.

As he silently cleared the outdoor area of the main deck, he made his way along the side and stopped when he saw blood staining the deck.

A lot of blood.

Someone had recently been badly injured—or killed—right here.

Abby said she was already in the water when she was shot so the blood wasn't hers. Was it Evie's?

Along with a healthy dose of fear there was also a deep-seated fury roaring inside him. Evie was his, and the idea of anyone laying a finger on her soft, smooth skin, harming a single blonde hair on her head, made him see red.

Using that anger as fuel, Fox quickly stepped through the doors inside, into a foyer with a lift and a spiral staircase. To his left was what looked like a dining room, it was empty although he could see the remains of dinner on the table, dirty dishes that hadn't been cleared away, and some of the chairs were shoved haphazardly into the middle of the room like someone had left in a hurry.

Bypassing the dining room, Fox turned right, cleared a powder room before finding a locked door.

Since he didn't want to make a lot of noise breaking down the door, he quickly picked the lock and eased it open.

In the middle of the room was a chair.

Tied to the chair was Evie.

Her head hung limply against her chest, and Fox felt his own chest tighten in response.

"Found Evie," he said softly into his comms.

"I've got half a dozen men on the hull deck," Abe said.

"Another three on the bridge deck," Cookie added.

"Any sign of Perez yet?" Wolf asked.

"None, but I'm guessing he's up in the master suite on the sundeck," Dude replied.

"I want Evie out of here, but we're not leaving without eliminating Perez," Fox said as he cleared the room and then went to Evie, touching his fingers to her neck. She had a pulse, but she didn't respond to his voice or his touch.

"As soon as we start firing everyone on board is going to know it," Benny said.

"We need to coordinate our attack," Wolf said. "Fox, get Evie down where we boarded, it should be easy to protect her there, and as soon as she's out of the line of fire we take out Perez's men."

"As soon as he hears the shots Perez will come out, then we can finally take him down," Mozart said.

"Perez will have at least one bodyguard with him, probably two," Cookie added.

"It would help if we knew exactly how many men are on board," Dude said.

It would, but they didn't so they were going to have to work with what they had. Right now, his priority was freeing Evie and checking her for injuries.

Turning his attention to Evie, he cradled the back of her head in his palm and eased her head back so he could see her face. When he got a clear look at her, Fox sucked in a pained breath. They'd beaten her badly not long ago, her blood was still wet and sticky, not yet dried. Both eyes were swollen almost closed, blood dripped from her nose, she had a split lip and two gashes, one along her left cheekbone and the other on her right temple.

"Baby, I'm so sorry," he whispered as he touched his lips against hers in a feather-light kiss. "So sorry I wasn't here to protect you."

She stirred at the kiss, her swollen eyes blinking open. Her entire body trembled with terror, and he hated that she was going to remember the fear and pain Luis had inflicted on her for the rest of her life.

"Evie, it's Owen. Are you with me?" he asked as he released her head and pulled out his knife, making quick work of cutting through the ropes binding her to the chair.

"Owen?" She sounded confused, but at least she was awake and talking.

"Right here, sweetheart." He knelt before her and carefully cupped her cheek in his hand, forcing back a glower at the black and blue marks forming on her perfect skin.

"You came." One side of her mouth lifted in a smile and then she hissed in pain.

"You doubted me?" he asked, brushing his thumb across the unmarked parts of her cheek.

"No. Never." The strength in her words stirred a million emotions inside him, none of which he had time to deal with right now.

"You ready to get out of here, go home?" he asked as he very carefully slipped an arm under her knees, his other behind her back, and lifted her into his arms.

"More than. Owen, Abby jumped off the boat, Diego shot at her, I don't know if he hit her ... then Luis had Diego tortured, he's obsessed with Abby," Evie explained.

"I know, honey, I found Abby. She's with Spider and the rest of the team, they're getting her help. Wolf's team is here with me, and as soon as I get you someplace safe we're going to take out Luis and his men."

"I'm glad she's safe," Evie said, resting heavily in his hold.

"Perez won't hurt her again. Or you," he vowed.

"He was so angry when he learned Abby was gone, he blamed me as much as he did Diego," she said. Her voice was strained, and he wondered what other injuries she had.

As much as he would love to strip her down and check every inch of her body, the priority right now was getting her off this boat. As soon as they took out Perez and his men, some of his team would bring the zodiacs in to pick them up.

Fox left the room Evie had been locked in and just as he was entering the foyer a man with a body draped over his shoulders appeared coming out of the galley.

So much for getting Evie safe before the bullets started flying.

For a second the man stood there, obviously shocked to see anyone who shouldn't be there on the yacht.

Aiming his weapon, Fox was about to fire, but the man threw the body at him, causing him to stagger backward. When the man then charged at him, he angled his body so that he was between him and Evie.

The man hit him like a raging bull, and the three of them

tumbled to the ground. Fox quickly shoved Evie forward. "Go, run, hide," he yelled.

She hesitated for a moment before stumbling unsteadily to her feet.

Fox swung at the man knocking him down, but he didn't stay down for long. The man rolled to his feet and aimed his weapon, only not at Fox. At Evie.

He didn't even think, just acted.

Fox lunged at the man, putting himself once again between Evie and the threat.

The sound of the gun tore through the otherwise quiet night.

The pain seemed to come a split second later.

It ripped through his side like a burning tornado.

Evie screamed.

The man aimed the gun again.

Fox grabbed him, and they tussled, trading blow for blow, his strength fading with each hit he took, each hit he gave.

The side of the boat loomed close.

He knew there were other threats on the boat, threats he would have to trust Wolf and his team to eliminate, but this one was his.

Latching onto the man who had tried to kill Evie, Fox tossed them both over the side of the boat and into the cold ocean.

\* \* \*

9:49 P.M.

Evie froze at the sound of the gunshot.

The bullet slammed into Owen, and she screamed.

She couldn't seem to stop screaming.

Couldn't seem to move either.

All she could do was stand there and watch in horror as Owen fought with Antonio who had dropped Diego's body when he saw them.

How many more bodies were going to fall because of Luis Perez?

Her heart seemed to stop when Owen and Antonio went flying over the edge of the boat. The sound of them hitting the water snapped her out of her stunned daze, and she started to run. She didn't really know where she was going just that she was terrified and the reprieve she thought she'd been given when she woke up to find Owen beside her was over, and she now doubted she was ever getting off this boat alive.

Evie found herself back inside. She ran through the foyer, through a hallway; the door to the bedroom where she'd been kept was open and she bypassed it and ran through another door. There was the galley on her left and a closed door on her right, she chose the closed door and shoved it open. She found herself in a room with chairs and a couple of tables, it was empty, and she didn't see any good places to hide so she kept going. There were two more doors, and she picked the one on her left and immediately wished she hadn't.

"Ms. Walter," Luis said his eyes wide with surprise as he turned in the direction of the opening door. There was a woman on her knees before him, and Luis had his hand tangled in her hair, holding her in place as he thrust into her mouth. The woman was dressed nicely in what Evie thought was a boat captain outfit, but she didn't know enough about it to be sure.

Before she could turn and flee, find somewhere safer to hide, Luis pulled out a gun, holding it pointed at her head as he continued to thrust into the woman's mouth.

She froze, unsure what she should do. From what she had seen, Luis didn't do his own dirty work, but he appeared to be in here alone with the woman, and she was pretty sure that he would shoot her if it stopped her from running.

He came with a grunt and shoved the woman aside. She fell onto all fours and then quickly crawled away from Luis. Although there was no fear in her eyes, she pressed her back against the wall and eyed the gun warily.

Against her will, Evie's gaze dropped to Luis' semi-hard length protruding from his unbuttoned pants.

He laughed—a horrible, blood-chilling sound—and grabbed hold of himself, stroking his length. "You ready for a turn?"

Her gaze snapped to his face and she shuddered at the expression on it. This man was pure evil personified.

Luis took a step toward her, the gun steady in his grip. "My men will take care of the intruders, your SEALs I presume. You and I can have a little fun while we wait for them to clean ship."

So he knew that Owen and the others were here, he was just arrogant enough to believe that nothing and no one could take him down.

"I will find Abigail, she will be mine, but I underestimated you, perhaps I will keep you as well." Luis reached her and stretched out a hand to touch her bruised and battered face. Instinct had her pulling away, and his face darkened as a storm of anger tore through him. "No one turns me down."

Shoving the barrel of the gun against her temple, he dragged her further into the room and pushed her down onto her knees. Evie fought against him, but her body was weak and uncooperative, and when he slammed the butt of his weapon into the side of her head he turned the entire world around her into jelly.

One hand kept the gun pointed at her head while his

other curled around the back of her neck as he tried to draw her face closer to his growing length.

"No, please," she slurred, trying to push him away, her fingers curled around the piece of wire from the bed that Abigail had given her earlier. It had been hidden in her pocket but now she pulled it out.

"You will learn you never deny your owner, you will obey my every wish." Luis hit her again and tried to force her to take him into her mouth.

She would *never* willingly submit to him.

Never.

He could beat her, he could starve her, he could threaten her, but in the end it wouldn't change anything. She would fight him every step of the way.

His tip brushed against her lips, and she shoved the sharp wire into his leg. Luis howled and then the next thing she knew something wet sprayed across her face and Luis dropped to the floor.

He was missing half of his head.

Bile burned her throat as she staggered to her feet.

What had happened?

Had someone shot him?

Who?

How?

Not wanting to hang around to find out, Evie managed to get her feet beneath her and staggered out of the room. She went to the closest door and found herself in a laundry room.

Her gaze fell on the washing machines, there was a line of four in a row, and it seemed like the perfect place to hide.

Quickly she scrambled inside and closed the door.

Quiet.

It was so quiet in here.

It was a tight fit, she was curled into a tight ball, but she felt safe like this, safe enough to let her tears start to fall.

Owen could be dead.

Abby might be dead.

Luis' men might kill the rest of the SEALs. If that happened, what would become of her?

With Luis dead, would one of his men take over? Would they sell her like Luis planned to or keep her like he had threatened to do?

The washing machine door was suddenly wrenched open, and Evie whimpered and scrunched as far back inside it as she could get. Her entire body throbbed with pain, and she was scared out of her mind. She just wanted to go home, but she held the piece of wire out between her and this newest threat.

"Evie? Evie, honey, calm down. It's okay, honey, you're safe now, they're all dead."

It took a while for the voice to penetrate the haze of terror that she was cloaked in, but when it did, she risked a peek at whoever was out there, just in case what he was saying was true.

The man who stood there was dressed all in black, a machine gun in his hands, but if he was here to hurt her, he would have just dragged her out and done it.

Right?

"Hey, sweetheart, you with me?"

Forcing herself to concentrate through her fear, she noted the dark eyes that watched her carefully, the scars on the man's cheek, and his large, muscled frame.

She knew him.

It was Mozart.

Relief washed over her, and she started to cry again.

"Shh, honey, it's okay, come on, can I help you out of there?" He held out a hand to her but didn't try to force her, just held his hand there, palm up, and waited until she was ready.

Her brain screamed at her to reach out to him, that it was over, that somehow the SEALs had taken out Luis Perez and all of his men and that now she could go home, but she couldn't seem to make herself do it.

It was like she had reached the end of her rope and she had nothing left to give, not even her trust to a man who had just saved her life.

"O-Owen?" she asked, not yet ready to leave this tiny space where she felt safe.

Something flashed across his face, but Mozart quickly schooled it. "Cookie pulled him out of the water, they're on a zodiac waiting for us."

"A-Antonio sh-shot him," she stammered.

"He did," Mozart agreed. And although he didn't say it, Owen needed to get to a hospital, and they were only waiting on her to pull it together so they could take him there.

Slowly, Evie reached out her shaking hand and placed it in Mozart's. He pried the wire from her grip, squeezed her fingers, and then very gently took hold of her upper arm with his other hand and pulled her out of the washing machine.

As soon as he had her free, he didn't hesitate to scoop her up into his arms and carry her through to the stairs, which he took down to the bottom deck, then out into the cold night. A small black boat was waiting for them at the back of Luis' yacht, and Mozart climbed onto it before setting her down.

"She okay?" Wolf asked.

"Shock, and she's been beaten pretty badly," Mozart replied, taking the blanket someone offered him and tucking it around her, but Evie's focus was on Owen.

He was lying in the bottom of the zodiac, his skin a

horrible white that made him look way too much like he was already gone. His eyes were closed, he wasn't moving, and one of the guys had bandaged his gunshot wound.

The bullet that was meant for her.

The bullet Owen had taken instead.

How could she have ever doubted that he loved her?

How could she have ever thought that this brave, strong, intelligent, caring man would callously use her?

Now it all seemed so silly. She'd allowed the way her parents had treated her, the way men in her past had treated her to affect the way she saw Owen. But he wasn't to blame for the bad things other people had done to her, and he was nothing like those people who had hurt her.

He was the best thing that had ever happened to her.

He was her heart and her soul.

He was supposed to be her future.

Tears streamed down her face, and she lay down beside him, curled up against his good side, and unable to hold back the pain, fear, and exhaustion, she slipped away into unconsciousness.

# CHAPTER 15

April 12th

4:25 A.M.

Fox woke suddenly.

One second he was out, the next, he was awake and worried about Evie.

He remembered every second from finding out Evie was missing to throwing himself and one of Perez's men into the ocean. Then his memories stopped. He had no idea what had happened after that, if Evie was okay, if Luis Perez was dead, if any of Wolf's team had been injured.

Ignoring the pain in his side, Fox shoved himself into a sitting position, determined to find out what had happened and where Evie was.

"Relax, man," a quiet voice said beside him.

"Shark," he said, turning in the direction the voice had

come from to see his friend rising from a chair, setting a book down. "Evie?"

"She's right over there." Shark pointed across to the other side of the room.

Fox turned in the same direction and saw Evie curled up on the bed beside the one he was propped up in. There was an IV running into the back of one of her hands and the other one was bandaged. Her face—what he could see of it as half was buried against the pillow—was a mottled mix of blues, blacks, and purples.

For a moment it felt like he couldn't breathe.

He'd known she was hurt, he'd been the one to find her, but seeing her battered and bruised in a hospital bed stole his breath.

"How bad?" he asked.

"Your injuries or hers?" Shark asked.

Fox turned back to his teammate and rolled his eyes. Was that really a question Shark needed an answer to?

"Hers then. She has two cracked ribs, a hairline fracture in her wrist, a broken clavicle, a concussion, and bruises. And even though you didn't ask, you were lucky, the bullet didn't hit anything vital, you lost a lot of blood, but Cookie got to you quickly, killed the man who shot you—Evie said his name was Antonio—and got you out of the water. You were both lucky it wasn't worse."

"Yeah, lucky," he muttered. If they were lucky they wouldn't both be in hospital beds right now. "How's Abby?"

"Okay, she was hypothermic and lost quite a bit of blood too, but they stitched her up, and she's sleeping in a room down the hall. Spider is with her and Lavender brought the baby in because Abby needed to see him."

"We're back in San Diego?"

"Yes."

"What happened after I passed out?"

"From what Wolf told us, Evie ran when you hit the water, only she ran straight into Luis. He tried to force her to perform oral sex on him, and Abe took him out. Evie freaked and ran, hid in a washing machine. Mozart found her, coaxed her out, and got her to the zodiac. As soon as she saw you she started crying, then passed out. Once she was out they triaged her, gave her a shot of morphine, a sedative, and an antibiotic, and she was out during the helicopter ride back here. Once they got her here the hospital administered another sedative, and she hasn't woken up. Her body needs the rest to heal. As does yours," Shark finished pointedly.

Fox knew he needed rest, but right now all he wanted was to hold Evie in his arms. Fury toward Luis Perez, what he'd done to her and what he'd tried to do to her, wasn't going to change anything. They were alive, and Perez wasn't, and that was going to have to be enough. Evie would need his support as she dealt with what she'd been through, she didn't need his rage at a dead man.

"Help me over to her bed," he said, throwing back the covers.

Shark's dark eyes assessed him in the quiet way the man always did, then without another word he slipped an arm around Fox's shoulders and helped him stand. This wasn't his first rodeo, and as far as bullet wounds went, this one didn't rank amongst the worst he'd had.

It only took a couple of steps to cross the space between the two beds, and Fox hooked his own IV bag up next to Evie's. Shark carefully slid Evie to one side of the bed to make room for him. Exhaustion was gnawing at him, and he climbed onto the mattress and gently eased Evie against his good side, holding her close with an arm around her shoulders. He pressed his lips to the top of her head, breathing in her scent and letting it reassure him that she was alive and here in his arms.

"I'll be outside," Shark said as he spread the covers over both of them.

"You don't need to stay," Fox said.

Shark just gave him a look that said he had to be kidding and strolled out the door to spend the night outside their room, watching over them. The threat might be eliminated, Luis Perez was dead, he could never hurt either Evie or Abby again, but his team looked out for each other no matter what, and he'd sat outside an injured teammate's hospital room before just as Shark was doing tonight.

With Evie safe in his arms, Fox stopped fighting the drugs in his system, allowed exhaustion to take hold, and drifted off to sleep.

Light was streaming through the hospital window when he next woke, Evie was still against him, her warm body draped across his good side. Fox took a moment to give thanks that she was here, she was safe, alive, and relatively in one piece because he could so easily have lost her.

Losing the only other woman he had ever loved had been a very real possibility, but he hadn't, Evie was okay. Maybe if he kept repeating that to himself it would eventually sink in.

"Hmm," Evie moaned in his arms and shifted slightly, and Fox realized he was squeezing her so tightly he was probably hurting her.

"Hey, fairy," he murmured, touching a kiss to her forehead then frowning as he realized she was hot. "Evie? You feeling okay?"

"Owen." As she realized she was lying in his arms she shot up, grinning at him, then threw her arms around him again and hugged him hard before kissing him. "You're alive, I was so scared that Antonio had killed you."

"He didn't, I'm fine, honey," he promised, reaching for the bed's controls to elevate it.

"You're not fine, you were shot," she contradicted, her

blue eyes going wide with fear once again. "Are you really okay?"

"Bullet missed everything vital. I'm so sorry I didn't keep you safe." Fox reached out and feathered his fingertips across the bruises on her cheek.

"It's not your fault, he tricked us," Evie countered.

"I promised you I would protect you and you got abducted and beaten." He suspected that guilt over what had happened to Evie was something he would be dealing with for the rest of his life.

"I'll heal, Owen, don't let this build into something that comes between us, please," she begged. "I just got you back, and I don't think I could survive losing you again."

He dragged in a deep breath, ignored the shaft of pain through his side, and focused on the woman sitting in the bed beside him. She was right, he'd just been blessed with the second chance he'd wanted for two very long years, he couldn't let anything get in the way of that, not even his guilt over not doing a better job of protecting her.

Taking her chin between his thumb and forefinger, he leaned down and brushed his lips across hers. "Nothing will ever take you away from me again," he vowed. "Nothing. I love you, Evie, and I want to spend forever with you by my side."

"That's what I want too," she whispered against his lips.

"I love you so much, Evie, and I hope you never doubt that again."

"I won't. I know you do, I wish I had never doubted it." There was regret on her face, but he saw her push it away and then she kissed him again. "Nothing but rainbows and sunshine for us from now on."

"Amen to that." Fox kissed her lips, and then gently touched kisses to every one of the bumps and bruises on her face. When his lips touched her forehead, he stopped and frowned, remembering what he'd asked her when she first woke up. "You feeling okay, Evie? You feel hot."

Her brow crinkled like she hadn't considered anything to do with how she was feeling yet. "I hurt pretty much everywhere, my chest, my head, oh, and my ankle is sore too, but I don't remember Jose hitting me there."

"The blister," he said, then laughed. "Trust you to be in a car accident, get shot at, abducted and beaten, and in the end the worst of your injuries turns out to be a blister from hiking through the woods."

Evie giggled too. "I didn't even realize it at first, but I do feel hot, like I have a fever, I guess we got distracted and forgot to keep treating the infection."

"I'll press the call button, get a doctor in here to check you out."

"Wait." Evie stopped him when he went to reach for the call button. "I want a moment more where it's just the two of us, and we're both alive, and you're holding me in your arms before the rest of the world intrudes."

More than happy to oblige, Fox snuggled Evie against his chest again, wrapped his arms around her, and held her like she was the most precious thing in his life, because she was.

# CHAPTER 16

April 15<sup>th</sup>

11:06 A.M.

"I wish the doctor would hurry up and get here with my discharge papers," Evie grumbled as she sat on the hospital bed, legs dangling over the side.

"He said he'd be right back with the papers," Owen reminded her. He was lounging in the chair beside her bed.

"Easy for you to say, you got sprung from here already. I can't believe *you're* the one who got shot and yet *I'm* the one who ended up being stuck here for three days." Owen had been released about twenty-four hours after being admitted, but the infection in her blister had kept her here for days because her weakened and battered body had taken a while to fight off the infection enough that she could go off IV antibiotics.

"Aww, poor baby," Owen teased as he moved to sit beside her on the bed and tugged her against his side.

Despite being discharged, Owen had only left her side for a little while when Abby and Lavender had come to visit her with baby RJ. When she'd seen Abby a floodgate of emotions opened and the two of them had clung together and cried for a solid ten minutes before they'd even been able to exchange a single word. It was the first time she'd cried about what had happened, and it had felt good to be able to discuss it with someone who had lived through it with her.

Abby had gone home the day before, and now Evie was well and truly ready to get out of here and go home too. Well, not home since she didn't have a house anymore, but the hotel was almost as good, at least it wasn't a hospital, and she and Owen would be able to be alone. She couldn't wait to get him alone, strip him naked, and have her way with him. It had been almost all she could think about. She wanted to erase the memory of Luis standing in front of her with his pants undone, trying to force her to perform oral sex on him.

"What's wrong? You just shuddered and then went all stiff," Owen said, sliding her over so she was sitting in his lap.

They hadn't really talked yet about what had happened. She knew they would at some point, she'd meant it when she'd told Owen she didn't want anything to come between them, and she knew that not dealing with her abduction would end up coming between them. Now wasn't the time though, now she just wanted to get out of here and start to feel normal, start the healing process.

"I'm okay, just anxious to be alone with you."

"Want to ravish me, huh?" he said, coaxing a chuckle out of her.

"Something like that."

"It'll be okay, honey, we'll work through it together, deal with it together, we're a team and we *will* get through this."

He kissed the side of her head, and she wrapped her arms around his neck and held onto him.

"Your ride's here," Shark announced as he opened the hospital room door.

Evie went to move off Owen's lap, but he held onto her and said, "We're just waiting for the doctor to come with her discharge papers."

Shark eyed the two of them and although he didn't say anything, nor did his expression change or hint at anything that was running through his head, Evie sensed that he was uncomfortable with them being all over one another. Actually, now that she thought about it, Shark often seemed uncomfortable when he was around Abby and Spider, and Lavender and Night. She didn't know anything about his past, but she guessed there was a story there, a reason why he was so stoic and seemed to have no emotions.

Before she could think of anything to say or try to alleviate his discomfort, the doctor came into the room. They discussed anything she needed to be on the lookout for with her injuries, treatment for her healing infection, and reminders to rest and not overdo anything to give her concussion and cracked ribs time to heal.

Once they were done, she was put in a wheelchair to be taken down to the hospital's entrance, Owen and Shark flanking her like they half expected a threat to appear in the hospital hallways. She knew it was because of their jobs, so many years doing what SEALs did, but she still didn't like that their life view was tainted like that. She wanted the world to be a wonderful place, and even though experience had taught her otherwise, she was clinging to that dream, that determination to not let anything that had happened to her change who she was.

"Up we go," Owen said as he helped her out of the wheelchair and across the sidewalk to the truck Shark had pulled up.

He sat in the back with her, his arm laying across her shoulders, his fingers tracing and stroking her arm. Delightful little cartwheels turned in her stomach, and she was all but counting down the seconds until they got to the hotel.

Because Owen had her all turned on and distracted it wasn't until Shark stopped driving that she realized they weren't actually at the hotel.

"Where are we?" she asked as she looked out the window at the nice residential suburb. There were large trees lining the road, the houses all had big yards, it looked like a lovely place to live, a great family neighborhood, she just had no idea what they were doing here.

"You'll see," Owen replied mysteriously as he climbed out of the car then came around to help her out.

Shark had pulled out his cell phone and turned off the engine, as Owen took her hand and led her toward a gorgeous stone two-story house. It had flower boxes under the large picture windows on either side of the front door, a cute little porch, and a huge oak tree in the front yard that bathed the front of the house in dappled shade.

They walked right up to the front door, and Owen opened it right up and then stepped back. The first thing she saw was the red ribbon, and her gaze flew to Owen's who was standing behind her, a huge grin on his face.

The last time he'd done the red ribbon thing he'd been proposing.

Was he asking her to marry him again?

But why here?

"What …? Why …?" she asked, not even sure what she was really asking.

"Follow the ribbon," was all he said.

Giddy with excitement, she followed the ribbon as it trailed through the empty house, wrapped around door handles, light fixtures, and windows because there was no furniture. The ribbon ended in what she assumed was the master bedroom. It was tied in a bow around the neck of a huge teddy bear that had to be at least six feet tall.

Laughter bubbled out of her. "I don't think I won that bet."

"You more than earned your giant teddy," Owen said.

Resting on the teddy's lap was an envelope, the end of the ribbon attached to it. Evie picked it up, untied the ribbon from the teddy bear, pulled the end of the ribbon from the envelope, and then carefully opened it and pulled out a stack of papers.

Scanning the front page of the document, her eyes grew wide and she spun around to face Owen to find he had picked up the end of the ribbon and tucked it into the front pocket of his shirt.

Her mouth dropped open. This day was going from good because she was getting out of the hospital, to great when she opened the envelope, to perfection when she saw Owen there with the ribbon.

Owen pulled a small velvet box from his pocket and then dropped to one knee before her. He took the papers, holding them along with the box in one hand while his other grasped her left hand.

"I made mistakes, Evie, hurt you, betrayed your trust, and tainted what we shared, but I want a chance to make it up to you, to do it right. No secrets, this time. Just me and you, our love, our future. This house is in the perfect neighborhood, it's close to our friends, has good schools, and there's space in the backyard for us to put in a pretty big swimming pool. If you don't like it, we can find something else, but I could picture us living here as soon as I saw it. They accepted our offer, but nothing is finalized until you tell me if you want to buy it or not."

"I love the house, it's perfect," she gushed. She could picture them here too.

"Evie, will you marry me again?" The ring was beautiful, a diamond surrounded by small bright blue sapphires. It was different than the ring he'd given her last time, which she had returned to him when she left, and while she wouldn't have minded if he'd given her back that ring she liked that this was a real fresh start.

"Yes, of course," she said. Tears streamed down her cheeks even as she laughed. Owen slid the ring onto her finger and then she threw herself into his arms.

\* \* \*

12:08 P.M.

Fox caught Evie as she threw herself into his arms.

Although he had been pretty positive she was going to say yes to his proposal—his only doubt had been that she might want to wait before jumping right back into being engaged given they'd only reconnected two weeks ago—he hadn't been sure she would like the house. It had everything they wanted, and when he'd seen it while looking through listings as he watched over her sleeping form, he'd been sure it was the house for them.

He was so glad that she loved it too and had accepted his proposal.

"I can't believe we're getting married again," she said, her face buried against his neck. "I don't want to wait to get married."

"We can get married as soon as you're healed," he

promised. As much as he couldn't wait to make her his wife, he didn't want to marry her while she was covered in bruises, he wanted them to be able to enjoy their day ... and their wedding night.

"I don't think I can wait that long," Evie said, kissing his neck and then lips.

There was no bed here or he'd take her right here and now, but Shark was still outside ready to drive them to the hotel, so without breaking the kiss, Fox stood, gathering Evie into his arms. There was a slight pull on his stitches, but the bullet wound was already healing, it wouldn't be long until he'd be back to PT, and then he and his team would be ready to get called out again. Fox intended to make it official with him and Evie before then. If the worst should happen and he didn't make it back alive, he wanted Evie to be his wife.

Still kissing her, he walked back downstairs, he only stopped when he had to lock up the house. Once he got Evie back to the hotel and made love to her, he'd call the real estate agent and have the sale of the house finalized.

"How did you get time to put the ribbon in the house?" Evie asked as they got into the backseat of Shark's truck and buckled their seatbelts.

"I had a little help," he replied, looking at Shark as he pulled out into the street.

"Shark did that?" Evie giggled. "I can't imagine Shark walking around with a long red ribbon." She giggled again. "When I think about it I picture him like a boy ballerina dancing around the house."

Fox choked on a laugh, and even though Shark just grunted and didn't change his expression, his dark eyes sparkled with amusement.

"Maybe Shark could take some dancing lessons from our resident ballerina once Abby heals and goes back to work," Fox suggested with a snicker.

That managed to actually shock Shark into looking horrified. "I think I'll stick to blowing things up and shooting them," the big man said.

Evie laughed, and the delight and joy on her face was too tempting to resist. Drawing her as close as he could while they were both wearing seatbelts, Fox framed her face with his hands and claimed her mouth. Her lips were soft, she tasted as sweet as sugar, and her tongue met his thrust for thrust as he ravished her mouth.

"H-hmm."

They both glanced up as Shark cleared his throat to find that they were pulled up outside the hotel.

"Our temporary home sweet home," he said to Evie, then clapped Shark on the back. "Thanks, man, for everything."

Shark merely nodded in acknowledgment.

"We really appreciate it," Evie added, undoing her seatbelt and leaning between the front seats to kiss Shark's cheek.

"Are you blushing?" Fox asked, amused.

"No," Shark growled.

Laughing, he slapped Shark on the back and then got out of the car. He scooped Evie into his arms despite her protest and carried her up to their room. He hadn't been back here since Evie and Abby had gone missing, he hadn't wanted to leave Evie's side and had been happy to sleep in a chair beside her hospital bed, but now he couldn't wait to get into bed.

As he was about to lie her down, Fox hesitated. Evie had cracked ribs, a head injury, bruises all over her face. Was it selfish of him to expect sex the second they were alone? Maybe he should let her soak in a nice hot bubble bath, then tuck her under the covers and hold her while she slept.

"If you even think about not giving me what I want I'm gonna be mad," Evie warned.

"Are you up to it?"

"I *need* it," she replied.

Since he couldn't deny her anything she needed, he laid her down on the bed and took a moment to just stare at her. She was really his, when they'd slept together at the cabin it had been different, they weren't officially back together then, but this would be their first time making love as a couple.

"You know how much I love you, don't you?" he asked as he let his fingers stroke through her curls.

"I know, Owen." Evie caught his fingers and squeezed. "I love you, too."

"We have to do this carefully, slowly, you're hurt and in pain," he cautioned as he eased her sweatpants and panties down her legs.

"Slow, fast, I don't care as long as you hurry up and get inside me." Evie shifted on the bed beneath him, her body squirming as it sought some sort of friction.

Happy to oblige, Fox put his hand between her legs as his lips found hers. She was already wet, and he was already rock hard, but he focused on Evie, sliding a finger inside her and making her moan into his mouth.

"You like that, baby?" he asked against her lips.

"More," she whispered, her hips thrusting against his hand.

Fox added another finger, stretching her and stroking deep, and he could feel her breathing pick up as her arousal grew. He curled his fingers around so they hit that elusive spot inside her and his thumb found her swollen bundle of nerves and he began to circle it with the pad of his thumb, increasing the pressure as he felt her losing control.

"Stop," she said abruptly, pushing his hand away. "Want to come with you inside me." Her hands fumbled at his zipper, but she managed to unzip it and shove his jeans down enough to free his rock-hard length from his boxers. She hummed her appreciation and stroked him with her nimble fingers.

"You want to come with me inside you then you better stop doing that." Fox nipped at her bottom lip.

Evie kept hold of him and guided him to her center. Fox inched inside her slowly, careful not to do anything to cause her pain, but Evie was impatient and curled her fingers onto his backside, pushing him down until he was buried inside her. She was hot and tight, and he had to cling to control so he didn't come before she did.

"What do you need, babe?" he asked and trailed a line of kisses along her neck.

"Need you to move," she said breathlessly as she moved restlessly beneath him.

Fox moved slowly, pulling up until he was almost out of her then thrusting back in just as slowly. Keeping the pace slow, he moved up and down, his mouth never leaving Evie's. When he felt her start to tremble, he adjusted the angle and increased the speed a little, and a moment later she shattered, crying out her release into his mouth as he refused to let up on the kisses. Hitting his own release with the next thrust, he surrendered to the vortex of pleasure, dragging out every molecule of ecstasy he could for both of them by continuing to move.

"Hmm, that was good," Evie murmured, pressing her face against his shoulder and touching her lip to the side of his neck.

"Only good?" he asked as he pulled out of her.

"Okay, amazing, fantastic, fabulous, awesome, wonderful, mind-blowing, hmm, that's all the synonyms I can think of right now," she said with a giggle.

"I'll take those. Here, sit up and let me get this off you." Fox helped her sit up and take off her t-shirt, then stripped out of his clothes. He went to the bathroom, ran a face washer under warm water, then returned and cleaned her down. "I hate these bruises on your skin," he said softly as he blotted at the mottled bruises on her chest.

"I know, me too, but you saved me, that's what's important," Evie reminded him, smoothing a hand over his hair.

"I'd still take these away if I could." Keeping his touch light, he ran his hand over her damaged face.

"I know you would, because you love me."

"Yeah, I do." Giving her a quick kiss, he returned the washcloth to the bathroom and then lifted Evie so he could pull the blankets down and tuck them both into bed. He laid her down so she was mostly resting on top of his body, wanting to feel her skin to skin. "My sweet, huge-hearted, little light in the dark, I'm never going to let you go again."

"Good, because I don't want you to." Evie snuggled closer and tucked her face under his chin.

Fox held her tight, he'd lost Maya, but by some miracle, he'd managed to hold onto Evie even though she'd almost been ripped away from him several times. Sometimes life gave you a second chance, and it was up to you not to waste it. This time he was determined that he would do whatever it took to keep his dark world illuminated by Evie's light.

**Find out how Logan "Shark" Kirk and a woman he survives a helicopter with stop a terrorist cell in the next book in this action packed and emotionally charged military romance series!**

# ABOUT THE AUTHOR

Jane Blythe is a *USA Today* bestselling author of romantic suspense full of sexy heroes, strong heroines, and serial killers! When she's not weaving hard to unravel mysteries she loves to read, bake, go to the beach, build snowmen, and watch Disney movies. She has two adorable Dalmatians, is obsessed with Christmas, owns 200+ teddy bears, and loves to travel!

To connect and keep up to date please visit any of the following

Email – mailto:janeblytheauthor@gmail.com
Facebook – http://www.facebook.com/janeblytheauthor
Instagram – http://www.instagram.com/jane_blythe_author
Reader Group – http://www.facebook.com/groups/janeskillersweethearts
Twitter – http://www.twitter.com/jblytheauthor
Website – http://www.janeblythe.com.au

ALSO BY JANE BLYTHE

*Saving SEALs Series*
SAVING RYDER
SAVING ERIC
SAVING OWEN

**Broken Gems Series**
CRACKED SAPPHIRE
CRUSHED RUBY
FRACTURED DIAMOND
SHATTERED AMETHYST
SPLINTERED EMERALD
SALVAGING MARIGOLD

**River's End Rescues Series**
SOME REGRETS ARE FOREVER

**Detective Parker Bell Series**
A SECRET TO THE GRAVE
WINTER WONDERLAND
DEAD OR ALIVE
LITTLE GIRL LOST
FORGOTTEN

**Count to Ten Series**
ONE
TWO

THREE

FOUR

FIVE

SIX

BURNING SECRETS

SEVEN

EIGHT

NINE

TEN

**Christmas Romantic Suspense Series**

CHRISTMAS HOSTAGE

CHRISTMAS CAPTIVE

CHRISTMAS VICTIM

YULETIDE PROTECTOR

**Conquering Fear Series**

(Co-written with Amanda Siegrist)

DROWNING IN YOU

OUT OF THE DARKNESS

**Other**

PROTECT

COCKY SAVIOR

# ABOUT THE AUTHOR

Jane Blythe is a *USA Today* bestselling author of romantic suspense full of sexy heroes, strong heroines, and serial killers! When she's not weaving hard to unravel mysteries she loves to read, bake, go to the beach, build snowmen, and watch Disney movies. She has two adorable Dalmatians, is obsessed with Christmas, owns 200+ teddy bears, and loves to travel!

To connect and keep up to date please visit any of the following

Email – mailto:janeblytheauthor@gmail.com
Facebook – http://www.facebook.com/janeblytheauthor
Instagram – http://www.instagram.com/jane_blythe_author
Reader Group – http://www.facebook.com/
groups/janeskillersweethearts
Twitter – http://www.twitter.com/jblytheauthor
Website – http://www.janeblythe.com.au

There are many more books in this fan fiction world than listed here, for an up-to-date list go to www.AcesPress.com

You can also visit our Amazon page at:
http://www.amazon.com/author/operationalpha

### *Special Forces: Operation Alpha World*

PJ Fiala: Defending Sophie
Nicole Flockton: Protecting Maria
Alexa Gregory: Backdraft
Michele Gwynn: Rescuing Emma
Casey Hagen: Shielding Nebraska
Desiree Holt: Protecting Maddie
Kathy Ivan: Saving Sarah
Kris Jacen, Be With Me
Jesse Jacobson: Protecting Honor
Silver James: Rescue Moon
Becca Jameson: Saving Sofia
Kate Kinsley: Protecting Ava
Heather Long: Securing Arizona
Gennita Low: No Protection
Kirsten Lynn: Joining Forces for Jesse
Margaret Madigan: Bang for the Buck
Trish McCallan: Hero Under Fire
Kimberly McGath: The Predecessor
Rachel McNeely: The SEAL's Surprise Baby
KD Michaels: Saving Laura
Lynn Michaels: Rescuing Kyle
Olivia Michaels: Protecting Harper
Wren Michaels: The Fox & The Hound
Annie Miller: Securing Willow
Kat Mizera: Protecting Bobbi
Keira Montclair, Wolf and the Wild Scots
Mary B Moore: Force Protection
LeTeisha Newton: Protecting Butterfly
Angela Nicole: Protecting the Donna
MJ Nightingale: Protecting Beauty
Sarah O'Rourke: Saving Liberty
Victoria Paige: Reclaiming Izabel
Anne L. Parks: Mason
Debra Parmley: Protecting Pippa

Lainey Reese: Protecting New York
KeKe Renée: Protecting Bria
TL Reeve and Michele Ryan: Extracting Mateo
Elena M. Reyes: Keeping Ava
Deanna L. Rowley: Saving Veronica
Angela Rush: Charlotte
Rose Smith: Saving Satin
Jenika Snow: Protecting Lily
Lynne St. James: SEAL's Spitfire
Dee Stewart: Conner
Harley Stone: Rescuing Mercy
Sarah Stone: Shielding Grace
Jen Talty: Burning Desire
Reina Torres, Rescuing Hi'ilani
Savvi V: Loving Lex
Megan Vernon: Protecting Us
Rachel Young: Because of Marissa

### Delta Team Three Series
Lori Ryan: Nori's Delta
Becca Jameson: Destiny's Delta
Lynne St James, Gwen's Delta
Elle James: Ivy's Delta
Riley Edwards: Hope's Delta

### Police and Fire: Operation Alpha World
Freya Barker: Burning for Autumn
B.P. Beth: Scott
Jane Blythe: Salvaging Marigold
Julia Bright, Justice for Amber
Anna Brooks, Guarding Georgia
KaLyn Cooper: Justice for Gwen
Aspen Drake: Sheltering Emma
Alexa Gregory: Backdraft

Deanndra Hall: Shelter for Sharla
Barb Han: Kace
EM Hayes: Gambling for Ashleigh
India Kells: Shadow Killer
CM Steele: Guarding Hope
Reina Torres: Justice for Sloane
Aubree Valentine, Justice for Danielle
Maddie Wade: Finding English
Stacey Wilk: Stage Fright
Laine Vess: Justice for Lauren

### *Tarpley VFD Series*
Silver James, Fighting for Elena
Deanndra Hall, Fighting for Carly
Haven Rose, Fighting for Calliope
MJ Nightingale, Fighting for Jemma
TL Reeve, Fighting for Brittney
Nicole Flockton, Fighting for Nadia

*As you know, this book included at least one character from Susan Stoker's books. To check out more, see below.*

## SEAL Team Hawaii Series
*Finding Elodie*
*Finding Lexie (Aug 2021)*
*Finding Kenna (Oct 2021)*
*Finding Monica (May 2022)*
*Finding Carly (TBA)*
*Finding Ashlyn (TBA)*
*Finding Jodelle (TBA)*

## Eagle Point Search & Rescue
*Searching for Lilly (Mar 2022)*
*Searching for Bristol (Jun 2022)*
*Searching for Elsie (Nov 2022)*
*Searching for Caryn (TBA)*
*Searching for Finley (TBA)*
*Searching for Heather (TBA)*
*Searching for Khloe (TBA)*

## Delta Team Two Series
*Shielding Gillian*
*Shielding Kinley*
*Shielding Aspen*
*Shielding Jayme (novella)*
*Shielding Riley*
*Shielding Devyn*
*Shielding Ember (Sept 2021)*
*Shielding Sierra (Jan 2022)*

## SEAL of Protection: Legacy Series
*Securing Caite (FREE!)*

*Securing Brenae (novella)*
*Securing Sidney*
*Securing Piper*
*Securing Zoey*
*Securing Avery*
*Securing Kalee*
*Securing Jane*

## Delta Force Heroes Series

*Rescuing Rayne (FREE!)*
*Rescuing Aimee (novella)*
*Rescuing Emily*
*Rescuing Harley*
*Marrying Emily (novella)*
*Rescuing Kassie*
*Rescuing Bryn*
*Rescuing Casey*
*Rescuing Sadie (novella)*
*Rescuing Wendy*
*Rescuing Mary*
*Rescuing Macie (novella)*
*Rescuing Annie (Feb 2022)*

## Badge of Honor: Texas Heroes Series

*Justice for Mackenzie (FREE!)*
*Justice for Mickie*
*Justice for Corrie*
*Justice for Laine (novella)*
*Shelter for Elizabeth*
*Justice for Boone*
*Shelter for Adeline*
*Shelter for Sophie*
*Justice for Erin*
*Justice for Milena*

*Shelter for Blythe*
*Justice for Hope*
*Shelter for Quinn*
*Shelter for Koren*
*Shelter for Penelope*

## SEAL of Protection Series
*Protecting Caroline (FREE!)*
*Protecting Alabama*
*Protecting Fiona*
*Marrying Caroline (novella)*
*Protecting Summer*
*Protecting Cheyenne*
*Protecting Jessyka*
*Protecting Julie (novella)*
*Protecting Melody*
*Protecting the Future*
*Protecting Kiera (novella)*
*Protecting Alabama's Kids (novella)*
*Protecting Dakota*

*New York Times*, *USA Today* and *Wall Street Journal* Bestselling
Author Susan Stoker has a heart as big as the state of
Tennessee where she lives, but this all American girl has also
spent the last fourteen years living in Missouri, California,
Colorado, Indiana, and Texas. She's married to a retired
Army man who now gets to follow *her* around the country.

www.stokeraces.com
www.AcesPress.com
susan@stokeraces.com

Made in the USA
Coppell, TX
15 September 2021